"Matchm_____ na chirped, sidling up to him with a smile. "When are you going to make me a match?"

Strange how Simon still wanted her to come to her senses and want *him*, even though he knew it was better if she *didn't* want him. He really needed to get his head on straight.

"I'm waiting for confirmation, but it looks like my first pick is going to be available soon." That was a bit of an exaggeration.

"Really?" she said. The surprise in her tone suggested she lacked faith in his skills.

Prompting him to exaggerate again. "Yep, I'm setting it up even as we speak."

"Wow. What's he like?"

"You'll see," he hedged. Because following through was not even the worst of his problems. The real issue was that no one he'd come up with was good enough for her. And the thought of any one of them dating Fiona made him want to confess the truth.

Dear Reader,

There's always that pesky grass-is-greener syndrome. The one that leaves us asking if we have the right job, house, car, clothes... When maybe the question should be, do we need to take a step back, stop wanting more and just be? Because maybe we already have everything we need.

Fiona is one of the lucky ones. She's happy. At least she was, before circumstances left her questioning her choices. Now she's turning her world upside down to get that happiness back. In her muddled state, a cross-country move, a new job, embracing her newly discovered family and finding a husband seem like a sound plan. What better way to start than online dating? And what better way to ensure a perfect Montana match than having her "new" grandfather Big E Blackwell and her well-intentioned but grieving father fill out her dating profile?

By now, I'm sure you can envision how this goes off the rails. Luckily, it happens in a funny and, I hope, endearing way. And, of course, the "wrong" guy turns out to be the best one. Because sometimes happiness really is as simple as letting it be.

Wishing you all happiness!

Carol

HEARTWARMING

Montana Match

—

Carol Ross

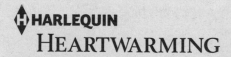

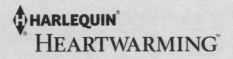

HARLEQUIN®
HEARTWARMING™

ISBN-13: 978-1-335-88993-5

Please recycle. This product is recyclable.

Recycling programs
for this product may
not exist in your area.

Montana Match

Copyright © 2020 by Carol Ross

This is a work of fiction. Names, characters, places and incidents
are either the product of the author's imagination or are used fictitiously.
Any resemblance to actual persons, living or dead, businesses,
companies, events or locales is entirely coincidental.

This edition published by arrangement with Harlequin Books S.A.

For questions and comments about the quality of this book,
please contact us at CustomerService@Harlequin.com.

Harlequin Enterprises ULC
22 Adelaide St. West, 40th Floor
Toronto, Ontario M5H 4E3, Canada
www.Harlequin.com

Printed in U.S.A.

Carol Ross lives in the Pacific Northwest with her husband and two dogs. She is a graduate of Washington State University. When not writing, or thinking about writing, she enjoys reading, running, hiking, skiing, traveling and making plans for the next adventure to subject her sometimes reluctant but always fun-loving family to. Carol can be contacted at carolrossauthor.com and via Facebook at Facebook.com/carolrossauthor, Twitter, @_carolross, and Instagram, @carolross__.

Books by Carol Ross

Harlequin Heartwarming

Return of the Blackwell Brothers

The Rancher's Twins

Seasons of Alaska

Mountains Apart
A Case for Forgiveness
If Not for a Bee
A Family Like Hannah's
Bachelor Remedy
In the Doctor's Arms

Second Chance for the Single Dad

Visit the Author Profile page
at Harlequin.com for more titles.

For Amy, Anna, Cari, Melinda & Kathryn

Thank you for your friendship and for making this cool thing possible once again.

You guys make me happy.

PROLOGUE

"SEVEN," PEYTON HARRISON declared from her position behind the flattened cereal box currently serving as home plate in the family's front yard. "Fiona gets seven strikes."

Seven? Grasping the bat and awaiting her turn behind the plate, Fiona gaped at her big sister. At thirteen, Peyton was the oldest in their family of five girls. Fiona was the youngest, which made Peyton her number-two all-time favorite hero, second only to her dad.

"Seven?" Ten-year-old Lily screeched in protest. As a triplet, Lily was technically tied with Amanda and Georgie for the title of second oldest. But, as the most outspoken and competitive of them all, it seemed to Fiona that she deserved some sort of special distinction. Like vice sister or second chair sister. "Are you kidding me? That is ridiculous!" Lily punctuated the assessment by stomping one sneakered foot, causing a puff of dust to whip up and dislodge the tattered scrap of blue tarp marking the pitcher's mound. Despite Lily's hands, which didn't always work as well as she wanted, she was still the best pitcher in the neighborhood.

"She's only eight," Peyton countered calmly.

"We *never* got *seven* strikes, not even when we were seven. How will she ever be a decent ballplayer if she doesn't learn to hit the ball in three strikes?"

"She's also tiny," Peyton added as if this definitively sealed the argument.

"So what? So is Titus."

"Who?" Peyton snapped.

"She means Titus Cole," brainy Georgiana explained from her spot at first base. First base was the best base in Fiona's opinion because it looked most like the ones on TV. An old throw pillow, it had been slated for the trash after Amanda used it as bedding for one of the stray dogs she'd brought home. Mom had washed it but declared that no amount of soap could get all the smell out. Lily had snagged the pillow, dubbing it the "ultimate bag." Genius, as far as Fiona was concerned.

Georgie added, "He's Lily's favorite professional baseball player. Shortstop for the Barons. He currently holds the team record for the most home runs in a season. He's also the lightest and shortest player in the league. Physiologically speaking, he shouldn't be able to hit home runs like he does."

"Oh, for Pete's sake," Peyton said, flipping her gaze skyward with a flourish that would make a roller coaster jealous. Fiona often practiced the gesture in the mirror but only managed to look as if she had something in her eye. "This is not the major leagues, Lily. Fiona gets seven strikes, and that's final." Peyton turned toward Fiona, who'd been standing on the sidelines waiting patiently for the matter to be settled. "Are you ready, squirt?"

Lily muttered under her breath and stared at the pitcher's mound for a second before looking back up, directly at Fiona. Planting her hands on her hips, she said, "You're not a baby, are you, Fee? Three strikes are enough for you to hit the ball, huh?"

"Um…" Fiona said nervously, and thought, *Please, don't make me decide how many strikes I get.* She would always side with Peyton, but she didn't want to upset Lily. She didn't like upsetting any of her sisters.

"Um, Lily?" Amanda broke in. "Does it really matter? It's just practice. We're going to win the championship no matter how many times she strikes out." The Harrison girls were undefeated in the neighborhood league, which Lily had started. Lily's friend Danny and his friend Will played on their team, too. The "big game" was tomorrow. Lily had made them practice three times every day, all week. Not including the extra batting practices she assigned her sisters.

"Why don't we vote on it?" Georgie suggested brightly.

"Because this is not a democracy," Peyton stated. "We all know you three will vote together. That's why I have to put my foot down."

Lily sighed. "If you baby her forever, she'll never learn."

"What won't she learn?"

All the girls turned at the sound of their dad's voice. None of them had seen their parents, Rudy and Susan, round the side of the house, intent as they'd been on the debate.

"How to hit the ball," Lily answered. "Peyton thinks Fiona should get seven strikes."

Rudy bobbed his head. "That seems reasonable. She's only eight."

"Ha! I told you!" Peyton cried.

Lily narrowed her gaze. "But I say she'll never learn to hit the ball in three strikes if she keeps getting extra chances. If I had to learn how to play with my messed-up hands, she can learn how to bat by the rules."

"Ah." Their dad nodded. "I see. Lily, that is a good point."

"Thank you," Lily said, tossing a satisfied grin at Peyton.

"But she'll never get better if she doesn't hit it at all," Peyton returned. "She needs the practice."

"That's an excellent point, too, Peyton," their mom said.

Fiona was certain that all the practice in the world would never turn her into an athlete like Lily. But she appreciated Peyton championing her cause.

Rudy glanced around the infield to Amanda and Georgie.

Lily, as if reading his mind, said, "Amanda doesn't think it matters since it's only practice, and Georgie thinks we should vote on it."

"Hmm," he said with a nod, looking extremely pleased by this answer. "All my girls are smart and fair."

"Statistically speaking, seven strikes could conceivably boost her confidence," Georgie added thoughtfully. "Because she would have a better chance of hitting it and—"

"What time is it?" Amanda interrupted. "I think practice is over now, right? You said an hour, Lily. It's been an hour, and I promised Mrs. Dailey I'd walk Truman for her today." Truman was a big, sweet golden retriever. Amanda took her job as neighborhood dog walker very seriously. Sometimes she'd let Fiona tag along.

"Six more minutes," Lily told Amanda.

Stepping closer to Fiona, Rudy said, "What do you think, Little Fee?"

What did she think? Fiona adored all four of her sisters, she truly did. That's why she wanted to please them all. But no matter how hard she tried, she would always be the youngest, always be outshined, always be just a little bit behind. She wasn't good at sports like Lily, or cool like Peyton, or smart like Georgie, or good with animals like Amanda. She was... She wasn't sure, but she did know that she wanted everyone to be happy.

Shrugging, she did her best to hold back unexpected tears. "I don't know, Daddy. I want to hit the ball, but I also want to be a good ballplayer like Lily... I guess I don't care."

"You can be a good ballplayer, Fee!" Lily declared. "You're strong for your size. You just need practice."

"Which is why she needs more strikes," Peyton reiterated with a touch of impatience. "So she can practice."

Gentle smile in place, her dad said, "I have an idea. I think you can do this."

"You do?" Fiona asked.

"In fact, I know you can. You just need a steady hand—or rather, arms—to guide you."

"Okay," she agreed bravely.

Fiona would never forget that moment, the feel of her dad's big, strong arms as they wound around her and took up the bat, positioning it just like Lily had taught her a million times.

"Ready!" their father called out as he stepped back. "Show us what you got, Lily bug. Fastball."

Lily went wide-eyed. "Dad…"

Fiona held her breath because Lily even held back with Georgie, who, as the second-best batter in the family, was really, really good. Not Lily good, but who was? Lily's fastball was legendary. It had once sent Tony Borzinksy to the urgent care clinic.

"I'm serious, Lil. Bring it. I want to see what you've got."

Oh, no… Fiona went cold. Because Lily would never be able to resist a challenge like that one. Especially not from their dad, who they all wanted to make proud.

Determination steeling her features, Lily punched the ball hard into the pocket of her mitt. "Don't move, Fee Keep your eye on the ball," she instructed. "Just like I showed you, okay?"

Fiona nodded and gripped the bat so tightly that her arms shook and her fingers began to ache. At the look of determination on Lily's face, she focused on not flinching and prayed that her sister's aim would be true. She was terrified of getting hit with the ball.

Peyton, as if reading her mind, lowered to a catcher's stance behind her and whispered, "Don't worry, squirt, I won't let her hit you."

"You got this, Fee," Georgie called. "A simple matter of physics is all it is."

"That's right, munchkin," Amanda agreed. "You can do it."

Lily wound up for the pitch. Fiona tensed, heart pounding like Peyton's rap music inside of her chest. She waited, unflinching. Trying to be a good ballplayer, a good sister, a good daughter... Then, suddenly, the ball was zinging toward her faster than a bolt of lightning. Fiona had no more time to catalog another thought or even register a sensation because the most incredible thing happened. Her arms swung forward, and she watched as bat and ball connected with an astonishingly loud crack. The feeling was...exquisite. It took her breath away. Laughter and cheers erupted from every quarter.

It was then that Fiona realized that her dad had stepped up behind her at the very last second and guided the bat and, with his help, and the encouragement of her sisters and her mom, she'd knocked it out of the park.

CHAPTER ONE

"WHAT CAN I get for you, ma'am?"

Fiona Harrison was aware that someone, the bartender presumably, had appeared behind the bar where she was seated. She heard the deep voice ask the question, but her attention was elsewhere. Bar stool angled slightly, gaze glued to the door, she would not look away. She wanted to memorize this moment, implant it in her brain forever. Should she video it? How cute would that be to show their kids someday? *Look, sweetie, this is the moment when I first laid eyes on your daddy...*

Because she was aware of the bartender still loitering, she finally murmured, "Um, coffee?"

"I'm sorry, I didn't quite catch all of that."

"What?" Irritating, this interruption of what could conceivably be her first glimpse of the man she was going to marry. Maybe. At least, it was a possibility if things went well. Every couple has their "meet-cute," and Fiona planned to savor hers whenever it finally arrived.

The same voice teased, "Are you calling me sweetie? Because I'm totally okay with that. Or are you asking if we have coffee? Or are you asking *me* if that's what *you* want? I hope it's not the last one because I could not begin to imagine what a pretty lady like you would like."

"Oh." Fiona felt her face go hot as she realized she'd uttered some of that kid video fantasy out loud. Still, she kept her focus on the door. "No, sorry. You're not my sweetie. I mean, I'm sure you're nice enough and all. But the…second option. I think. I mean, I'd like a cup of coffee, please."

"Do you want to order for your friend, too?"

"Friend? What friend?" Fiona whipped around on the bar stool, her gaze bouncing around the spacious room behind her. "Does this place have a back door?" The Silver Stake was both restaurant and bar, as well as a tribute to the town's Western roots and mining history. Vintage pickaxes, pans, hand tools, lanterns and assorted Western gear hung on the walls and from the rafters, and appealed to her love of history and all things antique. Even the security camera, she noted, was cleverly camouflaged inside a rusty sconce. But right now her focus was on the people inhabiting the space. There were exactly three other customers, all in the restaurant section—the same couple she'd spotted enjoying a late lunch in a corner booth when she'd arrived five minutes ago, and a lone cowboy working his way through a hamburger and a huge pile of French fries. The bartender had been nowhere in sight at that time, so she'd taken a seat and waited for the first of her promising PartnerUp.com dates to walk through the door.

The small town of Falcon Creek, Montana, and surrounding locale harbored a surprisingly plentiful pool of available men that fit her new and improved standards. Necessary standards, she reminded herself and tried not to think about the dating profile that, with the help of her dad and her "new" grandpa, Big E, she'd filled out. Big E, that's what everyone called Elias Blackwell, the man she and her four sisters had recently discovered was their biological grandfather. He'd assured her that he knew what men around here were looking for in a wife. Fiona tried to ignore the fact that she'd essentially placed her trust in her recently widowed, emotionally charged father, and a man she barely knew, who didn't know her. But Big E was family, she reminded herself. And family didn't let you down. At least, not in her experience. Plus, her older sister Peyton had helped as well, vetting the dating site and offering advice.

That didn't mean other people wouldn't let her down, though. Fiona had the ex-boyfriends to prove that. And from what she'd heard, people were notoriously dishonest on their dating profiles. The fact that she'd "tailored" hers—as Big E dubbed it—didn't count, though, did it? It's not like she'd *lied* lied. She'd just fudged a bit regarding what she was looking for. She was certain that she'd like a man who had a stable nine-to-five job with a retirement plan, drove a sensible car and was into settling down, if she ever actually dated one. Apparently, according to her dad and Big E, these were the same men who enjoyed watching contact sports in their man caves and eating "anything with meat in it."

The bartender's deep chuckle had her spinning back around to face him, scoping out the entrance again on the way by. "The friend you're obviously waiting for. Boyfriend?"

It was on the tip of Fiona's tongue to say yes, but she wasn't *that* far into her fantasy—she had a ways to go before any of these dates could be elevated to boyfriend status. The bartender's back was to her, and for a second she was distracted by the sight of wide shoulders and black wavy hair curling just above the collar of his denim shirt, the sleeves of which were rolled to the elbows on strong arms that were pouring coffee from a pot that looked freshly brewed. The thought popped into her mind that she hoped her date looked as nice as this guy did in faded jeans. Alarmed at her lack of self-restraint, she immediately reminded herself that she was on a mission. For far too long, she'd judged men on the wrong criteria. Out were looks, laughs, fun-loving dreamers with good intentions. In was respectable, serious, responsible men who were gainfully employed and career focused. She really needed to get this right.

But then he turned to face her, and the rational part of her brain slammed shut again. *Seriously, black hair* and *blue eyes?* She pried it open: *Fiona, you are absolutely done with good-looking, charming guys who talk a good game but have no plans past today.* Her dad hadn't specifically noted bartenders on his list of inadvisable occupations for a future husband, but she was pretty sure that was an oversight. Among those singled out were gambler, fire dancer, poet, professional jouster, ski bum and most any job that was prefaced with "aspiring" or "part-time." Okay, so she hadn't had the best luck, or judgment, where men were concerned.

Mischievous, appealing grin in place, the bartender tossed a coaster in front of her and followed that with a steaming mug. Fiona found that she now had trouble looking away; she was absolutely certain that the innumerable blue tones of the ever-changing Pacific Ocean had been the inspiration for the eyes now trained on her. They were twinkling with curiosity below deliberately arched eyebrows, reminding her that she hadn't answered his question.

"No." She cleared her throat and added, "Date."

"Ah." Was it her imagination, or did his eyes cloud over a bit? "Cream or sugar?"

"No, thank you."

He held out a hand. "Simon Clarke."

She reached across the bar and tried not to enjoy the feel of his big hand enveloping hers. "Fiona Harrison."

"You're new in town, Fiona. It's a pleasure to meet you. *Finally.*" There was a satisfaction in his tone, the "finally" implying he'd been waiting for way more than a few minutes for this introduction. Which was not only silly but impossible. Fiona would recall if they'd already crossed paths. She remembered pretty much everyone she ever saw and their names, a valuable skill in her former life as a professional server. Already, she could close her eyes and picture every member of the Blackwell family, her five newly discovered male cousins, their wives and children, people she hadn't even known existed until a few months ago. They might be strangers right now, but Fiona was embracing this opportunity to expand her family. If her new Montana life proceeded according to plan, they would soon view her like family, too.

"Yes, I am."

"First date?"

"How did you know?"

"When a person watches a door in a place like this, it generally indicates one of two things—waiting on a person or hiding from one. The manner in which you've been watching the entrance suggests to me it's the former."

"I can see how that might be a giveaway," she conceded wryly.

"First dates can be nerve-racking."

"That's for sure," she agreed, and chuckled. But not for the reason he thought. Usually, that wasn't the case for Fiona at all. Normally, she enjoyed meeting new people. This, however, was different. *Husband shopping.* She felt herself grimace at the term because she couldn't get past the notion that she was conducting interviews instead of fomenting romance. The thought depressed her a little, but she pushed that feeling aside. Peyton was right; internet dating was the most efficient and expedient means to achieve her goal. And she didn't want a husband just to make her dad happy. She wanted to make herself happy. Something had changed inside of her with her mom's passing. Shockingly, without warning or apology, an aneurysm had taken her and left her family—a husband and five girls—reeling with grief.

A difficult conversation with her dad had instilled a sense of urgency that she'd never felt before, a burning need to get her life together. He was right; she needed to "grow up and make some changes." Be an adult. Tied for first on his list, and of similar importance, was finding a "real" job and a "suitable" husband.

In her mind, a house and a dog would be next, with kids coming along soon after. Maybe even a horse. She'd like to have a horse. Maybe. She'd decide on that after she learned how to ride one. Both of which seemed like real possibilities here in Montana, especially if she made a rancher match. Rancher was near the top of her dad's list of best husband professions. No doubt, her sister Lily's recent engagement to a local rancher was fueling that option.

A wealthy rancher was number one on Big

E's list. "That way, you can settle right here in Montana," Big E had encouraged her just this afternoon via their pre-date online pep talk. Three months ago, if someone would have told Fiona that she'd be Skyping with her dad and her new grandpa while the two men traveled the country in Big E's motor home searching for her biological father, she would have… Well, she didn't know. She'd certainly never expected the two men would be giving her dating advice.

Big E had stared right into the camera lens so that it felt like his blue eyes were burning into hers. "Remember, Little Fee, it's just as easy to fall in love with a rich man as it is a poor one." After a pause, he'd added a hearty guffaw, but Fiona wasn't 100 percent convinced he'd been joking.

With a playful roll of her eyes, she'd said, "Great advice, Big E, or should I call you Grandpa now? You know what, I think I'm going to call you Grandpa E. Or wait! How about Big G? Yep, that's it. How am I supposed to know the difference, Big G?"

"Big G?" He chuckled. "I like that. You leave that part to me. Stick to the guys PartnerUp.com sets you up with, and you'll be all right."

Fiona had agreed. With her dad and Peyton

also advocating for this plan, it seemed the most sensible course of action.

"Just be yourself, Little One," her dad had advised, tipping his head so that his face was kitty-corner across the screen. "There's not a man in the world who wouldn't be lucky to have you."

Fiona thought about that. She loved her dad for the assertion, but she didn't want just any man. She wanted the perfect man. Not *literally* perfect, but perfect according to her new standards. Profile perfect.

"So, who's the lucky guy?"

"What?" Fiona gave her head a little shake and met Simon's gaze, probing hers with curiosity. "I don't..."

"I probably know him. Falcon Creek is a small town. Tell me his name, and I can give you the skinny."

"Oh. Well, um..." Fiona didn't want to tell him. She didn't want any preconceived notions where Randall Gemini was concerned. *Fiona Gemini.* That rolled off the tongue nicely, she thought. Randall wasn't a wealthy rancher, but he was a "well-off" insurance broker from a ranching family whose favorite foods included steak and cheeseburgers, both of which he enjoyed while watching football. She could learn to like football, right? Fiona couldn't think of a profession more stable and reliable than insurance. Except for maybe a database administrator. She had an upcoming date with one of those, too.

Fiona forced out a smile and said, "Thanks, but I don't need the skinny."

Simon glanced at the door and let out a sound like a cross between a groan and a growl, but when Fiona looked up at him, all she saw was a bright smile beneath sparkling eyes. He said, "Randall Gemini is a great guy and a fine catch for any woman who likes to study actuarial charts and discuss the most common types of accidental deaths."

"What? You know…" Fiona glanced toward the door, where a man was now standing, surveying the restaurant portion of the establishment. Of course, Simon was right about Falcon Creek being small, and, as a bartender, it was likely that he did know a lot of people.

Bar towel in hand, he leaned forward to polish the already spotless surface. His voice was low and soft, and she found herself holding tight to her breath as he whispered, "For an added thrill, don't forget to ask him about fire loss statistics. I'll keep you supplied with coffee to help you stay awake."

Fiona let out an indignant gasp. "That's a mean thing to say."

"Fiona." His expression went somber as he angled his head to snag her gaze. "One thing I am not is mean. What I am, however, is honest."

Fiona stared into his blue eyes now blazing with intensity and couldn't help but think that he was talking about something much deeper than his observations about her date. Then again, as a waitress, Fiona had known more than her share of bartenders and had even dated a few. She'd found the stereotype to be true—the best ones were wise and philosophical, at least when it came to other people's lives.

"It might be my only fault, though." Simon winked at her, then straightened and turned, lifting a hand to wave at her date, who was now approaching. "Hey, Randall, how ya doing, buddy?"

Randall greeted Simon, and Fiona was immediately heartened by the sight of her date's lovely, genuine smile. Introductions went smoothly. Simon brought Randall a beer, and Fiona suggested they move to a nearby booth. For some inexplicable reason, she didn't want Simon to overhear her first-date conversation. The words were barely out of her mouth when Simon slid her a grin that indicated he knew exactly what she was thinking. Irritating.

Which he obviously had, Fiona thought as she slowly sipped her coffee, wishing she'd requested it with a shot of whiskey.

Randall's tone was proud and held a hint of challenge as he said, "I bet you didn't know the very first insurance contract was signed clear back in the fourteenth century, did you?"

"Um, no, I did not know that." Fiona stared at Randall Gemini, who she'd learned in the seven short minutes—had it really only been seven?—she'd known him that he was licensed to sell insurance in six states. Equine, cattle, poultry, dairy, crops—he serviced all types of agricultural needs. And recently, he'd ventured into in agritourism, as well. He owned his own agency and employed three other people, none of whom were able to match him in sales.

Fiona stole another glance at the antique schoolhouse-style clock high on the wall, right in the center above the mirror that faced the bar and felt her mind wander. Had the clock once hung inside the town's school? Incredible that it still functioned. She wondered if Simon knew its origins. She tried not to look at him where he now stood behind the bar clear down at the other end, typing away on a laptop. Occasionally he'd look up and glance around the room. His knowing smile would find her and linger as if enjoying the sight of his own honesty. She ignored him. Or tried to, anyway.

"Yep, 1347, to be exact. So obviously," Randall said, finishing up his treatise, "this industry endures."

"Obviously," Fiona agreed with forced enthusiasm and took another sip of coffee. The final one. She stared dismally into her empty cup. What was she going to do now? She picked up her spoon and began polishing it with a napkin. "So, Randall, what else do you—"

"But," he interrupted because, apparently, he was just getting warmed up. "Interestingly, people only started insuring body parts in the early twentieth century. The word *insurance* is derived from the French language and originally meant engagement to marry."

"Really?" *Please don't ever ask me to marry you, Randall.* "That is interesting," Fiona lied politely and plucked another napkin out of the dispenser on the table and went to work on the saltshaker. The condiment holder was very disorganized, with the ketchup in front of the hot sauce and the pepper nowhere in sight. She'd tackle that next.

Randall sat back in his chair and ran a hand through his short sandy-brown hair. He did have nice hair. Good eye contact, too, with pale brown eyes that danced with excitement when talking about his work. That enthusiasm was undoubtedly a very desirable trait when it came to insurance sales. A career that obviously inspired him. And Fiona respected that. Yes, she absolutely did!

She redoubled her efforts to pay attention but couldn't quite follow the narrative because the set of spurs and the old wood-and-cast-iron oxen yoke hanging on the wall beside them had her speculating about how Falcon Creek must have looked in the old days. She'd noticed a hitching post out front when she arrived and wondered if it was original to the building. Exploring every crevice of this charming little town was at the top of her to-do list. Lydia, her new cousin Jon's wife, had offered to take her to lunch and show her around. Fiona was looking forward to that.

"Would you agree with that, Fiona?"

The sound of her name had her tuning back into Randall's discourse. He was grinning eagerly, and it was tempting just to say yes and make him happy, but she had no idea what she might be agreeing with, or to. A myriad of misunderstandings danced through her mind. What if he'd just asked her on another date or, worse, to drive to Billings this weekend for that insurance convention he'd mentioned earlier?

A nervous smile danced on her lips. She picked up her glistening spoon and studied it. "Um, well, I'd probably have to think about that one."

Randall's face scrunched with confusion. "You would?"

Simon materialized at that moment, coffee carafe in hand. "I would, too," he said. "It's a controversial subject."

"Controversial? How so?" Randall asked, eyebrows dipping into a low vee on his forehead.

"Imagine if your coverage-to-loss ratio was inverted at the time of loss."

Randall paused for a quick second, expression twisting with uncertainty. Then, with a loud guffaw, he slapped a hand on the tabletop. "Inverted ratio..." he repeated, along with an extended bout of laughter. Simon clapped him on the shoulder and joined in. Two buddies sharing an inside joke. Maybe she should have videoed their meet-cute, she thought with irrational resentment.

Fiona forced out a too-loud chuckle that sounded so fake it made her wince. Luckily, Randall was too busy enjoying the moment to notice.

Simon turned to Fiona. Innocent, inquisitive smile in place, he hefted the carafe, along with both thick black eyebrows. "More coffee, Fiona?"

CHAPTER TWO

SIMON CLARKE, temporary manager and bartender of the Silver Stake bar and restaurant, stared at the email on his laptop screen and tried to rein in his resentment. The message was forcing his attention away from the enchanting Fiona Harrison and her entertaining first date, and directing it back onto his real life. Specifically, his prop rental business in Los Angeles, where he'd left the day-to-day operations in the debatably capable hands of his younger brother, Mica. The subject line read: URGENT. And it was. Sort of.

In the month since he'd come back to Montana to help his cousin Ned and his wife, Valerie, with their restaurant business, Simon had rediscovered perspective where that term was concerned. Falcon Creek–urgent versus LA-urgent were two very different things. Although, if he didn't soon find at least one more server to hire at the Silver Stake, he might upgrade that matter to critical. Especially with the fundraiser only a few days away. Between running this place, managing his business in LA and helping Ned out on their ranch, he was fast approaching burnout. Which reminded him to retrieve the help wanted sign he'd made and hang it in the window. Posting the position online hadn't yielded any acceptable candidates. Attempting an old-school approach felt worthy of this old-school town.

Back behind the bar, he hit Reply to the email and tried to formulate a response. Too much to type. Better to just pick up the phone and call his sister/assistant, Colette. Colette's hands were infinitely more capable than Mica's yet justifiably distracted by the existence of her four tiny offspring, his adorable but rambunctious nephews. A situation exacerbated by the inattentiveness of the kids' apathetic father, his deadbeat former brother-in-law. Colette worked nearly full-time as it was, and he couldn't ask her to do more.

According to Colette, Mica, in Simon's absence, had taken to working nearly not-at-all. Colette had warned him that Mica wasn't cut out to manage his business, Clarke Props, Ltd., while he was away. But what choice did he have? With Valerie still recuperating, Ned needed him. And Mica needed a job.

Simon read the email again, his irritation with Mica spiking along with his blood pressure. At this rate, it would be a miracle if he made it back to LA without suffering a stroke. Double booking a prop was one thing, an inconvenience that required compromise and strategic smoothing of ruffled studio crew feathers. But, inevitably, it could be resolved. But triple booking? That degree of error would cost money and time and possibly future business. Especially when the prop rented was an antique airplane. Not exactly something you could throw into the back of one of the company vehicles and deliver at your convenience. Delivery required logistics, equipment, a crew to load the plane, a truck and trailer to transport, and then unloading at the destination. One of the shooting locations was at least a four-hour drive from their offices and storage facility.

Time to implement damage control. First, he needed to call Colette and discuss strategy since she would be the one contending with the situation on the front line. Dealing with Hollywood types, even ones who worked behind the cameras, could be challenging to the point of exasperating.

His hand reached for his phone, but he quickly realized the conversation might be a long one. Better to at least wait until the other bartender, Miguel, showed up. Tapping out a text to Colette, he briefly explained what had happened, told her to check her inbox and that he'd call as soon as he could.

Colette responded immediately: Mica! Along with the angriest emoji face in her arsenal. Just read the email. When can you call?

Simon glanced up to see Fiona and Randall emerge from their booth. Chatting amiably, they moved in unhurried fits and starts, pausing here and there while an animated Fiona gestured at assorted artifacts adorning the space. Randall laughed. Simon couldn't hear what they were saying due to the country music playing softly in the background.

Once they reached the door, they faced each other and exchanged a brief hug. Randall kissed her on the cheek. Fiona nodded and patted his shoulder. Simon felt himself frowning. Surely she wouldn't be agreeing to see the guy again, would she? The two were completely mismatched. Anyone could see that. Although, why else would Randall's smile be as bright as a Montana sunrise?

Waving at Simon, Randall called out, "See you later, Si."

"Looking forward to it, Randall. Take care."

Randall continued out the door. Simon waited for Fiona to turn, too, and give him a wave and a goodbye. When she didn't, he found himself staring at her back, waiting—wanting, if he was being honest—to see that pretty smile one more time. Several seconds ticked by while she stayed put, just standing there facing the door. After a long moment, she finally lifted both hands and tacked them to her waist. Then she rolled her head around on her shoulders in a drawn-out, careful way that usually suggested distress or frustration or possibly a kink in the neck. Simon felt an unexpected nibble of concern.

He was just about to call out, ask if everything was okay, when she spun a quick half circle and, keeping her head down, marched in his direction until she stood in front of him. Her chin came up, and her gaze collided with his, rendering him speechless. Because her expression, her demeanor, her entire bearing, was so completely at odds with how she'd appeared with Randall only a moment before that it caught him off guard. She looked...forlorn. His uneasiness increased about tenfold.

"Fiona, are you okay? What happened?" For the life of him, he couldn't conceive of Randall doing or saying anything offensive toward any woman, toward any *person* for that matter. He'd seen the guy blush at even slightly inappropriate jokes told around the bar. But if life had taught him anything, it was never to say never where predicting human behavior was concerned. Ever.

With a sigh, she hoisted herself onto a stool. Bringing both hands up, she arranged her long, dark blond hair to fall down her back. She waved a hand toward the exit and said, "I owe you an apology."

Ah. So, he'd been right about the compatibility thing. But she seemed awfully disappointed about it. It was just a date, after all, and there was no way this captivating woman had trouble getting dates. Still, he was relieved about her confession and suddenly itchy to make her smile again.

Straight-faced, he joked, "What did you do? Steal something off the wall? I noticed how you kept admiring all the antiques. Whatever it was, just put it back, and I won't call Scooter."

Gray eyes widening, her expression transformed with silent, openmouthed surprise. "What?" She barked out the word along with a laugh. "No, I didn't steal anything! Who's Scooter?"

And just like that, she was all sparkle and life again. Simon felt oddly, inordinately relieved for bringing it back so easily, and prouder of himself than the situation warranted.

"Scooter is the deputy here in Falcon Creek

and who I call in the event of illegal shenanigans. I'm glad you're not a thief."

"Are you?" she asked, her mouth fighting a smile as if she knew she was walking into a joke and couldn't stop herself. Simon liked that, too. A woman who enjoyed laughing so much that she'd risk a joke at her own expense.

"Yes, because I don't like being wrong about people."

"Oh." Her smile broke free as she absorbed the compliment. "That is sweet."

"Well, I told you I wasn't a mean guy. I may not be the mountain state's top insurance salesman seven years running, but I am pretty spot-on when it comes to reading a person's character…"

The words had barely left his mouth when her smile slid away like frosting from a too-warm cake. What happened? How could a person go from joy filled to dejected so quickly?

"No, don't frown." Simon reached out, realized he was about to touch her hand and then detoured, planting his palm on the bar instead. "What's going on? Randall didn't…upset you or something, did he?" He infused plenty of meaning into his tone.

"Oh. No! Nothing like that. He's a great guy, just like you said."

How great? Simon wondered and found

himself asking, "Surely, he didn't turn you down for another date?"

"No. I... We turned each other down. It's obvious we wouldn't be a good match." Nibbling on her lip, she threw a glance toward the door like she might be regretting the decision.

"It was very obvious," Simon reassured her.

"It was?"

She sounded so hopeful that he couldn't help elaborating, "Yes, even to me, and I haven't known you very long."

"Thank you. Oddly, that makes me feel better."

"Glad I could help."

"Which reminds me of that apology. I wanted to say that I'm sorry for calling you mean. You're obviously not mean."

"I appreciate you saying so." For the briefest, most impulsive of seconds, Simon considered asking her out. And then came to his senses. Not a good idea. If Valerie continued to heal he'd be heading back to LA at the end of the month after Thanksgiving. Or the beginning of December at the latest. Not that that mattered necessarily. Normally this time frame would make for ideal circumstances, because he didn't do long-term relationships and leaving after a month would give him the perfect out. But his gut, and his desire to keep her here talking, told him that his usual preference for short-term fun would not be enough with Fiona. That thought was disconcerting, too, and another reason to refrain. Best to keep things strictly friendly.

"There's always tomorrow, right?" she said, eyeing him curiously.

"Yes, ma'am. If we're lucky, we'll both have a long lifetime of tomorrows like this one to look forward to."

Grimacing, she muttered, "Oh, please, I hope not."

It was Simon's turn to chuckle as he watched her comprehend the absurdity of her statement.

Her mouth curled with a sheepish, utterly adorable grin. "Obviously, I didn't mean *that*."

"I didn't think you did."

They shared a quick laugh before she added, "I just meant that I hope it doesn't take me *that* many tomorrows to get this done."

Get this done? Before Simon could ask her to elaborate on that cryptic statement, his phone began vibrating on the counter between them. Colette's smiling face lit up the screen. Dread gathered inside of him because if his sister was calling him after the text he'd sent, the news could not be good.

Unfortunately, Fiona took that as her cue

to wrap up their conversation. Bailing off the stool, she said, "See you tomorrow, Simon."

"I hope so, Fiona."

Meeting his eyes, she smiled, transformed again, and it did something wonky to his heart knowing he was the cause.

"You know what, you might want to keep fresh coffee brewed anyway. Just in case." With a wink, she turned and headed toward the door.

As Simon reached for his phone to answer his sister's call, Fiona's final puzzling statements penetrated his brain. *Just in case.* What did that mean? She'd just told him that she and Randall were not a good match. And she hadn't said, *See you soon* or *goodbye,* but "See you tomorrow."

"Simon! Are you there? Can you hear me?" He didn't have time to think about it further as the sound of his sister's frantic voice transported him straight to LA and the myriad of problems awaiting him there.

FIONA EXITED THE Silver Stake onto the frosty sidewalk and immediately felt a shiver barrel up her spine like an iced-over freight train. Her attention caught and held on the sign in the window. Help Wanted—Server. Excitement spiked through her, and she took a step back toward the door before stopping herself.

"What am I doing?" she mumbled. The chime of her phone redirected her once again, and she dug into her bag. It would be so easy to head back inside and ask Simon if she could talk to the manager. With her experience and references, she knew she'd get the job.

"Waitressing is all well and good, but you have so much more to offer," she reminded herself, at least according to her dad.

Every time she thought about sticking with the familiar, what she both enjoyed and loved, she forced herself to remember "the talk."

"Fiona," Rudy had told her just weeks after her mother's death. "It's time for you to live up to your potential. You need to grow up, settle down and get a real job, you know, one with higher prospects. And quit dating these losers and find a husband, one who is suitable..." It had been difficult to hear because gaining her father's approval had never seemed to take much effort. Growing up, her sisters used to tell her it was because she was the baby, but Fiona always suspected it was because she made the least waves.

Locating her phone, she read the text from her sister Peyton:

How's it going? Do you like him? If you're still on the date and having fun do NOT respond! I hope I don't hear from you for at least three more hours. Xo

Fiona chuckled. One of the good things about husband shopping was the reconnection she'd forged with her sister Peyton. Fiona adored all her sisters, but Peyton had always been a bit extra special to her. Fiercely protective, devoted and helpful, she was like a second mother. Understandable, considering Peyton was the oldest and Fiona the youngest with their triplet siblings, Lily, Amanda and Georgie sandwiched in between. They'd been close when they were growing up, and the distance between them these last few years had been difficult. A distance, Fiona now understood, that had been due to Peyton's struggle with the secret she'd kept about the truth of their biological father.

She typed out a quick reply: Responding…

Peyton's reply was immediate: Seriously? Darn!

Chuckling, Fiona answered: Tell me about it.

Peyton fired back with a pep talk: I'm sorry, Fee. But don't be discouraged! This was only your first date. I want to know EVERYTHING so call me later. She'd added a kissy face emoji that made Fiona's heart swell.

Fiona sent a heart and a thumbs-up. Inhaling a deep breath, she took a moment to let the cold Montana air thoroughly expand her lungs. Growing up in San Diego meant she'd had limited experience with ice and snow. Another benefit of being a professional server was that, if you were a good one, you could get a job pretty much anywhere. A situation she'd taken full advantage of in the nearly ten years since graduating from high school, gravitating from one sunny enclave to another.

Santa Barbara had been her last and favorite place to reside, due in large part to Ivy. A pang of longing sliced through her at the thought of her best friend and longtime roommate. Ivy had recently gotten engaged and was making plans to move in with Andrew, which meant Fiona would have to find a new place to live or a new roomie anyway.

Those circumstances, "the talk," the discovery of her new family, and Lily's subsequent engagement and relocation, along with the positive experiences had here by Amanda and Peyton, made moving to Falcon Creek a natural fit for her new life goals. Except for the cold. The cold she had not fully anticipated. Or the decided lack of ocean and golf courses.

Okay, so she missed the weather, the beach, golfing and Ivy.

Since arriving in Montana, she'd been telling herself that she needed to give the wintry climate a chance. The snow was beautiful. If she could just shake the feeling that it was some sort of evil entity out to get her. It's only a season, she kept telling herself. Surely, there were delightful things about it she had yet to discover. Just like this charming town, the gorgeous ranch and her new family, the weather was an adventure to enjoy.

"I MISS THIS SKY," Simon told his cousin Ned early the next morning. They both paused to look up from where they'd been packing supplies into the horses' saddlebags. The horizon was painted in brilliant slashes of orange, purple, red and yellow across a shimmering blue canvas of sky. "The sun doesn't light the sky with color this way anywhere else on earth. At least, nowhere I've been."

"I don't know..." Ned gave his head a slow, thoughtful shake. "The sun setting over the ocean is an awfully pretty sight."

"That is true," Simon agreed, making a final adjustment to the saddle. He liked California, too. He'd liked it almost from the first day when, as a surly teenager, his parents had shipped him and his siblings there. That same surliness had teamed up with stubbornness and hadn't allowed him to admit it for way too long because, while he'd liked aspects of the place, it wasn't Montana.

He still felt guilty about the emotional torment he'd then proceeded to inflict upon his grandparents. Similar to the torture his little brother was putting him through. Mica, however, was far too old to be so irresponsible. Simon's rebellion had been deeply rooted in his parents' dysfunction and aggravated by homesickness.

At sixteen, Simon had been living with his family—sister, Colette; brother, Mica; alcoholic father, Philip; and champion enabler of a mother, Becca, on a ranch in a neighboring county. As the oldest, and because of his dad's drinking problem, Simon was already bearing an inordinate amount of the ranch's workload. He'd known they were barely scraping by, but he'd had no idea how deeply they were buried in financial trouble. Not until the day his parents announced they could no longer afford the ranch. They were selling the property and getting a divorce. Simon and his siblings would move in with their grandparents in California "until things were settled."

Things were never settled. For Simon, it

had felt like his soul had been torn apart and the biggest portion left behind. Summers in Montana working on his uncle Dean and aunt Jeannette's ranch, and other ranches where he could score work, had been the highlight of his teenage years, and his saving grace. Simon would do anything for Ned, as evidenced by the temporary pause he'd placed on his own life to help his cousin.

"Val is already talking about our next visit."

"That's fantastic. You know you're welcome anytime. Seems like a good sign that she's looking forward to things." Simon put one booted foot in the stirrup, hoisted himself up and settled in the saddle.

Ned quickly followed suit with his horse. "I think so, too. You sure you're okay riding her?" Ned nodded at the roan quarter horse mare Simon was riding.

"Absolutely. Val and I talked about her a lot. Tilly and I are ready to do this."

Six weeks ago, Valerie had been out trail riding on Tilly when the horse spooked and bolted. Thrown over a steep drop on the edge of the river, Valerie tumbled down and landed on the rocks below. The fall resulted in fewer injuries than one might imagine: three cracked ribs and a broken leg. Doctors credited the helmet she'd been wearing for avoiding brain trauma and the brushy embankment for slowing her descent.

At the time, Ned and Valerie had owned the Silver Stake for less than a month. An injury Ned had sustained during his time in the Marines had left him with an artificial knee and a bad case of arthritis in his ankle. Knowing his body couldn't handle a lifetime of ranching, they'd downsized their ranch, selling off a portion of the land and livestock, except for Val's horses. They'd borrowed, scrimped and saved, and then used every penny to buy the Silver Stake.

Simon had arrived the day after the accident and then stayed to keep the Silver Stake afloat and help Ned with the horses until Valerie was back on her feet. Valerie was a horse trainer, specializing in rehabilitating abused horses and breaking bad habits in troubled ones. Simon didn't possess the gift to Val's extent, but he was excellent with horses and possessed enough skill to help with exercising them while she recovered.

"Anything else you miss about this place, besides the sky?"

"Your parents. You and Val."

Ned snorted a frosty sigh. "You know what I mean."

"I do," Simon answered evasively, and urged

Tilly into a walk. Because the truth was a lot more complicated than he cared to discuss. He did miss specific aspects like the sky and the mountains, uncrowded spaces, horses and ranch life in general. But the good memories were tightly bound with the painful ones. Like trying to untangle fine silk that's been woven with razor wire, it was impossible to separate the two and come out unscathed. Not that he'd tell Ned that. And, honestly, the worst thing about being here, with Ned and Val, was how it made him yearn for things he'd never had. Things he'd long ago accepted that he never would.

CHAPTER THREE

TUCKED COZILY BENEATH the fluffy down comforter that topped the bed in her one-room cabin on the Blackwell Guest Ranch, Fiona reached for her phone and sent a text to Lily. Her sister currently divided her time between a nearby cabin and her fiancé Conner's ranch. Good morning! Do you want to have a spot of coffee and some sister time this morning?

Lily responded in a surprisingly prompt manner considering where she revealed herself to be: I'd love to! But Conner and I are working with the mustangs. Can we try for this evening?

Disappointment stole over her as she realized that wouldn't work. She had another date this evening—her fourth. So far, none had yielded the desire for a second meeting. Hopefully, with dates lined up for the next several days, that would soon change. She considered filling Lily in on her progress but didn't want to interrupt her any further. Fiona knew how hard her sister was working to learn to train horses. Besides, she'd called Peyton after each one and received enough sister sympathy and encouragement to carry on. There was no point wallowing in defeat. She much preferred sharing when she had news that was worthy of celebrating. Considering the promising lineup, that could be soon.

She typed out a quick answer: That's ok! Can't tonight. But we'll make time soon. Have fun!

Fiona stared at the time and marveled at how early life began on the Blackwell Ranch. The sun was barely up. Lily used to share Fiona and their sister Amanda's love for sleeping in. Apparently, those days were gone. She couldn't believe how well Lily had adjusted.

Fiona had dropped off résumés all over town the last few days, including Falcon Creek National Bank, where they were hiring a teller. Yesterday she'd met briefly with the assistant manager, who said they'd email her an interview time. That felt encouraging. But she doubted she'd hear back from anyone quite this early. She adored her cozy cabin, especially the soft bed, and gave another hour of sleep serious consideration.

She'd hoped that staying temporarily on the ranch would enable her to get to know her new Blackwell kin. So far, that hadn't happened. Understandable, she told herself, considering how busy they all were. Life on a guest ranch, especially one that was an extremely popular wedding venue, gave the word *busy* a whole new meaning. And she'd been preoccupied, too, what with the simultaneous job hunting and husband shopping.

Determination to change those circumstances had her up and moving. Thinking about the experiences her three sisters had had on the ranch over the last few months provided further encouragement. In addition to Peyton falling for her hot bodyguard, Matteo, Amanda and her sweetheart of a best friend, Blake, had finally declared their love for each other. And Lily! Lily had started it all by running out on her wedding day and meeting a sexy cowboy named Conner—instead of marrying her best friend. And now she was *marrying* that cowboy. A holiday wedding was in the works. So romantic.

Finding out how to help out around here seemed like a good start, and a way to earn her keep. Quickly she got dressed—or as quickly as one could when outfitting for an arctic expedition—base layer, outer layer, hat, gloves, down jacket, thick wool socks and boots. In the end, it was more of an exercise in sweating and cursing. Finally she bravely forged her way out the door to face what she'd not-quite-fondly begun to refer to as the Great Wall of Cold.

The icy air stole her breath and flagged her recurring concern about the long-term health of her lungs. At least it wasn't snowing at the moment. And, admittedly, the sun hovering lazily above the snow-covered landscape made for a very picturesque sight.

Taking a chance that one or more of her five new Blackwell cousins and/or their wives would be inside the guest lodge, or that someone would know where to find one of them, she trooped across the frozen ground and entered the guest lodge's spacious lobby. Finding the reception area empty, she began peeling off layers as she traveled deeper inside the building. The delicious aroma of strong coffee and the sound of animated voices had her veering toward the kitchen.

"Have you seen Ethan?" a pregnant Katie Blackwell, her new cousin Chance's wife, asked as Fiona came through the door. Katie was foreman of the cattle ranching portion of the Blackwell enterprise. Ethan was also a cousin, a veterinarian with a large-animal practice here on the ranch.

Fiona started to answer when an also pregnant Hadley Blackwell emerged from the pantry holding a giant container of hot cocoa mix. Hadley was the wife of cousin Tyler. Hadley and Tyler operated the guest ranch, complete with a lodge and guest cabins, full spa, a bar featuring an ax-throwing space and a wedding venue. Business slowed for the guest ranch activities in the wintertime, so most of the current lodgers were here for weddings.

Hadley answered, "No. Tyler told me he took off in the middle of the night for Zach Carnes's place. Pregnant mare, I think? Good morning, Fiona," Hadley tossed a warm smile at her. "Coffee is fresh if you'd like some."

"Good morning," Fiona said. "I would like that very much." Crossing the kitchen, she helped herself to a cup.

"Yes, Zach does have a pregnant mare. Two, actually. One of which I'm hoping he'll sell to me." Katie's brow scrunched thoughtfully. "That explains why Ethan hasn't answered my text. I've got a sick heifer segregated out in the barn that I need him to take a look at. You haven't seen him, have you?"

Now Katie *was* talking to her, Fiona realized after she'd lowered her cup from taking a sip. "Oh, no, I haven't." She gestured at herself. "Just got up."

Hadley said, "Jon is stopping by this morning to pick up the beef for Ned and Valerie's fundraiser. He might be able to help?"

Katie nodded. "Good. Yes, he might. He's seen about every type of ailment there is. I'll text him, too. But if you see Ethan first, tell him I need to talk to him."

"Will do. Are you guys going to the fundraiser?" Hadley asked.

"Planning on it. Val Clarke is one of my favorite people. I consulted with her on that gelding that was skittish around the ATVs, remember him?"

"Of course. Juniper, right?"

"Yeah. She spent hours with me and that horse and then tried to tell me I didn't owe her anything beyond the initial consulting fee because it took so much longer than she estimated. Seriously, who does that?"

"Tyler says Ned is about the nicest guy around."

"Oh, he is! That whole family is good people. The Dean and Jeanette branch anyway. Not so much the Phil and Becca branch, but they've been gone a long time."

"But Simon is Ned's cousin, right? Isn't Simon from the Phil and Becca branch?"

"Yes, but apparently he's reformed. He's organizing the fundraiser."

"Reformed?" Hadley asked.

"Mmm-hmm. A bit of a, um, wild one in his youth. Big E will tell you a story about Si Clarke," Katie added with a shake of her head.

Fiona thought Katie's expression suggested

more amusement than disapproval, but she didn't know her well enough to be sure.

Hmm… Fiona smiled to herself, wondering how Simon would feel about being the subject of that same small-town grapevine service he'd offered to her. Either way, this information about him did not surprise her. An image of the bartender's mischievous smile and flashing blue eyes danced before her. She could easily picture him as a wayward teen. Why did she have such a soft spot for misfits and troublemakers? Correction, she *used* to have a soft spot for them.

"Where is this fundraiser?" Fiona asked, intending to make sure she stopped by.

"At the Silver Stake—it's a restaurant and bar in Falcon Creek."

"I know the place." Fiona didn't add exactly how familiar she was with it or its handsome bartending, troublemaking, fundraising organizer. "Excellent coleslaw."

"I agree! It's Chance's favorite, which reminds me," Katie said, glancing down at her watch. "Chance wants me to hear a song he's been working on before I check on the horses. Izzy is working with that mustang colt that Conner purchased at the auction, the one I told you about with the white star on its forehead. He's turning out to be a dream. And I have a doctor's appointment this afternoon." She added a little groan of frustration. "How is this morning getting away from me so quickly?"

Fiona tried not to gape as she imagined what it would be like to hear a song by Chance Blackwell before anyone else. She still couldn't believe she was related to the music star.

Katie asked Hadley, "Any chance you can tend the zoo this morning? Izzy is on her way to Billings to pick up those new cattle guards and I am running seriously short on time."

Fiona assumed she was talking about the petting zoo. Tyler had shown her the lovable menagerie a few days ago when she'd first arrived.

"Shoot, Katie, I'm sorry. I can't. I slept in an extra half hour, and now I'm running behind, too," Hadley said. "With the wedding today, I am absolutely swamped. We've got two people out sick and Tyler had to run into town to pick up a delivery from Brewster's. Stuff we need for the wedding. The flowers and cake are on their way, and I still need to set up more tables."

"Can I feed them?" Fiona asked.

"Oh." Katie frowned and shifted on her feet. "Um, I don't know… Do you have any experience with animals?"

"I love animals, if that helps?"

"You're our guest here," Hadley said. "We couldn't ask you to do that."

"This is a guest ranch, though, right?" Fiona countered cheerfully. "Isn't that the point? For guests to get a taste of real ranching life? I'd like to help out."

"It is, but our guest work is designed to be fun. We wouldn't ask our regular guests to do something like this."

"It can be kind of a chore," Katie added with a slight grimace, but Fiona thought she detected a hopeful edge to her tone.

But it was the guest comment that pushed her over the edge; she didn't want these people to think of her as a guest. She wanted them to think of her as family.

"I am not afraid of a little hard work, I assure you." This was true. She and all her sisters had adopted the strong work ethic of their parents.

Katie and Hadley exchanged one of those speaking-without-words kinds of looks that reminded Fiona of the silent communication she shared with her sisters. A combination of longing and envy had her determined to make a good impression. Luckily, making good impressions was one of her strongest traits. A skill she was counting on to land her a job, help her find a husband and ingratiate herself into this family of Blackwells.

"Seriously, you guys, I'm sure I can handle it. How hard can it be?"

"Obviously, since this is a petting zoo, every critter is used to people," Katie said a short time later as she finished giving Fiona brief instructions. "They're harmless and love attention. The goats can be a little demanding about getting the affection they think they're due. It's pretty cute if you know their intentions ahead of time."

They were standing in the feed room located inside a large barn. The barn contained the animals' stalls, adjacent to their corresponding outdoor pens. Katie explained how Tyler had installed solar-powered doors on the stalls that opened at daylight, saving the trouble of having to turn the animals out each morning.

"Clever," Fiona commented.

"It's been wonderful," Katie agreed, and then began to explain the animals' eating habits. The amount of detail made Fiona begin to wonder if she should be taking notes.

She must have given away a trace of her uncertainty because Katie added, "Don't worry if you can't remember all of this. Here's the important part." She pointed at a laminated sheet of paper on the wall above the light switch. "When we first started the zoo, Ethan's wife, Grace, was working here. She's a CPA. Very organized. She made this chart detailing what type of feed and how much they get, and if they need supplements or medication—that kind of thing. With recommendations from Ethan, she still updates it regularly."

"Got it," Fiona said, her appreciation for the well-oiled machine that was the Blackwell Guest Ranch rapidly growing.

"Everything is labeled, but if you have any questions, just shoot me a text. I'll have my phone handy anyway, waiting on Ethan or Jon to get back to me."

"Will do. Got it. Go and do your thing."

"Okay, great," Katie added with a relieved smile. "Thank you, Fiona. This is super helpful. You are saving Hadley and me a ton of precious time."

With a quick goodbye she hustled off, leaving Fiona to once again marvel at the stamina and agility of the pregnant Blackwell women.

Fiona studied the chart and decided to start with what she perceived as the easiest of the critters and work her way through from there. Hedgehogs and rabbits seemed the least intimidating, so she loaded the wheelbarrow with assorted hay, pellets and greens from the fridge, double-checked the list and went to work.

Which went swimmingly, if she did say so herself. The bunnies were adorable and friendly, the hedgehogs funny and cute. Moving on to the next pen, she found herself delighted by the inhabitants. Who knew goats had so much personality?

"Well, good morning to you, too, sir," she said with a laugh as a black-and-white one jogged toward her while bleating out an enthusiastic greeting. Bowing his head, he gave her an affectionate shove. She patted his neck, which then earned her an armpit nuzzle. Chuckling, she asked, "What'll it be, guys?" Another one nipped her pant leg. "Oh, your usual alfalfa and oat platter, huh? Coming right up…" Fiona served their breakfast along with a buffet of ear scratches.

The llamas were charming and polite if a bit standoffish. The mini donkeys instantly became her favorite. Crowding around her, they nudged her with their velvety muzzles, seeming more interested in back rubs than breakfast.

The pigs were next. And easy, Katie had informed her, because you could just dump their food in the trough without even going inside the pen. And that was her intention. Until they all lined up along the fence just as Katie said they would, snorting and sounding so darn cute she could barely stand it.

"Smitten after one snuffle," she said, as they seemed to eye her curiously. "Must love pigs. How would that look on my PartnerUp.com profile?"

That's when she noticed one smaller piglet on the far side of the pen. It was lying on its side, facing away from the crowd. A spike of concern shot through her. Thinking the smell of breakfast would rouse it, she dumped their special mix into the trough. The crew arranged themselves shoulder to shoulder and happily began munching on their feast. The prone pig stayed put.

That didn't seem normal, did it? Briefly she considered texting Katie. But bothering Katie would defeat the purpose of her helping. Instead, she grabbed a bag of the apples Katie said they liked and slipped inside the pen. Before she was even halfway to him, the small guy suddenly rolled over, sprang to his feet, sniffed the air and jogged over to join the others at the buffet.

"Sleeping in, huh?" she asked, and chuckled. "A pig after my own heart."

Assured that all was well, she scattered around some apples and exited the pen. When finished, she rolled the wheelbarrow back to the feed room where she stowed the tools she'd used, tidied up the surroundings, and made sure the lids were on all the various barrels and containers. Exiting the barn, she took a moment to proudly survey her handiwork.

"A veritable zoo of happy diners." She couldn't resist pulling out her phone and taking a quick video to send to her sister Georgiana. Georgie was the only one of her sisters who'd yet to see the ranch or meet their new family. Fiona was on a mission to change that.

"Look at me, rockin' the ranch life," she said as she typed her a message. "Clearly, ranching is in our blood!" That would make Georgie chuckle. And wow, it felt so good to finally feel useful.

Speaking of ranch life… Her gaze was drawn to the stunningly beautiful scenery around her. Jagged, snowcapped mountain peaks glowed in the distance. Two people rode horses in a nearby field. A perfect morning to explore, she decided, and wandered away from the barn.

It wasn't until later, when she finally made her way back toward the lodge, that she discovered the destruction she'd wrought.

RANCH EXPLORATION PROVED fascinating, and time passed like a flash. Enough time that she found herself considering whether to head to her cabin or venture farther afield. Funnily enough, she wasn't even cold. If she didn't feel such a pressing need to find a job, she probably would have opted for a longer outing. But she needed to check her email, take a shower and review her dating profile "ups." That's what PartnerUp.com called it when two parties both clicked the up arrow expressing their interest in each other.

The lodge came into view. Fiona could see the wedding preparations had shifted into high gear. A white van was parked next to the side entrance of the grand old renovated barn where receptions were held. The place was pure rustic chic, boasting tall ceilings with exposed rafters and refinished barn-board floors. A billion twinkle lights and strategically placed candle sconces created a warm, peaceful atmosphere. Lily was so lucky to be having her wedding amid such peaceful sophistication.

The van's back doors were open, giving her the impression that it had successfully transported one of those deliveries Hadley had mentioned. Clearly, everything was coming together, and Fiona felt relieved on Hadley's behalf. She couldn't imagine how stressful her job must be—shouldering the responsibility of ensuring the happiest-day-of-my-life for so many eager couples. Talk about pressure.

Fiona got close enough to note the cute bear on the side of the van, along with the business name, Maple Bear Bakery. She adored wedding cakes. She'd designed her own in her mind a thousand times—a three-tiered strawberry cake with lemon cream frosting. Real frosting, too, none of that dried out fondant for her special day. People were gathered around the back of the van. Must be some cake. She couldn't resist detouring to sneak a quick peek.

But as she neared the scene, it didn't take long to realize the mood was anything but blissful. Off to one side, an older lady had her arms wound securely around a younger woman who appeared to be crying. Three women whose scowling faces were at odds with their lovely updos huddled nearby talking in hushed tones—bridesmaids, she'd hazard a guess. Confused and bleary-eyed, two men stood closer to the barn, their gazes bouncing around helplessly.

The sight of such trouble in paradise made her uncomfortable, as if she were spying on a private moment. She turned to leave. That's when she noticed the white chunks and sticky goo smeared all over the ground beyond the van, near the door…

Cake! Her heart clenched as she realized she'd happened upon a wedding cake catastrophe. Undoubtedly, it was the bride who was crying. Fiona felt like crying herself. She'd stick around and see if there was any way she could help.

Hadley and another woman wearing a baseball cap with a bear logo matching the one on the van emerged from the building.

"Hadley—" the woman sounded near tears, too "—I don't know what to say. I know this is going to sound crazy, but it felt like a setup. They came out of nowhere like a…a gang. One of them clipped me right behind the knees. I went down, though I held on to the tray. But then another one just…grabbed the edge of it and I couldn't hang on… Then they were all over. It was a nightmare."

What in the world was she talking about? Who would come out of nowhere and destroy a cake? If this was intended to be a practical joke, it had taken a very bad turn. Someone was responsible and needed to pay! Of more immediate concern was how to fix it. Hadley looked stricken, with one hand braced on her lower back and the other flat across her forehead. There had to be something she could do… Fiona started to move closer.

"I wouldn't if I were you." The voice was

close to her ear. Fiona startled and glanced over her shoulder to find her cousin Tyler. "Hadley is really upset."

Well, duh, Fiona thought. She said, "I don't blame her! What happened? This is unacceptable. Someone screwed up big-time. What can I do?"

Stepping beside her, Tyler grimaced and shoved his hands in his pockets. "Yes, they did, but let's not judge too harshly. There is no doubt in my mind that it was an accident."

"An accident?" Fiona returned indignantly. "The bit I heard sounds like something way worse than that. Like a roving band of cake bandits."

Tyler made a sound like a cross between a snort and a chuckle. "You could call them that, I suppose."

"Tyler," Fiona said sharply, "this isn't funny. What are you talking about?"

"Believe me, I know it's not funny." He exhaled a loud sigh. "The pigs got loose."

"Are you telling me pigs did this?" The idea, while inconceivable, made the woman's story much more plausible. "They ate the wedding cake? But how…?"

"That's not even the worst of it." Tyler blew out a defeated breath. "You should see the reception hall. They got in there, too. Knocked over tables, broke some expensive bottles of champagne in the process, ate everything that was even remotely edible, including the appetizers, the birdseed baggies, napkins, even some of the flowers."

"But how…?"

Shifting his glance toward the horizon and then back to her, he explained, "It appears that someone went into their pen this morning but didn't quite get the latch closed on the way out."

"Who would…?"

"An accident," he repeated firmly, his eyes now firmly glued to Fiona. Her mind quickly worked through the scenario.

She gasped as the realization hit her. "I did this?" She squeezed her eyes shut and let the full force of her negligence wash over her. "I did this. I need to—"

Again she started to take a step forward, but Tyler snagged her elbow. "Nope. Let's not. Fiona, I can only imagine how you're feeling but, trust me, Hadley is worse. And she's, um, extra emotional these days."

"Of course." Fiona nodded, blinking away her tears. She had absolutely no right to cry here. "I wouldn't want to talk to me, either. But what do I do? There's got to be something I can do."

"Honestly, nothing. My advice to you would be to just lay low for a while."

CHAPTER FOUR

TINY FLAKES OF snow swirled and danced across the frozen sidewalk, making it difficult to tell if they were falling from the sky or blowing on the wind. Chilled but satisfied from taking care of business, Fiona emerged from Maple Bear Bakery the next morning, and, after gazing longingly into the window of Mountains Past Antiques, hurried down Back Street, where she ducked into the Misty Whistle Coffee House and hoped she wouldn't run into anyone she knew.

Not that she knew very many people yet. So far, she'd managed clandestine visits to the bank, Pots & Petals, and Maple Bear Bakery. The outing had left her with an emergency credit card strained to its limit and an envelope of cash buried in the bottom of her bag. After ordering a cup of coffee, she took a seat at a table in the back by the window.

Fiona adored the Misty Whistle. Housed in the town's old train station, the original bronze steam whistle was displayed out front. Stunning hand-drawn maps, faded newspaper clippings and engineering memorabilia decorated the interior. The hardwood floors were worn and scarred. The tall open-beamed ceiling and oversize windows gave it an airy feel. Café-style chairs upholstered in deep red leather were arranged around small round tables. Despite the purpose of the day's mission, she'd enjoyed the impromptu walking tour of the quaint downtown. Old brick buildings stood shoulder to shoulder with structures of wood and stone, all hinting at stories that she was dying to hear.

A check of her phone revealed a text from her best friend, Ivy:

Haven't heard from you for a couple of days… Should I be afraid of what that means? Here's a fuzzy dose of happy. Just in case.

Tears pooled in her eyes, which she blinked away. Fiona didn't like to complain. Rather than vent, she tended to retreat when life went less than smoothly. Ivy knew this about her. She also knew her weakness for turning to cute and uplifting videos in times of despair. Fiona realized it was no coincidence that this one featured kitten hijinks, one of her favorite subjects. Tapping the play button, a montage of tiny, adorable fur balls napping in places where they didn't quite fit, like in shoes, cookie jars and houseplants, or sprawled on top of things where they shouldn't be, like computer keyboards, guitars and giant dogs.

Grinning, she texted Ivy:

You know me so well. This video could not have come at a better time. You made me smile when I didn't think it was possible.

The phone rang in her hand. Fiona answered, "Hey, you."

"I knew it!" Ivy said. "I knew something was wrong. What's going on? I told you that name, *Blackwell*, sounded menacing. They're jerks, aren't they? Do I need to come out there and adjust some attitudes? Kick some cousin butt?"

Ivy's concern pierced her heart. Fiona stifled her tears and told her friend everything, starting with her round of failed dates, moving on to her unsuccessful job attempts, and ending with yesterday's pig fiasco that had stalled her attempts to bond with her new family.

"I am so, so sorry, Fee." Ivy's tone oozed sympathy and immediately made her feel better. "Those pigs are the jerks. That's why the only pigs I socialize with are the ones I order as part of the breakfast special," she joked.

Fiona snorted out a weepy laugh.

"Your cousin was right, it was an accident. You know that, don't you?"

"Yes. Sort of. I don't know… Accident or not, it was still my fault."

"What are you going to do?"

"Tyler told me to lay low and not do anything, but that's not possible. I already paid for the cake and the flowers. The food is next." It had taken half of her remaining savings and her emergency credit card, but she'd done it. She'd gone to the bakery and the florist, and, fearing Hadley would protest the gesture, Fiona had asked that the ranch not be notified. And if—when—Hadley inquired about the credit to their account to please not divulge the source. A careful calculation of the remaining food costs had totaled almost the rest of her savings. She'd withdrawn the amount in cash, which she'd slide under Hadley's office door tonight when everyone was in bed. "Or, at least, I paid for part of it. I had to put the rest on my credit card."

"Oh, jeez. That is so…nice. And so *you*, Fiona. You're such a sweetheart."

"I had to. I couldn't live with myself if I didn't at least try to make up for it a little.

Imagine how upset you'd be as the bride. Thinking about the fact that I'm responsible for ruining some bride and groom's special day makes me sick."

"I don't even want to know how much that all cost."

"Me, either," Fiona managed to joke. "Believe me, the irony is not lost here that I came to Montana excited about the idea of paying for a wedding. I just didn't realize it wouldn't be my own."

Ivy laughed. "Do you know how much I love you for joking about this? Speaking of money, still no luck with the job hunt?"

Fiona ground out a frustrated sigh. "No. I have an interview at Falcon Creek National Bank for a teller's job. I have no experience, but it's in this great, really old brick building with the original vault inside. The place is absolutely jaw-dropping, so you know, fingers crossed."

Ivy chuckled. "Of course you're going to tell me all about the old building. Where else did you apply?"

"The town is super cute. Everywhere. The school, the library, White Buffalo Grocers, a dentist and other office-y places I can't even remember right now... The problem is experience. I don't know how to do anything but waitress. I'm sure I could get a job at a couple of different restaurants." Which was getting more tempting as each day passed. It was harder than she'd thought it would be, fighting the familiar.

Speaking of which, noises were now coming from Ivy's end, which made hearing her more difficult. A car door closing, the sputtering static of wind in the phone's speaker and finally a muffled roar. Familiar sounds, they spiked a twinge of yearning that felt suspiciously like the ones she'd experienced the first year she'd gone away to golf camp and nearly quit due to an acute case of homesickness.

"Where are you?"

"Don't ask." A dog barked.

"Are you at the beach? Is that Alistair?"

"I told you not to ask. Alis, please don't roll in that… Good boy! What about your family's ranch? Could you get a job there? Maybe work off the cake and stuff?"

"Maybe. But it's wintertime so there's not as much going on. And honestly, I'd rather not. They already won't let me pay for the cabin where I'm staying, which is wonderful and incredibly generous. But it also creates a sense of urgency to get a job and find my own place. I don't want to be the family freeloader, in addition to the wedding destroyer."

"I understand. You'll find something. You are the most adaptable person I've ever met. Not only that—everything you do, you do with a smile on your face."

"I know. I just…" Her throat went tight, cutting off the rest of her words. Uncertainty swept through her with the force of an ocean wave, knocking her off balance and leaving her head swimming. "It's just… This is so much different than I expected."

"Oh, Fee…" Ivy said. "It's okay." Mad Alistair barking ensued. "Alis is telling off a seagull for trying to steal his… I'm not sure what that is, but I am certain that I don't want to touch it."

Fiona laughed.

"Seriously, listen to me, sometimes things don't work out like we plan, but that doesn't mean they don't work out. Besides, you can always come back to Cali."

"Thanks, Ivy. You're right. I can do this. Kiss that adorable mutt for me."

"You can. I will. In the meantime, I'll keep the videos coming your way."

"Wow." Fiona's latest "up," Drew Ramos, leaned in to rest his forearms on the table between them. "This is going really well, don't you think?"

"I do." Fiona smiled as a combination of relief and hope alighted in her chest. Because it was. Incredibly so. Was it too much to wish that she'd finally found a potential second date on this, her fifth attempt?

She and Drew had been at the Silver Stake for nearly an hour with the conversation flowing nonstop. Drew was intelligent, told engaging stories and had a sense of humor. He wasn't Simon funny, but he had a quick smile and laughed at her jokes. A successful computer hardware engineer, he enjoyed his job, but the overview he'd given was quick, suggesting he wasn't obsessed.

In addition to horseback riding, Drew enjoyed woodworking, canoeing and archery. All of which she found very interesting. He seemed to like her, too, asking questions and taking the time to listen, ponder and comment on her answers. Plus, he was very attractive with sandy blond hair, a neatly trimmed beard and shimmering dark brown eyes that he trained on her in an appreciative but not leering manner. Fiona was fast becoming a believer in the power of the profile.

Feeling Simon's gaze on her, she glanced at him and delivered a quick, reassuring smile. They'd developed a pattern over the last several days. She'd arrive early to the Silver Stake and hang out with Simon until her date arrived. They'd talk about nothing and make each other laugh. Thrilled to discover his knowledge of antiques surpassed hers, Fiona quizzed him about Silver Stake's treasures and the part they'd played in Falcon Creek's history. The clock, she'd learned, had come from a schoolhouse in a nearby town where he'd attended elementary school. Visions of Simon as a precocious, mischievous kid with ripped jeans, tousled hair and a crooked smile left her smiling inside.

The chat sessions, she'd discovered, helped calm her pre-date jitters. Sometimes, there was a hint of flirting on Simon's part that admittedly left her buzzing with awareness and boosted her confidence. Possibly, she was getting a little too fond of that. But she stayed the course, and always made a point to tell him she was here for another date. The information didn't seem to faze him. Of course, he was a bartender. Flirting was part of his job. Probably, he didn't even realize he was doing it.

Not to mention that her fondness for him only proved her dad's assertion that her attraction to not the most ambitious guys was real, and it was a problem. One she was determined to overcome. That didn't mean she couldn't like the guy, though, and Fiona felt relieved to have made her first friend in Falcon Creek.

All week, with the pig debacle delaying her plans to get to know her new family, she'd focused on her objectives—job hunting by day and husband shopping by night. With their opposite schedules, she'd only managed one quick coffee date with Lily. Despite her renewed attitude, enhanced by Ivy's daily video inspiration, encouraging chats with Peyton and her inherently open mind, neither venture had panned out. Her interview at the bank had gone so well and she'd been so hopeful. But they'd ended up going with a woman with seven years of experience. Fiona couldn't blame them for that. Admittedly, a week of failure was making this date success that much sweeter.

Drew went on, "Please, don't think this is just some cheesy line. I swear, I don't say this to women all the time or anything, but you have the most beautiful eyes."

"Thank you."

"They are the exact same color as my mother's."

"Are they?" Fiona queried, tensing slightly as she wondered if that was a good thing or a bad thing.

"Yes," he said, his gaze now lost in hers. "It's uncanny." Fiona felt her heartbeat kick up its pace, but she wasn't sure if that was good or bad, either.

"What is your mom like?"

"She's going to love you." Sitting back in the booth, Drew shook his head while performing one of those can't-quite-believe-my-luck chuckles.

"Is she? That's nice. You and your mom must be close?"

"Heck, yeah, we are!" He delivered the declaration with a little scowl. Almost like he was offended by the question. "You should probably know that my last girlfriend, Debbie, didn't like my mom. It was a serious problem. Ultimately, it came down to my mom or Debbie." He shrugged a shoulder. "And, well, you know, obviously she had to go."

Uh-oh. "Does your mom live nearby? Do you see her often?"

"She lives with me."

Was it her imagination, or had he said this like he couldn't quite conceive of a world otherwise? "Tell me about her," Fiona felt compelled to request, bracing herself for she had no idea what.

"My mother—" Drew's lips curled up into a dreamy smile "—is the most beautiful woman in the world."

What in the actual...what?

"Don't think I'm weird or anything, but she's a total knockout. All my friends are in love with her. It's pretty intense. She literally picked you out for me on the PartnerUp site. She said you seemed 'genuine and down-to-earth.' But she told me if you were overweight, I had to come home to her immediately."

And...game over. Fiona glanced over Drew's shoulder to discover Simon watching her from his spot behind the bar. The panic must have been evident on her face because Simon went wide-eyed.

Lifting one hand, he mouthed, *On my way.*

Seconds later, he was approaching their table. "Hey, Fiona, sorry to interrupt, but your husband called. He wants you to know that he picked up the kids, but the younger three have lice again, so he needs you to stop and get some of that special shampoo on the way home. The three older ones are all clear."

Drew opened his mouth, shut it quickly and then visibly shrank back as if trying to meld into the cushioned booth behind him.

Fiona cleared her throat to cover the bubble of laughter. "Thank you, Simon. I'll do that." To Drew, she said, "Sorry, but it looks like I've gotta run."

"Yeah, sure," he said, and bolted out of the booth like his pants were on fire. "Me, too. I need to, um, get Mom's dinner..." he mumbled, already backing away. "Yeah, look, uh, maybe I'll see you around." Then he turned and power walked toward the exit. Fiona held it together. Until he reached up and scratched the back of his head while he busted through the door like an outlaw on the run.

Satisfied grin in place, Simon slid into the spot he'd vacated.

When she'd gathered herself, Fiona said, "Thank you. How did you know...?"

"The look on your face. What happened?"

"What did I look like?"

"Well, you went from smitten to horror stricken in pretty quick order."

Fiona felt her cheeks heat with embarrassment. "I was not smitten."

Simon chuckled, and that only made it worse. "You liked him. I could tell. And then you didn't."

She sighed. "It's not that I *liked* him, it's that he wasn't...disappointing. At least, until he was."

"Not a love match, then?" Simon inquired, unsettled by the enormous sense of relief he felt at her admission. Watching her on these dates was testing both his resolve and his sanity.

Despite the myriad of distractions and complications from his business in LA and his current work for Ned, thoughts of Fiona were increasingly getting top billing in his mind. Every afternoon, he found himself hoping she'd be back as promised. Without fail, for the last several days, she'd arrived during that lull between lunch and dinner when the place was always the least busy. She'd walk through the door, grace him with that warm, sweet smile, and he'd immediately feel this irresistible pull. They'd settle in for a chat. He'd flirt a little. She'd almost flirt back. Always, they'd laugh. It was the highlight of his day.

Until her next mismatch of a date arrived, and he'd watch as she struggled to get through it and then listen to how it went wrong. Brutal.

"Ha. Not even close."

"You made it a whole hour, though. That's a new record." When that didn't produce a smile, he asked, "Was it really that bad?"

"Hmm." Her gaze narrowed as she pressed her lips together into a thoughtful frown. "That depends, I suppose, on what you think is healthy," she joked. "Because I'm pretty sure the only love match that guy will ever have is the one he already shares with his mother."

"Yikes." Simon laughed. "I'm sorry."

"It's not your fault." She brushed it off like it was nothing, but the disappointment emanating from her suggested it was anything but. "Pretty sure it's mine."

"What are you talking about?"

Her painful sigh seemed extreme, considering the circumstances. "I'm discovering that I'm not great at this."

"I take it by *this* you're referring to online dating?"

"Yeah, have you done it?"

"No. I prefer the old-fashioned way of meeting someone. You know, non-virtually, where I can see my date's unfiltered face in clear focus and feel confident that her skin does indeed have pores and is not actually a plastic mask. Maybe we even have a conversation where I get a sense of whether she can string enough words together to make sentences. And maybe then, if those sentences are interesting, I'll ask her out."

"Me, too!" she cried, and slapped a hand on the table. "This is torture. Don't ever try it."

"Then why in the world do you keep doing it?"

"Because I need to—" Abruptly she cut off the sentence, making Simon wonder what she'd been about to say. She started again, saying, "It seems like an efficient way to meet people."

"Efficient?" he repeated uncertainly.

"Yes."

Simon thought about this for a second, reminded himself that her love life wasn't any of his business and then butted in anyway. Because, seriously, who could resist that kind of allusion? "Why do you need to meet someone *efficiently*?"

"I'm new in town?" she said like it was a guess instead of an answer.

"So? Come on, Fiona, you're…" *Beautiful, smart, kind, funny…* He only barely stopped himself from listing all the things he liked about her. He liked too much about her, he realized. He needed to be careful. Because if she returned the sentiment, that would only complicate matters. He wasn't willing to follow through, so what was the point? "Let's just say that you don't strike me as the type of woman who would have trouble meeting men."

Despite what he told himself about keeping his distance, Simon liked how his compliment made her blush. "Thank you. That's sweet. And true. I don't. I've never had trouble meeting men and finding dates. It's the relationship part where I struggle."

Simon gave her a sympathetic shrug. "Me, too."

She eyed him thoughtfully, but before she could ask any questions, he said, "Why do you think online dating is the answer?"

"Well, my dad thinks I should…" She trailed off and then said, "My grandfather agrees and… Wait, this is difficult to explain."

"Are you sure?" Hitching a thumb toward the door where her date had gone, he joked, "Because it sounds like it's a family event for you, too. I can probably still catch Oedipus Rex. You two might be perfect for each other, after all."

Fiona agreed with a laugh and tried again. "My sister Peyton advised me to try online dating. She's engaged."

Her tone and those carefully chosen words once again prodded Simon's curiosity. Everything about her stirred his interest. "So, your sister met her fiancé online, and you thought it would work for you, too?" That made sense. Simon knew people in LA who'd had good luck with internet dating. He's heard plenty of nightmare stories, too.

"Not exactly." Fiona squirmed a little in her seat, confirming for Simon that she was not being entirely forthcoming.

"What then?" he urged.

"My sister tried to use a matchmaker but ended up engaged to her bodyguard."

"Your sister has a bodyguard?" he asked, not bothering to hide his surprise. "What is she, a rock star?"

"Yep. Well, she did for a while, but like I said, now they're engaged. She's not a rock star. Well, she is to me, but not in the literal sense. But she has an important job, and there were some threats and concern about her safety."

"What sort of threats?"

"It's a long story."

"Lucky for me, I have just enough time for…" Simon paused to look around. There were currently no customers seated at the bar. Three other tables contained diners, but Riley, the Silver Stake's newest and very efficient server, was taking care of them. "One very long story."

Fiona glanced around as if confirming his observation. A slow smile spread across her face. "Okay…" Then she glanced down at the seat beside her and reached into her bag. "Hold on. I'm sorry, I need to check this. I've got a lot going on." Phone in hand, she swiped the screen. "I'm looking for a job, so I'm constantly checking my email."

"You're looking for a job?"

"Yes."

Offering her a job was not a good idea on more than one level. What if she was terrible? More than that, how would he ever be able to stay away from her if she worked here? He was supposed to be keeping her at arm's length. Neither of these concerns stopped him from blurting, "We're hiring servers here at the Silver Stake if you're interested?"

Brow furrowed, she sounded almost disappointed as she said, "I know. I saw your sign and I… Don't be offended, but I'm looking for something else."

"Why would I be offended?"

"You know, because you work here and you're a bartender. Not that there's anything wrong with being a bartender."

"Ah." This struck him as funny, but he managed to squelch his laughter. It would probably be a good time to tell her his bartending gig was only temporary, but first he wanted her to continue with the long story. "I appreciate your sensitivity."

"I wish—" She stopped herself mid-wish. Wide-eyed, her gaze latched on to his, and Simon decided there wasn't much he wouldn't give to hear the rest of that statement. Because he had the sense that her wishes were running along the same lines as his. The question was, why wouldn't she say how she felt? He knew why he didn't. But what was her story? At that moment, he decided that if she admitted to having feelings for him, he wouldn't be able to lie to her about his own.

"What, Fiona?" he prodded gently. "What do you wish?"

Head shaking, she sighed. "It doesn't matter. I appreciate the offer, but I'm going to have to decline."

"Oh-kay…" he drawled in a lighthearted tone despite the letdown he felt. "But working here, you'd be able to hang out with me. And just think, you could try speed dating during your breaks. You could get paid to date. Wait, that doesn't sound very good, does it?"

"No!" she belted out with a laugh. "It does not."

"Okay, scratch that. Maybe you could meet a guy the old-fashioned way. Lots of people meet in bars." At her dubious expression, he added, "But if you insist on persevering with these online meets, I'll be here to rescue you."

Scowling, she asked sharply, "What makes you think I'm going to need more rescuing?"

"Fiona, I—" He started to apologize, but before he could get the words out, she erupted with another bout of laughter.

"I'm kidding, Simon. At the rate I'm currently bad-dating my way through this town, you're going to have to start charging me for your services."

"I am happy to offer you my date-saving expertise for very little charge."

Fighting a smile, she repeated, "Very little?"

"I'll trade you for that story."

"Oh, right." She grinned. "Okay, well, a few months ago, my sisters and I learned that our dad, Rudy, the man who raised us—my four sisters and me—is not really our biological father. We have this whole new family that we never knew about. Soon after that, Peyton started receiving weird threats, so she came here to Montana to hide out on our new family's ranch. My sister Lily was already here because she fell in love with a local cowboy. Amanda *was* here for a while—she came to help Lily with her wedding planning—but now she's back in San Diego. Big E, our new bio grandpa, and our dad, Rudy, are off somewhere in Big E's motor home trying to track down our bio father and—"

"Hold on." Simon stopped her with a hand, palm up and out. "Your new family's *ranch*? Elias Blackwell is your biological grandfather?"

"You know him?" Fiona brightened.

"Yes," Simon said. "Well, I knew him a long time ago. I know his grandson, Jon, a lot better." Good thing she turned down his offer. He could only imagine what Big E would think about his granddaughter working for Simon. He didn't even want to imagine what he'd think about Simon dating her. Not that it would stop him necessarily, but it was an altercation he'd rather avoid. If he needed another reason to keep his feelings to himself, Fiona had just handed it over. With any luck, Simon would be good and gone before Elias and his motor home cruised back into town.

"How well did you know him?" Fiona urged.

"Not that well, although he was a friend of my uncle's. I was a, um, sort of a wild teen. This one time, my best friend and I—" Simon laughed, because really the story was funny now, although he doubted Big E would agree. "We… You know what, that's another long story. Kid stuff, we'll save it for another time. Let's finish your story first."

CHAPTER FIVE

"I'M STILL NOT sure I'm comfortable with this. Looks like you have everything in order, though…" Ned told Simon, glancing nervously around the Silver Stake, where employees were scurrying about, moving the pool tables, and setting up extra seating for the evening's fundraiser. All proceeds were going to Ned and Valerie to help defray the costs of Val's medical expenses.

Simon looked around, too, and decided that everything *appeared* to be proceeding smoothly. The clash and clatter of pans drifted from the kitchen and mixed pleasingly with the sounds of cheerful chatter. Spicy barbecue scent permeated the air. Behind the bar, Miguel and Riley were laughing and polishing glasses. Now, if he could just get Ned out of here before he realized just how deceiving appearances could be.

"Too bad. Too late." Simon grinned and clapped his cousin on the shoulder. "It's going to be so great."

Ned groaned at Simon's lapse into his childhood fondness for rhyming, which he still did on occasion primarily to irritate his cousin. He hoped it would get him moving toward the door. "Okay, stop. You know how I hate that. You sound like a cheerleader."

"I will. If you stop giving me a hard time about this."

"You've already done so much for Val and me. I don't know how we'll ever be able to repay you."

"Come on, Ned, I'm seeing red…"

"Simon, I'm serious."

"Me, too." Simon blew out a sigh. "Ned, if I stayed here in Falcon Creek for the rest of my life and helped you out, I wouldn't be able to repay you and your parents for everything you did for me when I was a kid."

"You're family."

"Exactly," Simon returned quickly. "Thank you for making my point. And for keeping me out of prison."

Ned chuckled. "You're welcome. But prison is kind of an exaggeration—you were a minor. Besides, Dad had more to do with saving you than I did. You're lucky he and Big E were friends."

Speaking of prison, and the Blackwell who'd wanted to send him there, reminded him of an important point. He said, "And just so you know, I'm not the only one grateful to your family. Every bit of the food costs have been covered with donations. The Blackwells donated all the beef—Jon at the JB Bar Ranch, and the rest came from the Blackwell Ranch." That was a relief on more than one level because, clearly, Elias Blackwell did not hold Simon's past misdeeds against his cousin.

Then again, inadvertent updates from Fiona assured him that Big E was still off searching for his son, Fiona's biological father, and might not even know that Simon was back in town. Although Simon doubted it, since the man had always seemed to know everything that went on in this town. "Frank and Cody Goode donated the pork. Maple Bear Bakery made the rolls for the sandwiches. White Buffalo Grocers supplied condiments. Pots & Petals made these centerpieces. Speaking of which, did you see what Riley and the rest of the staff did?" With permission from everyone, Riley had designed the flower arrangements with a donation box as the base and a sign asking that all tip money be deposited there. "The list goes on. You, my friend, are beloved in this town."

Ned swallowed and looked away, clearly choked up by the generosity of his employees and the community. Meeting Simon's gaze again, he nodded. "Do you need any help? You know, with logistics and stuff? You've got enough staff and all that?"

"Don't worry, I got this," he hedged. He did not have enough staff, but he wasn't about to confess this to Ned.

"Are you sure? Because I could—"

"Get going, get out of here. Be a pal, go home to your gal, Val."

Ned scowled and shook his head in disgust. "That's it, you idiot. I warned you. We're no longer family."

"Ha. You can't get rid of me that easy." Simon spread his arms for a hug. "Now, bring it in for a big ol' squeezy."

"SO, FIONA…" JACK QUISP glanced down at the copy of the online application she'd filled out a few days ago for a job at Quisp Brothers Enterprises. It had been less than an hour since he'd called and asked how soon she could come in for an interview for "the job." Since she'd been at the Misty Whistle with her laptop drinking coffee, browsing job postings and checking out her latest "ups," she'd offered enthusiastically, "How about now?" And then she had driven straight to the large, square, attractively faded gray clapboard building located on the edge of town.

A woman with long, dark, straight hair wearing blue jeans, a cool funky-printed sweater and combat boots had met her at the door. She'd introduced herself as Lauren, given Fiona an encouraging smile and directed her into a suite of offices right inside the front door. A cheerful man with silver-gray hair and that wiry muscled look she'd already noted in a lot of cowboys stood from where he'd been seated behind a desk. Fiona shook his hand, and a bout of small talk ensued.

Then he looked up and met her gaze. "Let's chat about the job."

"That would be great," Fiona said, and meant it on more than one level. She wasn't exactly sure what the duties of this "junior technician" position entailed, but she'd been attracted to the salary and the "will train; room for future advancement" aspects. Also, the part where it was a job for which she earned money, something she now needed even more desperately than before.

In addition to the wedding expenses, driving back and forth from the ranch to Falcon Creek for interviews and dates was eating away at her remaining funds at an alarming rate. During the day, she'd taken to hanging out at the Misty Whistle to save on gas. The delicious complimentary breakfast in the lodge had become her main meal of the day. For lunch, she'd pilfer a bagel and a piece of fruit from the morning's buffet and stuff it in her bag for later. At this point, she wasn't much better than those pigs stealing food, was she? Somehow, she'd have to make up for that, too.

Shuffling the stack of papers in front of him, he asked, "What's the best way to deal with snakes, in your opinion?"

Snakes? Fiona thought fast. The posting had said, "Busy, fast-paced environment dealing with a variety of entities and stressful situations." What in the world did they do here that his first question would be about dealing with dissatisfied customers? Possibly, she should have done her homework on the Quisp Brothers. But the listing also said experience preferred and, truthfully, she hadn't counted on getting an interview.

But she was tough; she could certainly handle "snakes." Working in food service meant regularly dealing with all types of people from the gentlest of lambs to the most vicious of snakes. Defusing angry diners was one of her special gifts. She doubted the skill varied all that much from one industry to the next.

"In my experience, I've found that if you ignore them, or more specifically, ignore their bad behavior, and show them kindness they'll usually calm down and leave happy, or *happier*, at least."

"Hmm." Jack peered at her thoughtfully and scratched his cheek with one thumb. "Well, that strategy might be prudent under certain circumstances, but we can't really ignore them around here. We have to deal with them directly. Zero tolerance. Are you okay with that?"

That philosophy appealed to her on a certain level. Although, at least in the restaurant business, unhappy customers usually responded best to kindness. Unless they were just the naturally belligerent type or the drunk type or—worse—both, but, obviously, Quisp Brothers Enterprises was not a restaurant or a bar. A vision of Simon with his disarming sparkly-eyed smile danced before her. Something told her that when dealing with problematic customers, he'd opt for the charm tactic, too.

"Sure, yeah. I'm not *afraid* of confrontation. Whatever your protocol is, I'm up for executing it."

"That's the spirit. Of course, we won't be turning you loose in any dangerous situations right away. Me or Isaiah or one of our experienced techs will train you until you're ready to engage with them yourself. Most can be dealt with fairly easily if you know what you're doing. And our training process is the best in the business, in my humble opinion. But, of course, there's always some risk involved."

Dangerous ones? Hmm. She supposed working with the public could be considered dangerous under certain circumstances. But what type of business was it that this interview led with the topic? She asked, "What kind of risks?"

"Oh, you know, bumps and bruises, bites and scratches, which can cause infection and, on the rare occasion, disease. Then there are those real unruly ones who require extreme measures to be subdued, level fours, we call 'em. You'd be surprised how clever some of these guys can be."

Were they bail-bond agents? Or maybe prisoner transport of some sort? Was that even a thing? "Bites and scratches?" she repeated.

"Occasionally, although we wear protective gear. To be perfectly honest, getting sprayed is the worst. Unfortunately, it's also the most common."

"Sprayed? What kind of spray?"

"Skunk."

"Skunk?" Fiona repeated flatly. This must be something new. She'd heard of pepper spray and bear spray, even carried the former in her bag, but never skunk.

Jack grimaced. "Yeah, it's nasty. Despite what you hear about these tomato juice or vinegar or lemon concoctions, nothing really removes the smell one hundred percent. Or, at least, I haven't found it yet. It's oil based and it lingers."

"So, this spray is like a weapon?"

"For the skunk, I suppose." Jack looked confused now. "But I'd say it's more of a defense mechanism, you know? Like porcupine quills or an armadillo shell."

Oh, jeez... He was referring to the literal spray of an actual skunk. Real animals. Jack lifted his coffee mug, drawing her eye. There was a cartoon skunk with the iconic thick red circle and line drawn through it. The words "Got Stink?" were inscribed above the image with "Call Quisp" etched below. Yep, she was interviewing for an exterminator job. She barely resisted reaching up to scratch at the prickles of embarrassment tingling across her scalp.

"Um, Mr. Quisp, this might be a good time to explain to me exactly what this position entails."

"Sure! What we do here at Quisp Brothers is humanely trap and relocate problem animals. Mostly. There are some, uh, unfortunate exceptions, but we'll get to those later. To start with, as a tech assistant, you'll be out in the field assisting a senior pest control technician."

"Trapping snakes and skunks?"

"Yes, ma'am. And bats, raccoons, porcupines, squirrels and the occasional opossum or coyote."

Bats? A block of ice formed in the pit of her stomach and radiated outward. She was stone-cold terrified of bats. "How interesting," she somehow managed to wheeze through her frozen lungs.

"I think so!" he agreed enthusiastically. "But it's also, you know, not for the faint of heart. It can get pretty…intense. Sometimes the animals we deal with are sick or old or injured— or protecting their babies. That's the worst. And, of course, they don't appreciate being locked up, even though it's temporary. In most cases."

"I understand." Trapping animals. Of course she knew someone had to perform this unpleasant chore, and she was eternally grateful there were people like the Quisp brothers willing to do it. She just wasn't sure she could be one of these brave souls. Could she? She needed to think. The pay was so very good, and she was so very broke.

"Mr. Quisp—"

"Great—"

They spoke at the same time, and when Fiona didn't continue, he went on enthusiastically, "That's great. And please call me Jack, because the job is yours if you want it."

Fiona prodded herself to smile and be grateful. A feat that turned out *not* to be that difficult because, on one level, she was. At least someone had finally seen her potential. She found herself thinking hard about the offer. How bad could it be? Maybe this would help her to get over a lifelong debilitating phobia around bats? Like some kind of being-thrown-into-the-deep-end therapy. That sounded like something Georgie would encourage her to try. Amanda would probably befriend the bats and gently convince them to relocate. Peyton's order that they leave promptly would be obvious.

"Thank you so much, Jack. Can I get back to you tomorrow?"

"Sure. It's not like I got candidates lined up for this job, you know?" He added a chuckle. "Our last three trainees didn't even last a week."

"Really?"

"It's been a real bad year."

"For skunks?"

"Bats." He shook his head. "Ever since that rabies incident out at the Walker ranch, people are skittish…" He continued on with the story. Fiona pretended to listen while an image of a bat entangled in her hair and gnawing on her scalp produced a fresh rush of adrenaline.

They said their goodbyes, and a cold-sweating Fiona promised to call the next day. Remarkably, she made it all the way to her car and was driving on the main road headed toward the ranch before breaking down.

"What am I going to do?" she whispered through her tears. No job. Zero husband prospects. Almost out of money. Which reminded her once again of how badly she'd screwed up with her new family. Loneliness squeezed her insides like a vise. Pulling the car over into a mostly deserted parking lot, she dipped her head to rest on the steering wheel and reassured herself that regrouping occasionally involved crying. She felt hollow inside and just so…incredibly sad. She missed her mom.

Not long ago, she would have called her parents, her mom for consolation and her dad for advice. She could do neither now. Her dad would only be more worried and disappointed. She thought about seeing if she could meet up with Lily, or calling one of her other sisters, but couldn't bring herself to do it. They were all so cheerful and blissful and *happily-ever-aftered*. The last thing Fiona wanted to do was bring them down. Except Georgie, who was so busy Fiona couldn't imagine bothering her with her boy troubles and bat fears. Georgie was busy curing diseases, for goodness' sake. Literally, that's how smart and good her sister was, which offered a tiny bit of perspective but didn't really make her feel any better.

Her reality was still, unfortunately, her reality.

Ivy had heard it all already. And a video, no matter how cute or funny, would not help matters right now. Nor would the suggestion, the temptation, of moving back to California. As if to torment her with that last thought, pellets of snow began tapping against her windshield like tiny frozen crisps of rice cereal. Reminding her that she was hungry, too, and couldn't afford to eat. Inhaling deeply, she attempted to pull herself together.

Mopping her tears took up a whole tissue, blowing her nose used another three, which left her with one to wipe the mascara off her face. For reasons she didn't want to examine, she could only think of one person she wanted to talk to right now. Maneuvering the car back onto the road, she drove toward the center of town.

EVER SINCE HIS senior year of high school, when Simon had decided to get his act together, failure had not been a problem he'd had to contend with. Neither was overconfidence. Tonight, however, the two were on a collision course with his name written all over it. He most definitely had not "got this" as he'd claimed to Ned. Scanning the overcrowded restaurant, he took a moment to call himself every kind of fool as he tried not to panic.

"Simon, what are we going to do?" Riley said, scurrying over to join him behind the bar where she began filling beer mugs from the tap. "We'll never be able to keep up. Michelle called—her son is sick, and her husband is stuck at work. She's trying to get a sitter. But have you seen the line? It's already out the door and down the block."

"I know, Riley. We're just going to have to do the best we can. Hopefully, people will be patient since it's a good cause."

At least Ned had gone home and wasn't here to witness the looming disaster of a fundraiser in his name at the restaurant and bar he owned, but hadn't even had time to run yet. On the one hand, Simon was thrilled and grateful for the incredible turnout. What he'd told Ned was true the community adored the Clarke family. Ned's branch anyway. His own father's not so much. Memories were long in small towns, and that fact had him wondering how many of these people would enjoy witnessing his humiliation. Like Elias Blackwell. Simon threw up a silent thank-you that the man was still out of town. Funny, how those youthful insecurities could arise at the most inopportune moments to chip away at your confidence.

Enough self-pity for one day. He wasn't that same troubled teenager anymore. He could handle this. He was a successful business owner in LA. The problem was that a month ago, when he'd settled on this date for the event, he'd been counting on the notion that by now he'd have hired more employees. The uptick in the economy meant there were job postings all over the surrounding area for experienced restaurant help. Competition was fierce. He'd hired Riley and Vaughn, but then they'd lost two servers to a steak house that had opened in Livingston, a hostess to a nearby pizza kitchen, and a busboy to the new burger place a few miles east just off the highway.

"I'll see if Olivia can come in and help," Riley said, placing a final beer on the tray. She pulled her phone from her pocket and tapped out a text.

"That would be amazing." He knew that Riley's younger sister, Olivia, waited tables at the Clearwater Café. "Tell her I'll pay her."

"Simon!" a familiar voice called from his other side.

He turned to find Fiona beside him and looking…off. It hadn't taken Simon long to learn that Fiona smiled with way more than her mouth. Normally she seemed to light up from within, but right now, a dull flatness had settled over her, replacing the usual glow. And why were her eyes red? Had she been crying? The addition of tight lines around her mouth gave credence to his fear.

"Something is wrong. Are you okay?"

"What?" She seemed taken aback by his assessment. "No. I mean, yes, I'm fine."

She was lying. He thought about calling her on it but decided to see if he could tease her troubles away, instead. For now. At least, until he had more time to talk. "I hope you're not here to meet a date. As you can see, we're a little busy tonight. I don't think I'll have time to keep you supplied with the appropriate amount of coffee and escape plans."

She gave her eyes a respectable roll but couldn't quite squelch her grin. "I can see that. Nope, no date tonight. I actually came here to talk to you, and then when I got here, I remembered the fundraiser was tonight. This is fantastic, right? Did you anticipate this big of a turnout?"

"Not exactly," he said, the statement heightening his anxiety. But despite the chaos raging around him, he felt a sense of joy at her reason for coming here. Especially as it was fueled by her own desire—and not to meet a match.

Forehead bunching, she frowned and scanned the room. "Do you have more help coming in?"

"Nope. Well, maybe—Riley called her sister." Simon hefted the loaded tray. "You came to talk to me, huh?"

"Yeah, to be honest with you, I did kind of have a bad day. I came here hoping you would cheer me up. And you did. So now, I'm going to help you out."

"Oh, really? And how are you going to do that?"

"If you tell me where to find an apron, I'll show you."

CHAPTER SIX

SIMON TRIED HARD to think of a time when he'd felt anything approaching this depth of gratitude for a single act of kindness. Certainly, the time that Ned's dad, his uncle Dean, had bailed him and his best friend, Luke, out of jail. When he was fourteen, he'd decided to try his hand at bull riding and cracked three ribs. Aunt Jeannette had taken care of him while his own parents went off on a bender. Summer before senior year, Ned had driven all the way to Bozeman to pick up him and Luke after they'd run out of gas.

There were many similar deeds he could list and credit to Ned and his family. But Ned was right: they were family. And Uncle Dean's devotion was also due in part to his love for his own alcoholic brother, Philip, Simon's father. Fiona had no idea what she'd done for him here. Which was exactly the point, wasn't it? She was being nice solely because…because that's who she was.

In addition to this, she was also an accomplished waitperson. Like expert level.

How had he missed the fact that she was a professional server? In all their conversations, she'd never mentioned it, not even when he'd offered her a job here. Keeping in mind all the job hunting she'd been doing could only lead him to conclude one of two things: she no longer wanted to be a server, or she didn't want to work here. Or, he felt himself frowning as another option occurred to him. Maybe she didn't want to work with him.

Regardless, this was a mystery he needed to solve because she already looked like she could run the place. No doubt, the time she'd spent here had given her some familiarity with the way of things. Still, she was something to see. Dashing here and there, taking orders without writing down a word, and then delivering them all exactly where they belonged, carting heavy trays loaded with drinks and plates and fulfilling requests for sauces, dressings and condiments without batting an eye. All while smiling, chatting, calling people by their names, and generally looking friendly, composed and unhurriedly efficient—if that last one was even possible under the circumstances.

At that moment, as if she could feel him

watching her, Fiona glanced up from behind the bar where she was loading yet another tray with waters and met his gaze. The look she gave him felt both reassuring and familiar, and yet it was also charged with something else. Something…electric. He couldn't seem to take his eyes off her. Because she also looked… happy.

She winked, and Simon felt himself smiling goofily in return. At least, he felt a little goofy. Off balance and out of sorts, like he'd suddenly been smacked upside the head with what had been staring him in the face all along. He was extremely attracted to his winsome savior, but that wasn't exactly a revelation. He'd been aware of that fact from the second she'd first stepped through the door. What had him reeling now was that his attraction to her went beyond her obvious traits of being witty and beautiful and full of life. How far? He wasn't sure. He just knew that he wanted her to stop this silly dating and choose him. Hefting the loaded tray, she then traveled to the back of the restaurant, where a large group had pushed several tables together. Laughter floated in Simon's direction. Interesting, how easily he could now identify her husky tone through the boisterous din.

On her way back, she detoured to stop in

front of him. "Hey, if you're done making sure I know what I'm doing, you might want to get behind the bar and give Miguel a hand. That group came in not knowing about the fundraiser. They're celebrating a birthday and ordered a bunch of fancy cocktails. I have a feeling the drinks are going to be flowing for a good long while."

"I'll get on it."

"Good." She turned to go, but he stopped her with a hand to her elbow. "Fiona, thank you is inadequate."

The smile she gave him was radiant, and it traveled straight to the center of his heart. "You don't need to thank me."

"Oh, but I do. You have no idea how much I need to do just that. But first, why didn't you tell me you were a professional server?"

With a little sigh, she covered his hand with her own. The feel of her skin pressed to his was like a further balm to his anxiety even as the contact sent a jolt of heat through his bloodstream. He had to concentrate on not pulling her into his arms and wrapping her in a hug.

Riley approached them. "Hey, table four and six need drinks. Fiona, can you get to them? I have got to use the restroom. Simon, where's Vaughn? We've got three tables that need bussing."

"I'm on it," Fiona assured her, "We've got this."

"I'm going." Simon nodded, his confidence strengthened by Fiona's declaration.

"Oh, good, there's Vaughn," Riley said, and scampered away.

Fiona gave Simon's hand a gentle squeeze. "How about we talk about all of this later? I'll stay and help you clean up."

THE FUNDRAISER OFFICIALLY stopped serving dinner at nine that night. It was nearly ten thirty by the time the last of the customers finished their meals and headed out the door. Around midnight, Simon thanked the remaining Silver Stake staff who'd stuck around to help clean: the head cook, Roy; Roy's second in command, Anita; busboy Vaughn; and Miguel, Riley and her sister, Olivia. Michelle had already gone home to her ill son after managing to come in for the busiest hours between six and eight. To make up for being late, she'd brought her mom to help, ensuring the second half of the evening went even smoother than the first. Simon walked to the door and locked it behind them.

Fiona poured herself a glass of water and waited for him to return. As he approached, she lifted a glass in question, and he nodded.

She filled it, too, and headed for the empty booth nearest to the kitchen.

Simon slid in across from her and took a long drink. He set the glass down, and said, "I cannot tell you how much your help meant tonight. This evening was very important to me for a lot of reasons, and I don't know what we would have done if you hadn't shown up when you did. You saved me from disaster."

Fiona smiled, partly because she knew it was true and partly because she felt exhilarated in a way she hadn't since arriving in Falcon Creek. She'd done nothing but struggle and fail since she'd gotten here, and it felt amazing to have this triumph. "Because I know you're not going to let this go, I'll say you're welcome. I was happy to do it. I enjoyed every minute. Besides, you've bailed me out enough around here—it was the least I could do."

"My hovering around your dates with a coffeepot in one hand and a tall tale at the ready hardly compares."

"It does to me," she said, and laughed.

"Which reminds me, what was bothering you earlier when you came in?"

"It doesn't matter now."

"You changed your mind about telling me?"

"I don't know. Maybe. It's embarrassing."

"More embarrassing than arranging a fundraising dinner for my cousin and his wife and not being prepared?"

"Okay," she conceded with a grin. "I had a job interview earlier and finally got my first offer."

"Second. And congratulations, although I'm getting the impression it's not good news."

"Second what?"

"I offered you a job already, so that's your second offer."

"Oh. That's true." And Simon had offered her the job before he'd known she could do it. No matter the reason behind it, that belief in her felt good. Nearly as good as being a key part of the evening's success.

"Why didn't you tell me then that you're an experienced server? I'd like to extend the offer of employment once again, along with a raise."

"Because I've waitressed for a very long time and I've been looking for a change. But you know what? This time, I accept."

"Seriously?"

"Yes, because I don't think I'm ready for a change quite as extreme as the one I was offered."

"What do you mean? What's the job?"

"Put it this way, it's either stinky, possibly rabid animal–trapper or server. And I cannot adequately convey to you my fear of bats."

"Ah," he said with a knowing nod. "The Quisp Brothers. I heard they were hiring."

"I need a job. As tempting as the challenge of becoming an expert bat ninja might be, I'm going to choose the option that I know I can do and that I enjoy." Meanwhile, she'd keep looking for something else. "I can't promise how long I'll stay. But I can work as many hours as you can give me. I *really* need the money. Do you have any idea how expensive a wedding cake is?"

"I do not," Simon answered with a sympathetic smile. He'd already heard her pig tale of woe. "And I can honestly say I hope to never find out."

IT WAS THE darkness of the morning that took Fiona by surprise. Once she left the area illuminated by her cabin's front porch light, it was surprising how quickly the blackness curled in around her, stealing her perspective. Where was the road? Running late because she'd struggled to get out of bed, she'd forgone some of her winter gear, telling herself she'd only briefly be subjected to the cold. Cutting across the field instead of following the path would be a shortcut and had felt inspired in the moment. Not so much now. It seemed like she should have already reached the road.

Picking up her pace, she continued walk-jogging in the general direction of her destination, Hadley and Tyler's house. She could see the lights, which gave her a modicum of comfort. But only the mental kind. A fresh dusting of snow crunched under her feet and the cold air seemed desperate in its attempt to seek out and transform every patch of uncovered skin into ice. This weather was a serious drain on her fortitude, and she was pretty sure Jack Frost had it in for her.

A flashlight would have been a good idea. Wait! She had a flashlight app on her phone! She pulled it from her pocket. Of course the app wasn't on her home screen. With stiff, partially frozen fingers she was trying to locate it, and then, exactly like in a horror movie just before the creature swoops in and carries off the one woman dumb enough to tramp off alone in the dark across the snowy field, a god-awful screech split the air.

"Crikey!" she screamed, flinching and crouching defensively, the phone flying from her hands like a hot potato. Lunging forward to catch it, her feet slipped out from under her and she fell—hard—landing on her hip and the side of her head.

As if mocking her, another screech followed. Lying on the cold ground, the source of the sound occurred to her. Screech owl. Simon had actually mentioned them, asked if she'd heard one yet. He was going to love this.

Taking a deep breath, she forced herself to calm down. Pushing to her hands and knees, she crawled around until she found her phone. Activating the flashlight app, she then climbed to her feet and did her best to brush the snow and grit from her flannel pj's bottoms, all while hoping she didn't lose a finger to frostbite. Why hadn't she at least put on some gloves? And a hat? There was a solid chance her ear had chipped off in the fall because she could no longer feel it.

"Because I didn't plan on crawling around an ice field in the middle of the night," she whispered into the darkness as she hobbled toward the lights of the old house. Relief surged through her when she realized she'd finally stumbled onto the road. Briefly she considered turning back toward her cabin, but even staying on the road it would take forever to walk back, change clothes and drive to the house.

Car defrosting, she'd discovered, was another Montana time suck she hadn't anticipated. And this was not a mission she could abandon. Best to soldier on.

A group text had arrived from Ethan late the night before explaining that Jon's wife, Lydia, had been rushed to the hospital, where she'd undergone an emergency appendectomy. Jon and Lydia lived nearby on their own ranch, the JB Bar. Fiona had met the couple and their four adorable children the first day she'd arrived. In the text, Ethan had invited whoever could make it over to the old house for an early breakfast of pastries and coffee so they could devise a schedule to help Jon and Lydia with the kids while Lydia recovered.

Fiona was both honored and relieved to be included in the message considering her current standing within the family. More than that, she'd felt an instant connection to Lydia and wanted to help. A thing had to be this important to rouse her at such an ungodly hour and prompt her to make this trek.

Shivering, hip throbbing, she finally made it to the house. From the number of vehicles parked in the drive, it appeared that the Blackwell troops had rallied. When her knock on the front door went unanswered, she twisted the knob, found it unlocked and stepped inside. Voices sounded from the depths. Slipping off her boots, she removed her down coat and hung it on a peg next to a bunch of others and headed for the action. As she entered the dining room, she spotted Lily seated at the long, rectangular table and felt a rush of relief. Her sister waved and pointed to the empty chair beside her. A grateful Fiona tried her best not to hobble the remaining distance and slipped into the spot.

"Are you limping?" the always-observant Lily softly asked, her expression growing concerned as it traveled over her. "Why are you all wet? Your cheek is red. And…" Lily reached toward her and patted around the side of her head. "What is this?" Pulling her hand back, she held a liberated object aloft like a piece of evidence. "Why are there bits of hay in your hair?"

"Good morning, sunshine." A smiling Conner appeared and placed a cup of coffee in front of her. "Here you go. Careful, it's really hot."

Conner took his seat beside Lily. Fiona whispered to Lily, "Because there's snow all over the ground and ranch life is hard." Tipping her head, she paused a beat, and added, "And so is the frozen ground, in case you were wondering." Then she leaned forward and smiled gratefully at Lily's fiancé. "Thank you, Conner. If you weren't already marrying my sister, I would propose to you right now." She curled her chilled hands around the mug and took a sip. "And I would return the salutation, but within those words you raised a very important point. Because the decided lack of sunshine, or even ambient light from the sun's attempt to rise, tells me it is the middle of the night and not morning, your greeting does not yet apply. So, I'll just stick with hello, Conner."

Conner chuckled. Lily snickered and patted her shoulder. "Ranching hours do take some getting used to, don't they?" To Conner, she added, "Fiona enjoys getting up early as much as Amanda does."

Fiona snuffled out a mirthless laugh. In a low tone, she joked, "Early does not do this justice. To me, it will still be early in three hours."

Squinting, she then studied with genuine wonder the bodies gathered around the table. Four of her five Blackwell cousins were here, Ethan, Ben, Tyler and Chance along with three of their wives. Hadley and Katie, she'd expected, but Ben's wife, Rachel, was present, too, seated beside him. Like Hadley and Katie, Rachel was pregnant, but not quite as far along. And, like Ben, the woman was wearing a neatly pressed outfit and looking ready to tackle a day of important legal matters.

In fact, everyone appeared ready to ride, so to speak. Even Grandma Dorothy was all smiles as she bustled around the kitchen passing out plates, napkins, utensils, spiced liber-

ally with compliments and "Good morning."
As if, at any second now, she might decide to
burst into song while dancing a jig. How they
could all be so bright-eyed and eager so bless-
edly early in the morning was an absolute mystery to Fiona.

Their attitude reminded her that she'd shown
up wearing a thermal top and her kitty-cat pj
bottoms, now uncomfortably damp and dirty
from her roll on the gritty, snowy ground. Not
to mention the bruise likely forming on her
cheek or the fact that she'd pulled back her
snarly hair without the aid of a brush or a mirror, making her wonder what else had become
entangled in the Velcro-like mass. Under the
influence of sleep deprivation, she'd charged
over here like a kid on Christmas morning
instead of a grown adult meeting to discuss
a family emergency. Seriously, her dad was
right—she needed to grow up.

Lily slid a sheet of paper in front of her.
"Grace made a spreadsheet, so you can sign up
to make a meal for Jon and Lydia or help out
with the kids or drive Lydia to the doctor, et
cetera." Grace, she recalled, was Ethan's wife,
inventor of the petting zoo's master schedule.

Fiona studied the options. Names were already written in a bunch of the spaces. The
sight cheered her, reminding her of the real

reason for the gathering and filling her with a mix of warmth and awe. Emergency notwithstanding, this was what she'd fantasized about when moving here. *This* was family. She scrawled her name in a few empty boxes.

Ethan stood. "Okay," he said, then paused a beat to let everyone settle in to listen. "Now that we know Lydia is going to be okay and we have a plan in place to help her and Jon, we have another problem to discuss. And in case you think I'm being insensitive here, it was Lydia's idea to raise this topic. In fact, she insisted. Thanksgiving is a little over two weeks away, and, as you all know, Lydia had graciously offered to make dinner again this year. Obviously, she's not going to be able to do that now."

Hadley said, "I can—"

"I will—" Katie started talking at the same time.

"Nope," cousin Chance stated. "No way. Neither one of you expectant mothers is going to host this shindig. You're both supposed to be making an effort to stay off your collective feet." He pointed at Rachel. "That goes for you, too, Counselor."

"That's absolutely correct," Tyler concurred.

Fiona had already observed that neither woman seemed inclined to follow this directive.

"Can't we just go out for Thai food?" Ben inquired from his spot at the far end of the table. "You know, like regular people do."

"What *regular* people?" Tyler returned drily. "Who goes out for Thai food on Thanksgiving Day?"

Ben shrugged. "People in New York. When I lived there, I used to work on Thanksgiving Day every year, and I'd have Thai food delivered to the office for everyone. It was a tradition."

"So that would be what? Pad thai and sticky rice for two?" Tyler joked. "You and the doorman."

"Tyler, don't be insensitive," Chance chided in a tone oozing sarcasm. "The order was for three. Don't forget his paralegal, who I'm sure was nothing but grateful to spend her Thanksgiving working alongside the brilliant legal mind of Ben Blackwell rather than enjoying a dinner at home with her family."

Tyler fist-bumped Chance, and they spent a moment laughing together.

"Ha-ha," Ben returned flatly. "You guys are a riot. You'd be surprised how many people work on Thanksgiving Day in New York. For your information, we celebrated. We could see the parade from our building's windows."

"Ooh, the parade!" Tyler exclaimed, clapping with exaggerated excitement. "That totally makes it okay then."

"Ohh..." Ben's wife, Rachel, cooed at him with playful sympathy. "You were so sad and lonely before I came along and saved you."

From the heart-melting look Ben gave his wife in return, Fiona decided that must have been true.

"We don't even have a Thai food restaurant here in Falcon Creek, do we?" Lily asked.

"No, we do not," Ethan answered in a tone that suggested he was ready to get the conversation back on track. "Grace and I briefly discussed going out, not for Thai food obviously, but for Thanksgiving food. Grace did some research, and no restaurant in Falcon Creek is going to be open on Thanksgiving Day."

"Seriously?" Ben asked. "Not one? Someone is missing an opportunity here. I bet if you offered them enough money—"

"That's the way it should be," Chance said, interrupting his brother. "People should not be working on Thanksgiving. They should be home with their families eating a delicious meal."

"And watching football," Tyler added. "Or the parade, in Ben's case."

Ethan got back on track saying, "Both the

Clearwater Café and White Buffalo Grocers will do a heat and serve meal."

Fiona shook her head. Heat and serve for her first holiday meal with her new family? No. Surely, they wouldn't...

"Works for me," Ben said.

"As long as there's mashed potatoes and gravy," Tyler said.

"I know for a fact they make pumpkin pie," Hadley added, laying a hand on her belly. "Which is what this baby loves, so yes."

"White Buffalo's fried chicken is delicious," Katie said. "I don't know why the turkey would be any different. We can—"

"Wait, no!" Scooting forward, Fiona raised a hand. "I'll do it!" This was it! This could be her chance to elevate her status with the family, while saving herself and everyone else from a Thanksgiving takeout meal. "I'll make dinner for everyone."

The room had gone silent, every pair of eyes focused on her. Was it her imagination, or were there varying shades of doubt and skepticism reflected there? How could she blame them? She hadn't exactly burst onto the Blackwell scene in the positive, heartwarming manner she'd imagined. She could only guess what they thought of their unskilled, uneducated, unemployed, perpetually single cousin who couldn't even manage to properly feed the pigs. And now, here she was, in her pj's, wet and dirty, looking like she'd been dragged through the hayfield, offering to organize a holiday gathering. For a second, she wanted to laugh. She might have if everyone wasn't still staring.

Nervously she cleared her throat. "As long as we can eat the meal here, or maybe the lodge? I don't think my cabin is quite big enough for everyone," she attempted to joke.

Tyler, bless him, broke the silence with a chuckle. "No, it is definitely not, you are right about that. And the TV is too small for proper football watching."

Chance added, "We'll need two TVs so Ben can watch the parade."

"Hey, those floats are veritable feats of engineering," Ben said.

Fiona grinned at the playful banter designed to help smooth her way. She loved her cousins, she decided at that moment, even if some of them didn't quite return the sentiment. Yet.

Speaking of which, Hadley answered, "Of course we could have it at the lodge. But, Fiona, are you sure? That's an awful lot of work and—"

"Are you sure you can…" Katie started to ask, then switched courses. "Are you sure you have the time?"

Their uncertainty, no matter how well deserved, made her want to do it even more. She *needed* to redeem herself. She would earn a spot in this new family if it was the last thing she did. "I'm sure."

Hadley frowned but wouldn't quite meet her eyes. Katie wore a worried expression. Grandma Dorothy did meet her gaze, wide-eyed and fearful, not bothering to squelch her obvious and extreme concern. Rachel had gone stone-faced and offered Fiona an out. "There will be a crowd of at least twenty people."

Hadley opened the door a little wider, and said, "More, probably. Our family seems to have a way of growing."

"Can you cook?" Ethan the Practical asked.

"Nice," Tyler said drily. "Jeez, Ethan."

Ethan frowned and said, "I didn't mean it like that. I meant, is this something you've done before? We don't want you to take on more than you can handle. And then feel obligated."

"This is a very generous offer, Fiona, thank you," Sweetheart Chance said.

Straight shooter Ben was watching her with a proud expression that suggested he was impressed that she'd offered at all. Fiona liked that—it boosted her confidence a bit.

"Yes, I can cook." Just wait until they tasted her corn bread stuffing.

"She can definitely cook," her darling of a sister Lily happily confirmed. Under the table, she felt Lily take her hand and give it a gentle squeeze. Lily, who was learning to train wild horses, for goodness' sake. Fiona could certainly handle cooking for this crowd.

This prompted her to boldly toss her gaze and a good dose of eye contact around the table, along with a promise she knew she'd do anything to keep. "I've got this."

CHAPTER SEVEN

GARY BIERMAN WAS a car salesman from Billings. Technically, car salesman was an understatement. He owned three luxury car dealerships—one in Billings, another in Bozeman and a third in Helena. Not a rancher, although he'd grown up on a ranch and now had a stable full of expensive horses. In addition to skeet shooting, bird hunting and collecting cars, riding happened to be one of his favorite hobbies.

"I can teach you how to ride," he said confidently. "I grew up in the saddle."

"That is such a generous offer," Fiona answered carefully, knowing it was way too soon to commit to a second date. Plus, something bothered her about Gary. She couldn't quite put her finger on it and was trying to resist forming a hasty opinion.

She'd just finished her shift at the Silver Stake. Not surprisingly, she loved her new job. It had only been a few days, but she enjoyed the atmosphere, the people she worked with and getting to know the locals. And while she hadn't taken to speed dating during her breaks as Simon had joked, the locale was convenient.

In the short time since she'd clocked out, she'd changed her clothes, fixed her hair, applied a touch of lip balm and settled across from Gary in the "dating booth." That's what Simon had taken to calling the table that had turned into the regular spot where she met her dates.

As if on a schedule, Simon emerged from the back room. After a quick scan of the crowd, his gaze homed in on her, shifted to Gary and then narrowed perceptibly. When he looked back at her, she gave him the "all is well" signal—a quick one-fingered brush to the tip of her nose. Normally he'd respond with a nod and take up residence behind the bar with his laptop. Tonight, though, he ignored her sign and strode straight over to their table.

"Excuse me," Simon interrupted Gary, who was droning on about how powerful the engine was in his new "sport model convertible." She couldn't imagine owning a convertible in this climate and was pretty sure her eyes had glazed over. "Fiona, I need to see you in my office." His features were stark and unreadable. That and his urgent tone caused her a rush of distress. "I'm afraid there's a situation." To Gary, he added, "Sorry, Gary. Date's over."

Heart pounding, head spinning, Fiona followed Simon through the restaurant, down the hall and into his office. For the life of her, she couldn't imagine what could be wrong. Had Lydia suffered a complication?

Ranches could be dangerous. Had another family member suffered an accident? She'd been reading about horseback riding.

Or her dad? A vision formed of Rudy and Big E puttering around the country in that motor home, a venture she'd always had reservations about. They weren't exactly young men. No! Surely, if it was a medical emergency, he would have already said so. Was it work related? Had she offended a customer? Was she getting fired? She couldn't think of a single thing that had gone wrong in the past few since days since she'd started.

Once inside the room, he shut the door behind them, turned toward her and didn't utter a word. Wearing a stony expression, his arms stiff at his sides, tension radiated from him as he inhaled a deep breath. Then another. He seemed…angry? She wasn't sure. She'd never seen him like this before.

"What is wrong?" Fiona asked, shifting to

stand a little closer to him. "Simon, you're scaring me. What's going on?"

He exhaled with a whooshing sound of frustration and gestured in the direction of the restaurant. "You are not dating Gary Bierman."

"Whaatt?" Fiona shook her head, shock and relief coiling inside of her and rendering her momentarily speechless. "My *date* was the 'situation'? Simon, you scared me!"

"Yes." Nodding, he raked a hand through his hair. "I'm sorry, but *that* scares me." He pointed and clipped out his words. "You, out there, flying blind."

"What in the world are you talking about?"

"Fiona, I've been patient, but I've had it. I can't do this anymore. It's like watching a train wreck that I know is coming and yet I can't stop. Or like that movie where the guy lives the same day over and over again trying to get it right. You need to stop this dating thing."

"I need to stop this dating thing?" she repeated flatly.

"Yes!"

"For your information, I *plan* on stopping this dating thing as soon as I find someone suitable to be with. But that's going to be difficult if you send my dates away before I can determine that for myself."

"I…" At least he had the good sense to look

uncomfortable, Fiona thought, as she watched him shift his weight from one foot to the other like he'd just realized the wider implications of what he'd done. The line he'd crossed. "I should have explained better. But I know Gary. He's not right for you."

"He seems very nice," she countered calmly.

He scoffed. "Of course he *seems* nice, Fiona! This was your first date. Even serial killers are notorious for being nice on first dates."

"Are you saying Gary is dangerous?" she queried in the same even tone.

Squinty eyed and impatient, he scuffed a foot and asked, "Are you purposely misunderstanding me?"

"Are you purposely trying to irritate me?" she countered quickly. "You just ended a date for me, Simon. You ran that poor guy off without even consulting me. Don't you think that's overstepping?"

"I'm watching out for you. Fiona, I…"

And just like that, her anger cooled. This was her fault. She'd allowed this. Encouraged it, if she was being completely honest, what with the signals and the strategic interruptions. She'd relied on him too much. They needed to set some boundaries. "Okay, I see where you're coming from and I appreciate your concern.

I've also appreciated you watching out for me. But I never asked you to decide on a date's *rightness* for me."

"I know. Fiona, I know what you're saying. And you're right. I apologize for my…execution. It was presumptuous and maybe a little rude."

"Thank you. Apology accepted. I think maybe—"

Hands out, palms up, he interrupted as if he couldn't contain his frustration. "But why do you keep dating these men who are so obviously and completely wrong for you? I was right about Randall Gemini, wasn't I? Trust me, Gary Bierman, with his expensive Thoroughbreds, Italian loafers and fleet of BMWs, is *definitely* not your type."

That touched a new nerve. She folded her arms over her chest. "What is that supposed to mean? Are you saying I'm not good enough for him?"

"What? No! Everything about him is pretentious and pompous. What I'm saying is that if I didn't know you better, I'd think some uptight social-climbing sorority girl filled out your profile for you." Clearly aggravated and fighting to rein it in, he looked at the ceiling for a few seconds before focusing on her again. In a slightly softer tone, he said, "Gary

Bierman is an overbearing chauvinistic igno-
ramus who thinks women shouldn't work outside the home. Seriously, I've heard him use
the term 'barefoot and pregnant' in reference
to his ideal woman."

That was a valid concern, but for some reason, she could not let this go. A part of her
wanted this protectiveness from him. Another
part of her, the part she couldn't seem to quiet,
wanted it to mean something.

"He's got a good job," she countered.

"A good job? That's your criteria?" He
moved toward her, and Fiona felt her entire
body react, pulse racing, skin tingling, breath
accelerating. Along with rapid confusion as
her brain attempted to make sense of what
was happening here, because it was like she
could feel his body reacting to her, too. Like
a magnetic field was drawing them closer. "In
finding someone..." He tipped his head with
exaggerated thoughtfulness. "What did you
call it—suitable?"

Fiona could only nod because he'd taken another step, right into her space. His gaze thoroughly searched hers before traveling over her
face and neck, and scorching a trail of heat
across her skin. He was so close now that the
intoxicating scent of him surrounded her, en-
veloped her in a mix of spicy cologne with

a hint of the alcohol that she knew he never drank. Why, oh why, could she not have felt even a fraction of this kind of attraction with at least one of the PartnerUp.com men she'd dated?

He cursed softly and then solidly merged his gaze with hers again. Blue and stormy, his eyes were flickering with desire but also curiosity. "What is going on here, Fiona? What woman wants to date a man who is *suitable*?"

"Uppft..." Fiona's muttered response was unintelligible and barely audible. The sound of her rapid, shallow breathing was much, much louder and told Simon everything he needed to know. Her gaze drifted to his mouth and remained there, the same way his had lingered on hers.

Was he "suitable" by her standards? He had no idea. Certainly he would never be good enough according to Big E. He couldn't even begin to imagine all the ways kissing her would complicate things between them. Obviously he wasn't thinking clearly, because he was considering it anyway. No, he was a bit past the thinking phase. Because she needed to get this ridiculous notion of "suitability" out of her head.

Simon brought one hand up, fingers threading into her hair, palm cradling the back of her neck. The other hand he placed low on her hip. Slowly he dipped his head, giving her plenty of time to change her mind. Instead, she moaned softly, shifted closer and wrapped her arms around his shoulders. Nice and tight, so they were chest to chest. It was his turn to moan because she felt even better in his arms than he'd imagined. They fit together perfectly.

And then their lips were meeting in a kiss so flawless it left him reeling. No awkward head-turning or uncomfortable lip crushing, just a seamless fiery meeting of affection and desire. Like they'd both finally accepted the inevitability that had been simmering between them.

Then she deepened the kiss, and Simon felt his world shift. And alter. His pulse rippled through his veins, almost like he could hear his blood sing. Even the beat of his heart felt different, thumping in time to hers. *This*, Simon thought, this was what she should be looking for. This was what he was looking for. Except, he wasn't looking. He was just…showing her that she should want more.

Fiona drew back, and Simon almost protested until he realized her intent. Fingers gripping his biceps above his elbows, she whispered, "Move," and pushed him toward the desk. He stepped back until his legs met the object behind him. Sitting on the edge, he pulled her between his legs.

"That's better," she whispered, and kissed him again. Better than he'd ever been kissed in his life. Simon knew he needed to think about the ramifications, but he really didn't want to. He couldn't, not when he was holding her like this. While she held him right back. And that fact in itself, that someone could make him stop thinking, was completely addicting.

When Simon's phone began to buzz in his back pocket, Fiona shifted enough to whisper, "Do you need to get that?"

Simon grinned against her lips because she sounded as out of breath as he felt. "Ugh. Only if it's my sister." Keeping one arm curled around her so she wouldn't be tempted to move away, he reached into his back pocket with his other hand and removed his phone. "Not my sister," he said, reading a text from his best friend, Luke, who was currently on a golf course in Arizona. "My friend, complaining about his golf game. So interested in how you fixed that slice, thank you, Luke," he said in a wry tone, discarding the phone on the desk behind him.

Adjusting to look at him, she said, "Oh. I love to golf. Do you golf in LA?"

"I do," he said, momentarily distracted by

the news that she liked to golf. He'd never dated a woman who enjoyed golfing. Neither had Luke. They'd discussed many, many times what it would be like to be with a woman who not only tolerated their golf habit but also participated. And now he was holding her in his arms. How much temptation could he withstand?

Luke, his oldest friend from Montana, had a house just outside Falcon Creek. But his job as an airplane pilot meant he traveled a lot, including the regular route he flew to California, where he often stayed a day or two or more at Simon's house. As a result, he saw Luke more than he did his friends who lived in LA. Which was super convenient because he liked Luke more than he liked anyone else. His friend had been out of town working, and golfing, for the last two weeks.

"I also have a good job there," Simon added, fully intending on segueing into a conversation about his business to further convince her of his suitability. He would only be in Falcon Creek for a few more weeks, but he didn't care because they were weeks he would not have to spend watching her date men who were so clearly not right for her. He would love to take her golfing. Not feasible in the middle of a Montana winter, of course, but...

"I wish," Fiona muttered with her face tucked against Simon's neck.

"What?"

"I wish you had a good job so I could just date you."

"You can just date me." Cupping her shoulders, he angled both of them so that she'd look at him. "Tell me that kiss wasn't suitable."

She smiled, but the sadness in her eyes alarmed him. "That kiss was way more than suitable, and you know it. That's not the problem."

"Fiona, I do have a good job. I have another job in LA. I—"

Frantic fingers clasped the front of his shirt. "I know! Simon, *I* know that. If anyone believes that bartending is a good job, it's me. I've been a waitress my entire life. It's just… I'm not sorry that I kissed you, but I can't date you." Expression beseeching, her eyes latched on to his like she was willing him to understand something important and profound. The problem was he had no idea what that was supposed to be.

Then it dawned on him. "Because I'm a bartender?"

"Yes, and no. When I came here to Falcon Creek, I made a promise to my…self that I wouldn't date—" She stopped abruptly. After taking a deep breath, she started again. "That from now on, I'd only date men who are stable and responsible and…"

"Stable and responsible *and*…?" he repeated, urging her to finish. Because if these were her suitability requirements, *check* and *check*.

She nodded toward the sofa against the far wall. "Can we sit?"

"That is a great idea."

Taking his hand, she led him to the sofa. They sat, and Fiona immediately swiveled to face him, drawing one leg up and tucking her ankle under her knee. "Remember when I was telling you about my family the other day?"

"Of course."

"What I didn't mention is the reason I moved here to Falcon Creek."

"To get to know your new family."

"That was a part of it, for sure. But also, I came here to start over. After my mom died, Dad had this talk with me about growing up and getting my life together. I've always been a bit of a…wanderer, I guess you could say. My sisters call me a free spirit, but I'm not even sure what that term means exactly. I've never really known what I wanted to do with my life. I tried college, but it wasn't for me. I had a few very boring office jobs and quit those. I always gravitate back to waitressing. I like it. It allows me to move around and explore new places. And, honestly, it never bothered me. I thought I would eventually figure something out, find my thing career-wise. I enjoy living in the moment, and I never thought that was a problem. I didn't realize how worried my dad was about me. Anyway, during that talk, he pointed out that I need to quit spinning my wheels, focus, find a career and settle down."

"Fiona, that doesn't mean—"

"Hold on, let me finish. I'm getting to the important point. The dating is a problem. I have a history of relationships with men who are…"

"Losers?" Simon supplied, feeling slightly offended but mostly amused.

"That's the exact term my dad used. But I don't really care for that label. Let's go with underachievers." She paused and nibbled on her lip. "Okay, maybe unstable and even unscrupulous or scheming would apply to a few. I think you get the idea." At his nod, she went on, "I tend to listen to my heart and not my head. I also tend to be a bit too supportive. Turns out, this can be a problem in that helping a person too much financially can sometimes lead to a lack of motivation on their part."

"That is true." Simon thought about his own

upkeep of Mica. "How many guys have you supported, Fiona?" Anger coursed through him at the idea of these deadbeats taking advantage of her kindness. He could only imagine how difficult that would be for her father to witness. He thought he understood the intent of this father-daughter talk, if not the result.

Fiona fidgeted with the throw pillow next to her. "Um, I don't think that's relevant other than to say that at one point I had three extra people on my cell phone plan, none of whom I was dating. The point is, I promised my dad I'd get serious about the men I see. My hope was that online dating would weed out these less-desirable qualities ahead of time, allow me to specify what I'm looking for. Peyton assured me it would work, and it has to a degree. All the men I've been matched with have seemed promising."

"Promising?" he repeated, not bothering to stifle his disbelief.

"Yes," she said, her tone a little defensive, "in certain specific ways that I've learned are important."

What in the world was she talking about? He hadn't seen even one guy he thought might be a good match for her. "Did Peyton fill out your profile for you?" That would explain a lot, a sister's good intentions, and "specific ways" not quite translating to the right guys.

Fiona hesitated for a beat before answering. "Peyton made a couple valuable suggestions where I asked for them. But honestly, Big E and my dad did most of it, to tailor my profile toward finding the right guy here in Montana."

"Your dad and Big E filled out your profile?" That explained even more. A man's notion of the perfect man for his daughter might differ significantly than said daughter's. Especially when the dad was a classic military man, as Fiona had described Rudy, and the daughter an independent free spirit like Fiona. Elias Blackwell would also want a certain type of man for his granddaughter—wealthy, well connected, successful. Certainly not the delinquent teenager who'd once been arrested for stealing from him. This would be funny, except that it wasn't. It felt like manipulation, as if Rudy and Big E were coercing Fiona into something she didn't want.

"Fiona, this is messed up. Surely you can see that, right? Allowing someone else to dictate what you want in a partner?"

"No, I do not see it that way! I haven't had any success doing it on my own. I am attracted to the wrong men, Simon. Men who are directionless and financially insecure."

"You think I'm directionless and not secure financially?" he asked, growing increasingly annoyed by this assumption on her part. And with the assumption itself. She already knew him well enough to know that he would never use her in any sense. Worse than that, though, was the notion that she thought she needed to put herself through this to find a boyfriend.

"No. I'm not saying that. What I am saying is that I need to stick to men from the dating site, men who are already preapproved."

"What are you...what?" He could hear the frustration in his tone, and he didn't care. "Are you kidding me?"

"I am at a point in my life where I want to date a man who wants the same things I do. I need to know what they want going into it."

"What things? Fiona, you do not need to subject yourself to this...dating gauntlet to find a good guy."

"Well, what do you suggest I do, Simon?" Frustration had seeped into her tone, too, and he could see it on her face, feel the tension in her body. It reminded him of every bad date he'd witnessed her suffer through, which was beyond exasperating.

"Go out with me! I have to go back to LA in a few weeks, but we could have a lot of fun until then."

"Are you—" She stalled midsentence. "I don't want a guy to *date*, Simon! I don't want to have fun for a few weeks! I am the champion of dating fun, that's the problem. You are not hearing me. Don't you get it?"

"No, I do not see how dating and having fun is a problem." Unless… *Oh no.*

"I want…"

"You want what?" he urged, even as a part of him feared the answer.

"The next guy I date, I plan on marrying." *Marrying?*

Simon felt his entire body go cold. He'd been expecting a word like relationship or commitment or…boyfriend. Which were all bad enough but could be dealt with, especially with the miles that would eventually be between them. But this…this was much, much worse.

When Simon didn't respond, she went on. "Or, at least, I want that to be an option for the future. That means I want to date someone…"

"Suitable," Simon finished for her. "You're right. That's not me." Because he was no longer suitable. Not if marriage was what she wanted.

"Simon, I—"

"It's okay, Fiona." He forced a smile. "I understand. There's no future with me, you're right. And you deserve to have that. You deserve everything you want. I'll see you tomorrow for your shift." And with that, a dazed Simon fled from his own office. Instead of heading back into the bar, he scaled the stairs up to the one-bedroom apartment that currently served as his home away from home, where he tried to sift through the odd combination of relief, anger and disappointment he felt at his own admission.

CHAPTER EIGHT

LYDIA BLACKWELL LOOKED remarkable for a woman who'd undergone surgery only a few days before. "Fiona, I'm so sorry," she said the next morning from the sofa in her cozy living room. She was wearing sweats, but her dark brown hair was swirled and piled on top of her head in a stylishly messy updo that accentuated her lovely features. Her bright smile managed to convey both warmth and remorse as she added, "Looks like I'm not going to be able to show you around town for a while yet."

Fiona placed a cup of herbal tea on the table next to Lydia before taking a seat in the adjacent comfy armchair. She'd arrived early at the JB Bar Ranch for her babysitting gig. Jon and Lydia's twin girls, Abby and Gen, had spent the night with their neighbors, Sofie and Zach Carnes, but Lydia had informed her they'd be home soon. The twin boys, Marshall and Brendan, were staying with the same friends for another night to give Lydia a little more time to heal. She was under strict orders not to lift anything that required much effort, especially her two busy toddlers.

"Please, Lydia, it's not necessary to apologize for your wayward appendix."

"You're right," Lydia said, and grinned. "As women, we do that a lot, don't we? Apologize for things that aren't really our fault. At least, I do." Before Fiona could respond, Lydia provided an example, "Like naughty pigs eating wedding cake."

Fiona felt her cheeks heat with embarrassment. "That was my fault. I left the pen open."

"You mean you didn't get the latch closed all the way. Just so you know, it's not the first time it's happened. That they've escaped. Katie is blaming herself for not telling you about the wonky latch. Hadley is upset because if she hadn't been running late that day she would have fed the animals. Tyler is feeling bad because he asked someone else to fix the latch on the pen and they hadn't gotten it done—and he knew it but hadn't gotten to it himself. Plus, pigs are smart and known for being escape artists. I wouldn't put it past them to have opened that latch themselves." Lydia added a wink.

Fiona knew all of this was supposed to make her feel better; instead, she felt responsible for upsetting even more people than she'd realized.

"Stop it," Lydia admonished with a chuckle.

"I know what you're thinking. It was an accident. Have you seen Hadley lately?"

"Only briefly." And not since the morning she'd volunteered for Thanksgiving duty. After the meeting, she'd hightailed it out of there. "I've been working late, and then by the time I'm up and around everyone is busy working. Then I've been gone during the day for job hunting." *And husband shopping during my breaks*, she added silently.

"I understand. Hadley brought us dinner last night and told me that the bride and groom have turned the whole thing into this hilarious social media story. Some of the hashtags are cracking me up, #countryweddingproblems, #uninvitedguests, #hammingitup. I guess there's a photo of one of the pigs with wedding cake all over its face and snout with the caption Pigging Out on Our Wedding Cake. It's pretty funny. Hadley is relieved. Tyler is thrilled. New bookings are going like crazy. At least two people have messaged asking if one of the pigs could be their flower girl."

This information did make her feel a tiny bit better. Hearing it from Hadley would help even more. Maybe she was ready to listen to Fiona's apology in person. Fiona would have to ask Tyler.

Lydia smoothed a hand across the blanket

on her lap. "Let's talk about something else. How's the job hunting going?"

She hadn't thought there could be a worse topic than the pig blunder, but Fiona felt a fresh mix of red-hot humiliation and nerves swamp her at that question. Job. Simon. Kiss… Sweat broke out on the back of her neck as she thought about what came next: The Insult followed by The Declaration of Marriage. How could she have been so stupid? How desperate had that sounded?

She may as well have said, *Sorry, Simon, I can't date you because I'm looking for someone better to marry.* Poor Simon. She hadn't meant to insult him. What she'd wanted to do was stay wrapped in his arms for the next three weeks and not think about what would happen at the end of that time. But she was supposed to be breaking her pattern. Besides, her gut told her that three weeks with Simon would be just long enough to get too attached. And he'd made it very clear that three weeks was all he was willing to offer. He hadn't even bothered to suggest there could be anything more. In truth, she respected him for that. At least he'd been honest. And, realistically, she wasn't in the market for a long-distance relationship, either.

Fiona coughed in an attempt to clear the ball of shame from her throat. "I found a job."

"You did? That's fantastic. Where?"

"At the Silver Stake. I started a few days ago."

"You're working for Simon? That's great! He's a friend of ours."

"He mentioned that."

"Such a sweetheart."

"He is." And an excellent kisser. She couldn't stop thinking about it. "I'd actually gotten to know him a bit before he hired me." At Lydia's questioning glance, she quickly explained, "I volunteered at the fundraiser for Ned and Valerie. And I'd been there before with…" She didn't want to talk about the dating that had been going on before that. "Friends."

Lydia brightened at the comment. "I heard there was an amazing turnout. I bet he's a great boss."

"Things are going well so far." If I can only figure out how to hypnotize him so he'll forget how badly I insulted him. She had to see him tonight. She needed to call Ivy or one of her sisters and talk this out, get some encouragement. Maybe Georgie, if she could get a hold of her. Georgie was so calm, so logical. She always helped Fiona see things more clearly. This was important enough to warrant seeking out her busy doctor of a sister. Georgie's schedule might be packed, but Fiona knew that her family meant the world to her.

Anxiety must have shown on her face, because Lydia said, "Don't worry. You're going to be great."

"Thank you, Lydia," Fiona said, purposely letting her misread the source of her unease. "I appreciate your faith in me."

"Speaking of faith, I also heard you signed up to cook Thanksgiving dinner?"

Fiona nodded, happy for another topic shift. "I sure did."

"That is really sweet of you. I wish I could help."

"Well, I'll be honest, it was partially a selfish act," she joked. "There was talk of Thanksgiving takeout."

"Oh, boy. Jon would have…mutinied." Lydia snickered at the thought. "The man loves his food."

"Ben wanted—"

"Let me guess." Lydia held up a hand. "Ben's solution to every food dilemma is to order Thai."

"Yep."

"Sometimes, I think he likes to bring it up just to irritate Jon."

Fiona laughed. "Hey, you can help—you can

give me advice. I want to make some favorite dishes. You know how everyone has that one thing that the holiday wouldn't be the same without?"

"Yes!" Lydia brightened at the suggestion. "Like Nana's rolls. Finally, something I can help with. In fact, there's this salad the guys have talked about for years that their mom used to make…"

"WOW, JON, GOOD CALL." Simon felt his pulse tick with excitement as he slowly circled the old stagecoach sitting in the barn at the JB Bar Ranch. Jon's dog, Trout, joined him, stopping occasionally to perform a sniff check. It felt good to be doing what he loved, hunting for antiques and vintage items for his business. "It's in excellent condition."

Jon nodded slowly. "I thought so, too."

Years ago, professional disagreements had prompted Jon, the eldest of the Blackwell grandchildren, to quit working for his grandfather, Big E, at the Blackwell Ranch and establish his own cattle ranch, the JB Bar. Big E's disdain for Simon hadn't mattered to Jon; he'd often hired Simon as a ranch hand during the summers of his college years. When Simon started Clarke Props, Ltd., he'd purchased his first Western pieces from Jon, who now regularly kept an eye open for objects that might be of interest. Like this stagecoach he'd scored at a farm equipment auction.

"Price is right. I'll arrange for delivery."

The men shook hands and then chatted about the logistics of safely moving the coach. They soon went on to discussing other pieces Simon might be in the market for in the future.

They were heading for the door when Jon asked, "How're you liking your bartending gig?"

"Believe it or not, I kind of enjoy it." If he didn't have a business to run in California at the same time, he'd enjoy it a whole lot more. Hiring Fiona had already eased a significant portion of his professional anxiety concerning the Silver Stake. Now, if only he could figure out how to ease the post-kiss personal awkwardness looming between them. They were working together again tonight. "Ned and I bartended our way through college. That's what I was doing when I wasn't working summers for you on the JB Bar. That's how Ned fell in love with it."

"Hmm." Jon scratched his chin as if giving that notion serious consideration. A rancher to his core, Simon knew Jon could not conceive of anyone ever wanting to spend their nights inside a crowded barroom, or a crowded room of any kind, for that matter.

"I will confess that I prefer my real job, though." Under these circumstances, the reminder of his life in LA was a welcome relief from fretting about Fiona. He respected her for being honest about her intentions even though he believed the means she was employing were ridiculous. And ineffective. But he couldn't very well talk her out of it, could he? Not without offering a solution. And *he* was not the solution. He wasn't even willing to be the possibility of a solution. Briefly he'd considered telling her that, and about his business in LA, but what was the point?

His parents' toxic relationship, bitter divorce, and the subsequent marriage-and-divorce cycles they'd both embarked upon had taken marriage off the table for him. Unlike his triple-divorced mother, twice-divorced sister, recently divorced brother and his father, the family divorce champ at five, he wasn't willing to take that gamble. He should be relieved that he'd learned about Fiona's matrimonial intent when he had. And he was. Except the disappointment cut deep, too. Deeper than he could have anticipated.

"Now *that* I can believe," Jon said drily.

"Lydia wanted me to ask if you could come inside and say hello when we're through?"

"Sure thing. I have to come inside. I ran into your sister-in-law Grace this morning at Brewster's. I signed up to bring you guys dinner for tonight."

FIONA WAS HAVING a ball. Tom, the JB Bar Ranch foreman and honorary uncle to Jon and Lydia's children, had brought the girls home from the Carneses' ranch. They'd come inside and spent a few minutes gushing to Lydia about their visit, which consisted of rebuilding a horse's stall with Zach, decorating cookies with Sofie and learning rope tricks from Zach's bull-riding brother, Matt. All in all, it sounded like a day Fiona wouldn't have minded getting in on. When Lydia's eyelids began to droop, Fiona helped her get settled in the bedroom.

The girls had then given Fiona the grand tour of their bedroom, where Fiona admired the animal photos and horse posters on the walls. They'd played several rounds of cards and two board games before deciding to play Kings and Queens. Using brightly colored building blocks, they constructed an elaborate castle. A jousting match ensued, where Princess Blackwell, disguised as a knight and riding a "massive destrier," which Gen informed her was a "super huge war-horse," bested all the other contestants. Her prize consisted of a stallion, a lance and pedicures for her and her "ladies in waiting." Fiona decided she was a fan of Kings and Queens, Blackwell style.

Then they'd headed to the kitchen for a snack. They first agreed on a radio station to listen to and then decided on a menu of quesadillas, apple slices and dill pickles.

"I like to do mine like this," Gen said, slathering butter on the tortilla lying on her plate. "I love butter so much. Grandma Dot does, too. Sometimes we eat butter and sugar sandwiches together."

"We have that in common then," Fiona said, spreading a healthy dose of butter on her own tortilla. "Everything is better with butter."

They were doing the prep work when Abby suddenly let out an excited shriek. "It's Uncle Chance!" She dropped the cheese she'd been grating and grabbed a wooden spoon. "This is my favorite song! Fiona, you gotta turn it up!"

"Gladly," Fiona said, and acquiesced.

Microphone-spoon in hand, Abby sang along to one of Chance's recent hits.

Gen said, "Did you know Aunt Katie is Rosie's aunt and also her mama because she married Uncle Chance? She calls her Mama K."

"I have heard that," Fiona said. She'd learned that Chance had once been married to Katie's older sister, Maura, who'd passed away when Rosie was just an infant. "Rosie is lucky to have Katie for a mom now, isn't she?"

"She sure is, Aunt Katie is the best. She says someday I'll be able to ride horses as good as her. I hope so. We're lucky, too, because Daddy married Lydia, and she's our mommy now."

Abby belted out a few more bars before announcing, "If I wasn't already going to be a veterinarian like Uncle Ethan, I'd be a singer like Uncle Chance."

"If I could sing, I would be a singer like Uncle Chance, too," Fiona said. "But don't let anyone tell you that you can't be a singing veterinarian."

Abby giggled.

"We're learning piano," Gen added, heaping cheese on her tortilla. "Daddy plays the fiddle. Sometimes he plays while Uncle Chance sings and it's super awesome. Uncle Chance wants him to get up onstage at his concerts, but he won't do it. He only plays *local*, that's what he calls the music jams around here."

Jon played the fiddle? Fiona decided she could probably discover the entire family history simply by spending an afternoon with these girls.

"I wish I could dance like Mommy," Gen said. "She's the best dancer ever. Me and Abby are taking dance lessons."

"How does this look?" Abby called loudly over the music, studying her tortilla now piled high with grated cheese. "Is it too much cheese? The cheese kind of sinks down when it melts, right?"

"Yes, it sure does," Fiona agreed. "I think that looks about perfect."

"After we eat, do you want to go out and see the horses?" Gen asked before taking a bite of pickle.

Fiona answered, "I would love to. What's the protocol for that? Do we need to ask your mom?"

Gen swallowed the bite. "Yep." Then she scrunched her face thoughtfully and added, "But Daddy said she needs to rest a lot right now. Kind of like at the end of the time when she was pregnant with our baby brothers. So we could ask Tom or text Daddy and let him know."

"Let me know what?" Jon asked, strolling into the room. Trout, his black-and-white border collie and constant companion, trotted by his side. The oldest of her Blackwell cousins, Jon was tall and leanly muscled with a square jaw and an unwavering, blue-eyed stare that reminded her of Big E's. Serious almost to the point of solemn, he moved in the confident, deliberate way of a man who knew exactly where he was going and what he was going to do when he got there.

"Daddy!" Abby jumped off her stool and ran to him. "Hi! How was your day? We didn't hear you come in. Hey, Trout." Kneeling, she scratched the dog and kissed him on the head. Trout returned the greeting with a nuzzle of her ear.

"I noticed," Jon said, and chuckled. His edges softened considerably when he smiled, which, thankfully, he did often when Lydia or the kids were around.

"Sorry." Fiona winced a little and turned the music down. "Uncle Chance," she added by way of explanation.

"No need to apologize," Jon said. "Lydia plays it like that, too. And trust me, Chance Blackwell gets blasted a whole lot louder than that."

"I wanted to," Fiona confessed, and sheepishly pulled up one shoulder. "It's a good thing she's napping."

Jon laughed, and then said to Abby, "My day was just fine, sweet pea. It's even better now that I've laid eyes on you girls."

Gen asked, "Can we show Fiona the horses after we eat?"

"Of course you can. But first, we've got company that you're going to be excited to see."

"Who?" Gen asked. She'd climbed off her stool, too, and had one hand on Trout while she hopped on her tiptoes next to her dad and sister.

"Who is it?" an only slightly more composed Abby asked.

"Hey, girls!" Simon appeared in the doorway, holding a large box in his arms.

"Simon!" Abby cried.

"Simon!" Gen shouted at the same time.

"Simon?" Fiona whispered in a strangled tone before she could stop herself. The music was loud enough that likely no one could hear the distress in her tone, but from the look he tossed to her, she was pretty sure Simon had seen it on her face.

WITH HER PULSE pounding erratically through her bloodstream and butterflies waging a violent protest in her stomach, Fiona decided horseback riding was possibly another Montana facet she'd heavily romanticized. Like snow. The reality was not shaping up to be quite like the fantasy.

Dazed from the stress, she stared at the saddled horse in front of her and wondered how she'd gotten here. One minute she'd been in Lydia and Jon's warm and cozy house drinking coffee and chatting while pretending there was no awkwardness between her and Simon, the next she was out in their barn freezing and gearing up for her first riding lesson. Why, oh why, had she gone on about how much she'd *love* to learn to ride a horse? Besides, wasn't that just something people said? Like traveling the world or bungee jumping. It certainly didn't mean she wanted to ride *right now*!

"Simon is an excellent teacher," Jon said.

"Great," she managed to utter with feigned enthusiasm. Simon was the last person she wanted to see right now, much less have *watch her* while she made a complete fool of herself. Or worse. Curious about the fundraiser, she'd asked about Valerie and learned how she was an expert with horses but had an accident, nonetheless. A quick internet search had informed her that riding accidents were more common than she'd ever imagined. Horseback riding consistently earned top billings on those "most dangerous sport" lists. Yet another reason to like golf.

"Are you okay?" Jon asked her.

"Just a little nervous," she answered honestly because there was no doubt in her mind that the terror could be read loud and clear across her face.

Even by children, apparently. "Don't worry, Fiona. Mesa is real sweet." This from Gen, who was already settled in the saddle of her own horse, Garnet. And, good gravy, the girls were cute in their helmets, puffy coats, riding gloves and miniature cowboy boots. Reins in hand, feet in stirrups, Gen radiated pure joy and laid-back confidence like the cowgirl she aspired to be. "Abby and I both learned how to ride on Mesa. She doesn't like snakes, but there aren't any out in winter. Abby fell off her one time, but she was fine."

"Abby fell off?" Fiona asked as her chest constricted with fear like a snake coiling tight around her lungs. "This horse?"

"Abby wasn't paying attention," Jon explained in a serious tone. "Which I know you will be doing."

"I was *too* paying attention, Daddy," Abby politely countered, who now, after a boost from Simon, sat atop her horse, Topaz. "Gen and I and Rosie were practicing being a roving band, remember?"

"Ah, yes, your roving bluegrass band."

To Fiona, Abby offered this helpful advice. "Just don't play the harmonica while you ride her, and you'll be good."

Fiona repeated the recommendations, "Avoid snakes, pay attention, no harmonica. Got it. Thank you, Blackwells, one and all."

Jon and Simon chuckled before exchanging a few quiet words. Jon smiled at Fiona and said, "You're in good hands, cousin. Have fun." She then watched as Jon smoothly mounted his horse, donned his hat and, with a barely perceptible shift of his body, signaled the horse to walk. Trout jogged ahead, confidently taking the lead. Under different circumstances, one where she wasn't suffering a heightened state of panic, she would have found the unintentional demonstration extremely cool. Her cousin was truly the epitome of cowboy.

Somehow, the girls imparted "go" to Garnet and Ruby, too, because they followed Jon's horse. They turned in their saddles, waved over their shoulders, and called out final goodbyes and encouraging words.

"Are you sure we have time for this? We don't really have to do this today." Fiona gulped in a deep breath, but the pungent odor of horse only reminded her of what she was up against. That, and the wall of horse in front of her. Great Wall of Horse suddenly made Great Wall of Cold seem warm and inviting.

Simon had his back turned, busy saddling another horse. "Change your mind?"

"Well, I, um, I recently started a new job, and I don't want to be late. I've heard my boss is a real bear about employee tardiness."

"Don't you worry." He turned to look at her now, his mouth curling up at the corners while he waged a valiant but losing battle with a grin. "I'll make sure you get to work on time. Nothing I hate more myself than a tardy employee."

"Really? Nothing?" she babbled nervously. "I find that difficult to believe. What about a guy who cheats at cards? Or your coworker who eats all the shrimp at the employee Christmas party? Don't you hate that guy? Or a woman who tells you she can't date you because she's looking for a husband and you don't have the right kind of job? You've got to think she's a real—"

"Fiona—"

"Shoot," she interrupted, dipping her head and pinching the bridge of her nose. "I'm sorry. I didn't intend to bring it up like this. I'm very nervous and also..." She searched for an explanation, but anxiety was interfering with the proper firing of word-locating neurons. Or whatever neuroscience phenomenon was required for proper speech. "Nervous," she finally puffed with a breathy sigh. "How 'bout that? One word to cover all the feels. Ha-ha, like one ring to rule them all..." He chuckled.

Why did he seem completely calm? Come to think of it, that composure of his was a little annoying. "Yep. Nervous about falling off this horse and about what happened last night."

"I'm glad you brought it up. I think we need to talk about what happened."

"I disagree. I think *I* need to apologize, and then let's move on. No need for rehashing." She *really* needed to get it together here. Inhaling deeply, she said, "Simon, I am so very sorry. You know I didn't mean it, don't you? I mean, it was all true. I do want to get married, but my explanation for not wanting to date you came out wrong. I don't have anything against bartending—you know that, right?"

He couldn't contain a chuckle. "You're extra cute when you're flustered, do you know *that*? You don't need to apologize. I get it."

"Do you?"

"Yes. I am not your type."

"But you are my type! That's the problem. You're exactly the kind of guy I would have dated a few months ago."

"You realize how that sounds? That you're essentially calling me a lovable loser. And possibly a freeloader."

"What?" she gasped. "No! That's not what I meant. Simon, I—"

"Fiona, I'm joking. Please, relax. I understand that I am not acceptable per your new standards. Or should I say Big E and Rudy's standards?" She started to argue again, but he added, "Seriously, Fiona, it's okay. I am most definitely not the man for you—on that point we agree. And your grandfather would most likely agree, too. Probably your dad, as well. Besides, I'm going back to California soon. So, we're good."

"Oh," she managed to say. "Good." She meant it—she wanted things to be okay between them. So why did it still hurt a little? The fact that he didn't even try to convince her otherwise.

CHAPTER NINE

IT WAS ALL Simon could do not to step forward and gather Fiona in his arms. Reassure her that she could trust her judgment where he was concerned, that he was both her old and new type combined. But how would that help? Because ultimately, what he said was true—he was not the man for her. The *husband*, he reminded himself, she was looking for a husband. But neither were these guys she was dating. Frustration twisted inside of him. To busy his tempted hands, he reached up and scratched Mesa between the ears.

He said, "Fiona, I like you. I don't want this awkwardness between us."

"Me, either. I like you, too, obviously. I wish things were different for both of us."

"Me, too."

Fiona groaned. "Now I have to go back to dating."

That moment, Simon recognized later, was his undoing. Specifically, that sound, the heart-wrenching sound of Fiona's sadness, weariness

and despair. It dug right into him and precipi-
tated his final descent into foolishness. That,
and the idea of watching her continue to waste
time on these mismatched "matches" via her
bogus family-influenced profile. What if she
grew so tired of the process that she gave up
and settled on someone? He couldn't handle it
if she ended up with some guy even weirder
than Drew or as domineering as Gary. If she
was going to go through with this husband
search, she deserved one worthy of her. He
needed to make sure of that.

"No, Fiona, you don't."

"Unfortunately, I do," she countered.

"You don't even like this internet dating
stuff."

Fiona gazed quickly and impatiently skyward before focusing back on him. "That's not
exactly news, Simon. I've already told you I
don't. On paper, however, it should work." She
executed a theatrical air punch and forced a
smile, and added, "It will work. Trying to stay
optimistic here, but it's getting difficult. I'm
beginning to think I'm the problem."

"You are most definitely not the problem."

"Yeah? Well, so far... Never mind, I hate
being negative. Ugh. Did you hear that? I just
did it again. I'm usually not a negative person, but since I've moved to Montana things

have not worked out like I thought they would and…" Her eyes widened as if surprised by her comment. "You know what? You don't need to hear this. I'll figure it out. I always do."

"Maybe I can help."

"That is highly unlikely."

"Neg-a-tive," he crooned in a singsong voice. "We're not doing negative anymore, remember?"

"Right." Twitching and extra cute, her mouth barely resisted a smile.

"I have a dating proposition for you."

"Very funny," she returned drily.

"I'm not talking about me," he said. Just gathering the words felt painful, but he forged on, "Shut down your dating profile, and I'll find you a guy."

Her eyebrows darted up as her mouth opened and then snapped shut, leaving an expression that reflected the pure bizarreness of the suggestion. "*You* are going to *find* me a guy?"

"I know a lot of people around here." Ned and Val knew even more. He would enlist their advice, he decided, growing more encouraged by his suggestion. "Let me be your matchmaker."

"Why would you do that?"

"Because I care about you. I can't stand to see you on these dates, disappointed over and over again." If that gave away more of his feelings than was wise, he didn't care.

When she didn't answer, he posed it another way. "How is my setting you up with a guy I think you'll like, and who I think is worthy of you, any different than your family helping you fill out your profile to attract a certain type of guy?"

"Are you saying that you think you can do a better job of finding me a potential husband than my own family?"

"Well, I know you *and* I know the guys. So…" He shrugged one shoulder dramatically. "What do you have to lose? I'll be leaving in a few weeks anyway. If it doesn't work, you reactivate your profile and go back to doing it your way."

"FINE." AN EMOTIONALLY exhausted Fiona found herself agreeing to Simon's matchmaking proposal.

"Really?" he asked. "Just like that?"

"Sure. Why not? Like you said, what do I have to lose?" *Not my heart.* She wasn't listening to that anymore. And, logically, he had a point. Maybe he could do better than her PartnerUp.com profile. Just the thought of enduring another bad date left her fraught with despair. The idea of being free from it filled her with pure relief.

At that point, she was also blessed with a pardon from her riding lesson when Simon received a phone call about a bungled order that had been delivered to the Silver Stake. Fine by her.

With relations between them if not entirely repaired then certainly mended, Fiona went back to the ranch, to the warm and welcoming sanctuary of her cabin. She texted Lily, but her sister wasn't home.

Since she had time to spare and was due for one of the regular updates they'd been sharing, she decided to try for a video chat with her dad and Big E.

"Hi, Dad. Hey, Big G." Fiona threw two kisses into the camera lens on her laptop. The two men were quite a sight, sitting next to one another on the sofa in Big E's motor home. Like two giants squeezed together on a piece of doll furniture. The sight warmed her heart.

"Fiona! How's it going, sweetheart?" Rudy asked.

"Great!" she gushed, and then warned herself not to pour it on too thick. She had absolutely no intention of telling the complete truth about her misery, but she didn't want to lie, either. Reciting the difficulties she'd faced here would only cause them worry. Her dad had enough on his plate right now. She could only imagine how he'd feel if he eventually found Thomas Blackwell. She had to make him see that no one, biological or otherwise, would ever displace him in her heart.

That thought renewed her determination to see this Montana plan through. All he wanted was to see his daughters happy and settled. This call was a good idea, Fiona decided, renewing her determination to do that for him.

"Settling in at the ranch okay?" Big E asked. "Everyone treating you right?"

"Absolutely," she answered, which was true on account of her new work schedule and the low profile she'd been keeping. "Everyone is so nice."

"Any progress on the dating front?" Rudy asked. "How did you like that last guy, the car salesman?"

"Unfortunately, that date got cut short," she informed him. Or Simon had felt the need to shorten it anyway. Probably, he'd been right. The guy had given her the creeps. But she wasn't about to mention any of that. "Circumstances beyond my control. But I'm definitely hopeful for my future prospects." She declined to mention that those prospects now hinged on Simon. It was way too much, and too personal, to explain. It seemed likely that both men would protest. Yet, if Simon's efforts worked, they'd both be thrilled. That's what mattered. They wouldn't need to know how she'd gotten there.

"Did you find a job yet?" her dad wanted to know.

"I did!" Fiona cried, grateful for the subject change. "I have a job. Don't get upset, Dad. I took a serving job at a restaurant here in Falcon Creek. I'm still looking for something else, but in the short term I need income. I don't want to stay on the ranch much longer without paying something. Big G, I realize that technically I'm a Blackwell but, Dad, I'm still your daughter. You taught us to make our own way in the world, and I can't live at the ranch forever. I know they are losing income by letting me stay there." Not to mention by her inadvertent wedding destruction. Another event she didn't want to divulge.

"I understand, honey. I'm proud of you for being so conscientious."

"Me, too!" Big E said, slapping a hand on his knee. Leaning forward, he winked into the camera. "Nothing wrong with good honest work, Little Fee. Besides, today's pig is tomorrow's bacon, right?"

Rudy looked a little confused by that comment, but Fiona knew exactly what he was referencing. Of course, Big E would have found out about the pig episode. Grandma Dorothy probably told him. Fiona had stopped by her house this morning to get the salad recipe. They'd had a lovely chat. Fiona adored her new grandma. Or Tyler could have told him. Everyone had probably told him. Regardless, she appreciated his support more than she could say.

"Indeed. Thank you, Big G. That means a lot to me."

"Which restaurant?" he asked.

Fiona was surprised he didn't know that, too. "The Silver Stake."

"So, you're working for Ned Clarke?"

"Nope. His cousin is running the place until the end of the month."

"His cousin?" Big E snapped out the question, and Fiona felt the force of his scowl. She could see who her cousin Jon had gotten his intensity from. She could practically hear the wheels spinning in that network of clever gears that made up his brain. "Si Clarke? Simon Clarke, delinquent son of Philip and Becca?"

"Yes," she said, "but I promise you he's not a delinquent. He outgrew his wild streak a long time ago. He's only here temporarily to help out Ned and his wife, Val. I'm sure you heard about her riding accident."

"I did." Which he followed with a frown and a flatly delivered "Hmm."

Simon had mentioned that Big E wasn't fond of him back in the day. What had happened, she wondered? "Kid stuff," he'd said, but they had yet to revisit the topic. As curious as she was about that, and Big E's opinion of Simon, for now Fiona wanted to steer clear of any discussion where he was concerned. Nothing that would lead to questions about the matchmaking she'd agreed to.

"So, guys, how's the search going?" Fiona asked brightly, knowing the question would steer the conversation in a new direction. "Any sign of Thomas Blackwell?"

As RELIEVED AS Simon was not to have to watch Fiona on another date, the problem, he'd realized almost immediately after hatching this harebrained matchmaking scheme, was that now he was expected to follow through. The details of which had left him sleep deprived and irritable. His current state as he prepared to open the bar for lunch.

"So, matchmaker, matchmaker," Fiona chirped, sidling up to him with a smile on her face that seemed too bright for the circumstances. "When are you going to make me a match?"

Strange how he still wanted her to come to her senses and want *him* despite the fact that she believed he was only a bartender, even though he knew it was better if she *didn't* want him. Okay. He really needed to get his head on straight.

"I'm waiting for confirmation, but it looks like my first pick is going to be available soon." Although that was a bit of an exaggeration, there was no reason to think that anyone he chose would be anything but thrilled to be set up with Fiona.

"Really?" she said. The surprise in her tone suggested she lacked faith in his skills. "How soon?"

This prompted him to exaggerate again. "Yep, I'm setting it up even as we speak."

"Wow. That's… I didn't expect… What's he like?"

"You'll see," he hedged. Because following through was not even the worst of his problems. The real issue was that no one he'd come up with was good enough for her. He could name several decent guys with jobs and no obvious issues or financial problems. But the thought of any one of them dating Fiona made him want to punch a wall.

"What? Simon!" She cuffed him lightly on

the shoulder. "PartnerUp.com at least gives me some stats."

"I know, but we're not judging guys on stats anymore, remember?"

She frowned before conceding with a thoughtful nod. "Fine. You're right. If you like him and think he's right for me then I won't ask any questions. Set it up."

"OH, THIS IS going to be fun!" Valerie exclaimed, immediately warming to Simon's matchmaking task. The gist of which he'd just spent the last several minutes relaying. Val's irrepressible enthusiasm was such a good match for Ned's quiet, thoughtful countenance. They were the perfect example of opposites attracting and then remaining that way. Even their physical appearances were in stark contrast. Like Simon, Ned had inherited the dark hair and blue eyes of the Clarke side of the family. Val had reddish blond hair and arresting amber-colored eyes.

"There are a lot of good guys to choose from around here."

"Really? You think?" Simon scratched his stubble-roughened cheek. Since he'd been up most of the night fretting, he hadn't taken the time to shave this morning. At the Silver Stake, he'd spent the afternoon agonizing. Fiona's "set it up" comment only aggravated his foul mood. When the lunch crowd finally thinned, he'd decided he had just enough time to drive out to Ned and Val's before meeting Luke for dinner.

Luke was back and, oh, man, it would be good to catch up with his oldest friend. He planned to introduce him to Fiona. Luke would understand his angst and possibly even have some ideas of his own.

"Guys you'd set your sister up with?" he asked.

"Absolutely," Val said, snatching the notepad off the table next to her recliner. "I'm making a list, in no particular order…" She trailed off, scribbling away.

"Great." Simon exhaled the word on a relieved breath, his anxiety already beginning to diminish. Val's optimism was contagious, not to mention it seemed to cheer her considerably, too. Simon knew she was getting bored being confined indoors so much. Consulting Val and Ned had been a good idea. Maybe there was hope after all.

A short time later, she looked up. "First name on the list, Matt Carnes. Nice guy, funny, great family, not to mention he looks like a Greek god on horseback, oh, and—"

"No!" Simon interrupted. He knew he was

scowling, but seriously? "Val, you know very well that Matt is a bull rider."

"I thought she wanted a rancher type."

"She does, but not one who's engaged in a profession as dangerous and financially unpredictable as bull riding."

Val frowned thoughtfully. "Okay, I see your point."

"I've got one," Ned said. "JT Brimble. Former bull rider."

"Stop it, Ned." Simon glowered at his cousin. "This is serious."

"What?" Ned said, unable to contain a snicker. "Women are crazy about him and all that long blond hair."

"Yeah, and he knows it. JT is a player."

"I think he's right, Ned," Val agreed hesitantly. "Deep down he's a good guy, but problematic. What about Martin Coulson? He's such a sweetheart. Volunteers at the nursing home on Saturdays. And he's excellent with horses."

"No. He comes into the Silver Stake all the time. Drinks way too much."

"Will Jackson?"

"Absolutely out of the question. He's mean to his dog."

Val gasped and then made a dramatic show of scratching him off the list. "How 'bout

Emmet Baker? I love how he plays chess with Pops at Brewster's all the time."

"Too old."

Ned peered at him with squinty-eyed confusion. "He's only thirty. Graduated the same year we did."

"Really?" Simon shifted in his seat. "Well, he *seems* older. He's boring."

"Cody Goode?" Valerie suggested brightly, tapping the paper as if to emphasize each point. "Nice, *nice* guy, smart, stable job. Did you know he's taking over his dad's farm equipment business?"

"No." Simon shook his head. "No way. Too nice."

"So that's a problem, too?" Val repeated slowly, her eyebrows drifting up high on her forehead. "Niceness?"

"Well, yeah. Fiona is...full of life--outgoing, witty and sarcastic. Cody would be no match for her. She needs someone more..."

Val and Ned exchanged a look before Val offered, "Confident?"

"Yes!" Simon emphasized, slashing the air with a pointed finger. "Assertive, you know, someone who would stick up for her. She has a history of being too nice, and guys taking advantage of that. Fiona has a huge heart. I can't stand the idea of someone not treating her right. He needs a sense of humor, too. Funny, but not cruel funny. Kind funny. He needs a good job, too, a steady job."

"I see," Val said, and nodded thoughtfully. "So, she's really a catch, huh?"

"Yes, she's pretty much perfect. I mean, she's not *perfect*, obviously. But she's really close. Any man would be lucky to have her. Like lottery lucky."

"Lottery lucky," Val repeated flatly. "My list is suddenly getting shorter."

"I know," Ned said, holding up a hand in a gesture that said the discussion was all but over. "I've got it. I have the perfect guy for your perfect Fiona."

"Who?"

"Simon Clarke."

Val laughed. Ned joined in. So, they weren't complete opposites—they shared the same annoying sense of humor.

"Very funny."

"I know," Ned agreed, and attempted to wipe the smile from his face. "But I'm not joking, Simon. You obviously like her, she likes you. Why are you doing this? Why don't you just date her?"

"It's not that simple."

"It pretty much is," he countered.

"Aside from the fact that I'm leaving in a few weeks to go back home?"

"That's plenty of time to get to know if you want this to go anywhere."

"Which is precisely the problem and you know it. She's looking for more and I am not fit to give anyone more, especially Fiona."

Ned shook his head. "Simon, just because your parents are all messed up relationship-wise doesn't mean you are, too."

Except that he absolutely was. "Think about it, Ned. It's not just my parents. That's the same advice I gave Colette before she married my nitwit ex-brother-in-law—the second one. We have some type of divorce gene in my family, and you know it."

"Oh, Simon," Val said, but didn't disagree. She sighed and handed him her list. "These guys are the best of the best here in Falcon Creek. You promised Fiona you would help, and that means you need to pick one."

FIONA'S SHIFT HAD ENDED, but she was still behind the bar filling saltshakers and assuring herself she wasn't stalling so she could see Simon before she left, when the hot guy sauntered through the door. She knew Riley noticed him, too, because she was next to Fiona and looked up. And then kept looking long enough to overfill the drink she was pouring. But it wasn't strictly his looks that caught Fiona's attention. Nope, what held her attention was the way he headed straight for the dating booth.

Standing beside the table like he knew he'd come to the right place, he peeled off his down jacket to reveal a version of what she'd silently termed the "off duty cowboy uniform" favored by locals: worn flannel shirt, stocking hat and blue jeans tucked into thick-soled snow boots. Reaching up, he tugged off the cap and ran a hand through thick reddish-brown hair. With a careless toss, he deposited both jacket and hat onto the seat and slid in after them.

As if his seating choice wasn't enough to tip her off, her phone chimed in her pocket. A text from Simon:

Hey, a friend of mine is showing up soon. I wish I was there to introduce you! You'll like him. Can you tell him I'll be there as soon as I can? He's not answering my text.

Fiona messaged back: No problem.

"Who is that?" Riley asked, wiping up the mess she'd made.

"That's my date," Fiona whispered, still not quite believing Simon had managed to set this up so quickly. Truthfully, she'd only raised the topic earlier because he'd been quiet and distracted, and all her previous attempts to make conversation had fallen flat.

"You have a date with *that* guy?" Riley whispered reverently.

"Yep." Fiona quickly washed and dried her hands, tucked a lock of hair behind her ear and inhaled a deep, fortifying breath. "Wish me luck."

"I would," Riley responded on a comically wistful sigh, "if only my jealousy would allow it."

Fiona chuckled, although she knew better than to be swayed by good looks. If physical attractiveness still ranked on her list, she'd be with Simon right now. Simon. Bless him. He'd come through for her. And she had to admit that he'd been right; there was already a degree of familiarity and comfort in the notion that he approved of this guy. If Simon believed this man could possibly make her happy, then she believed it, too.

"Hey," Fiona said, sliding into the seat across from him. "I'm Fiona."

"Hi, Fiona." The man smiled and extended an arm across the table to shake her hand. "Luke Bradley."

"How are you, Luke? Any trouble finding the place?"

"I'm just fine, Fiona." His gaze traveled over her in that lazy, roundabout way that all really good flirts seemed to master at a young age. Like Simon. Annoying, because Simon-on-her-mind was not how she wanted this potential meet-cute to go. "No trouble at all. I've been here plenty of times."

"Of course you have. What am I thinking? You're a friend of Simon's."

"Yes, ma'am, I certainly am."

"How long have you known him?"

"We met in first grade. We were inseparable until tenth grade when he moved away. Is he here?" Luke asked before she could formulate a response.

"Not yet, but he will be soon." Fiona was certain of that. Since he'd set up this date, she had every reason to believe he'd show up and watch it play out. "He asked me to introduce myself."

"You're a friend of Simon's, too?"

"I am. I've only known him for a couple of weeks, though." Unlike the situation with Big E where she knew the report on Simon would not be favorable, this guy had real insight, and she couldn't help but ask, "What was he like in school? You two get into a bit of trouble together?"

"A *bit* of trouble?" Luke repeated the words

while his mouth curled slowly at the corners. "You could call it that. Be sort of like calling a hurricane a *bit* of a storm, though." He chuckled and shook his head. "Si Clarke and Luke Bradley equaled nothing but trouble. In retrospect, it's probably a good thing his parents shipped him off to California. Although, we did our best to make up for lost time in the summers and assorted school holidays."

"I'm getting that idea," Fiona said, holding tight to her smile while considering yet another surprise. What did that mean, his parents had *shipped him off* to California? Come to think of it, Simon hadn't mentioned his parents much at all. Had he mentioned them? The only family she could recall him talking about were his sister, Colette, and her four boys, troubled brother, Mica, and grandparents, who were deceased.

Clearly this man seated before her was the key to unlocking all the hidden corners of Simon Clarke. Without thinking, she glanced around. Where was he anyway? And that's when she realized exactly what she was doing—waiting for Simon to show up and interrupt their date. So she could spend the rest of the evening lamenting to him about how it hadn't worked out. While mooning over him. Pathetic. Enough!

"I could spend all night telling you stories about Simon."

Fiona decided to change her strategy. If this first date had any chance of progressing to a second, she needed to get to know Luke Bradley without any trace of, or reminder about, her feelings for Simon.

Marshaling an enigmatic smile of her own, she said, "If it's all the same to you, I'd rather you didn't. I'd like to hear about Luke Bradley, instead." That's right, she could flirt with the best of them.

Luke's chin tipped up in a gesture that was slight but swift, as if surprised by the statement. His eyebrows vaulted high onto his forehead chasing that assumption. Then his expression settled, and the grin he delivered was pure appreciation. "That could most definitely be arranged."

"Is that so?"

"Yes, ma'am. In fact, since I just got back to town today after a rather prolonged work-and-play absence, I can tell you without consulting my calendar that my schedule is absolutely and unequivocally wide-open."

"Excellent," she gushed, and with a hopeful smile asked, "You want to get out of here?"

CHAPTER TEN

"YOU HAVE TO do something about Mica, Simon. Or I'm going to fire him. Or worse."

Simon fiddled with his Bluetooth headset and smiled at Colette's cool yet dramatic declaration regarding their brother. What was going on with his brother? He checked the time—he was supposed to be meeting Luke at the Silver Stake. He'd overstayed at Ned and Val's trying to decide which "nice guy" would be the best match for Fiona. He'd texted Luke to let him know he was running late, but when Luke was off duty, he was terrible about checking his phone. When his friend didn't respond, he'd decided to message Fiona, who'd agreed to keep him company until he arrived.

"Go ahead. But if you fire him, that means you're going to have to deliver the railroad cars to Indy Indies." Colette's first ex-husband worked for Indy Indies, the documentary film-making company who'd rented the railcars for their latest film project.

A low growl morphed into a string of muttered angry words followed by, "Don't think I won't do it, Simon. He's out of control. I've had it with him. He came in more than two hours late and almost missed the meeting today."

"*The* meeting?" Simon repeated, tensing as he realized what day this was. "Are you referring to the meeting with Enrique Hale and his team?"

"Yes. He would have missed it."

"What are you talking about, he *would have* missed it? Did it not happen?" This wasn't funny. Enrique Hale was an up-and-coming Hollywood director. Simon had spent two years trying to earn his business, a feat he'd finally successfully managed. Simon had personally arranged for the director and his team to come in and select items for their next project, a sweeping Western drama with a big fat budget. The only way Mica could screw this up was by not showing up.

"He is so, so lucky. Hale called and rescheduled."

"For when?"

"Day after tomorrow."

"Get me a plane ticket."

"Seriously?"

"Yes, fly me in tomorrow and I'll leave the next afternoon after the meeting." He could have Fiona pick up the slack at the Silver Stake for a couple of days; she'd be happy to have the extra income.

"Don't tell anyone I'm coming."

"Not even Mica?"

"Especially not Mica."

"Okay, I'm on it. That's awesome, but… Can't you just come home for good right now? I talked to Ned yesterday and he said Val is healing faster than expected."

"You know how Ned is," Simon answered ambiguously because what Colette said was true. Technically he probably could go back to California now, leave the day-to-day management of the Silver Stake to Fiona for the next couple of weeks until Ned was ready to return. Ironically, her presence would make it easier for him to go even as she was also the reason he needed to stay. He'd made her a promise and he intended to keep it.

"HEY, RILEY, WAS there a guy here earlier?" Simon asked when he arrived back at the Silver Stake. Like Fiona, Riley was new to Montana, having only worked there for a month or so. He was pretty sure she didn't know Luke.

"Sure was, boss. Believe it or not, there've been lots of guys here today."

"Funny. No, I'm talking about a friend of mine. Tall guy with brown hair most likely in need of a haircut." Luke only let June at Jem salon here in Falcon Creek cut his hair, and he'd complained about needing a trim before he'd left. Chances were good that he was looking pretty shaggy by now. "My age, friendly, smiley, probably wearing a red knit cap." His younger sister had knit the hat for his birthday and he was rarely without it.

"*Ohh*, him. Sexy, messy hair and brilliant green eyes to go with that killer smile? Flirty but not over-the-top, scorching hot?"

"Yes, to the green eyes," Simon returned wryly, very used to women fawning all over his friend and his eyes.

Riley's face erupted with a dreamy smile. "Yeah, he was here."

"Do you happen to know where he went?"

"He left with Fiona."

Simon's fatigued brain refused to process this information. "He left with Fiona?"

"Yep."

"Why?"

"I'm guessing to go make out." She shrugged. "Or maybe I'm projecting. But she said he was her date. And I gotta say, he seems way, way better than anyone else she's *interviewed* in here. Fiona must have thought so, too, right? Because as far as I know this is the first time any guy has made it out that door with her."

As if in slow motion, Simon swiveled toward said door, thoughts turning toward the unthinkable, his mind recalling the promise he'd made to her earlier and the subsequent text asking that she introduce herself to his friend... No! This could not be happening. An image formed in his mind, of his charismatic best friend with the woman he...liked. Followed swiftly by the unwelcome, unwanted horror of a thought—they would be a good match. A very good match. They had many similar and endearing traits: fun loving, cheerful, optimistic, free-spirited. Golf! Luke would date her for that alone.

Luke wasn't in any hurry to get married but, unlike Simon, wasn't fundamentally opposed to it, either. He'd just never met the right woman. Riley was right, Fiona had never met anyone she'd wanted to leave this place with. Until tonight. Until Luke. Fear seized him. A cramping pain made it difficult to breathe or speak.

"Simon, are you okay?" Riley asked. "You don't look so good."

He pulled out his phone and fired off a text to Luke:

Call or text me ASAP. Out of range of your current companion who you should NOT be with right now. Misunderstanding. Call me. I'll explain.

Luke would never pursue Fiona if he thought Simon was already interested in her. But his friend was as notoriously terrible about checking his phone as he was notoriously good at charming women. He looked at the text he'd sent Fiona and marveled at his stupid ambiguity: Introduce yourself! Keep him company! What in the world had he been thinking? A blast of adrenaline followed, leaving him in a cold, shaky state of panic.

All he could do was hope it wasn't too late.

"IT'S PRETTY, RIGHT?" Luke called to Fiona from his kitchen. His beautiful gourmet kitchen that was the perfect accompaniment to his gorgeous, newly constructed and stylishly decorated home. None of which held a candle to the stunning snow-swathed view spread out before her.

"Yes," Fiona conceded with a sigh, unable to tear her gaze away from the wonder before her, the setting sun and the river valley below. "Very, very pretty."

When they'd left the Silver Stake and Luke had asked her where she wanted to go, she'd responded breezily, "Somewhere that doesn't involve snow or, more specifically, me freezing in it."

She'd felt his eyes on her then, curious and

assessing. In a monotone that made it impossible to gauge his thoughts on the subject, he'd asked, "You don't like the snow?"

"Sorry, no." She was done avoiding unpopular topics and fudging her opinions, a feat she'd discovered was much easier to accomplish online. Not that that helped the situation. If anything, the consequences had been worse. It had wasted her time and the time of the guys she'd dated without finding anyone even close to a match. She smiled as she thought about how Simon had so aptly dubbed her online method the "dating gauntlet." He was so right. With any luck, she'd soon relegate that nightmare to the dustbin of the past.

"Don't apologize." His mouth had curved with a slow smile that she'd found adorable. "But I have an idea. I think I can change your mind."

"You're welcome to try," Fiona had said, liking his confident avoidance of the *I don't know. What do* you *want to do?* game often played on first dates.

Self-assured smile in place, he'd led her to his pickup and opened the door. "Climb in." Once inside, he'd started the engine, turned on her heated seat and adjusted the vents to blow her way. Then he'd maneuvered the pickup onto the road headed out of town. A few minutes later, he'd pulled into the parking lot of White Buffalo Grocers. Fiona had opted to wait inside the now-warm pickup while he'd ventured into the store. The sound of an incoming text alerted her that he'd left his phone behind. A few minutes later, he'd returned with two grocery bags in hand.

"Snow provisions," he'd said. "Don't worry, I promise you won't get cold."

Fiona had pointed at the console. "Your phone went off a couple times while you were inside."

Frowning slightly, he'd retrieved the phone. Face drawn with what initially looked like concern, he'd studied the display as if trying to make sense of something. Finally he'd emitted a short, sharp laugh, then chafed a hand over his jaw as if trying to scrub away the smile. Tucking the phone away, he'd given her a smile and shifted the pickup into Reverse. They'd continued on their way.

And here they were several miles outside of town at his home in the foothills. Giant windows made up the front of the structure, showcasing a spectacular view of the winter-kissed river valley below. Cows and horses foraged in distant fields. Closer in, tall pine trees stood tall and regal, brandishing their thick coats of snow. A sparkling blanket of matching white draped the yard and grounds.

Across the room, a fire blazed in the woodstove, the pop and crackle of the flames mixing pleasantly with the sound of Luke puttering about in the kitchen.

"Snow's not so bad from this angle, is it?" he called out.

Fiona chuckled. "Officially, the best snow experience I've had here in Montana. Probably the best ever, but in the spirit of full disclosure, I don't have a lot of snow experience."

"I knew I could change your mind." Carrying a mug in each hand, Luke crossed the room to stand beside her. He handed one over, his fingers brushing lightly against hers. They felt warm and slightly rough, and she held her breath, waiting for... Nothing. No spark. Not like when Simon... Disappointment flooded through her. Luke was every bit as good-looking as Simon. More so, if she was judging by traditional standards. He was also funny and sweet and clearly trying hard to make this evening nice.

"Well done." Curling her hands around the mug, she let the warmth seep into her.

"Dinner is in the oven. White Buffalo makes a very respectable lasagna. Not like my mom's but it's good."

"Sounds delicious."

Outside, something grabbed his attention. "Hey now," he said in a low tone and pointed off to the right. "There they are... See that?"

Fiona squinted at she had no idea what, until an elk stepped into full view. "No way!" she whispered as if they were right beside her. Another appeared and then another and still more until an entire herd stood fanned out across the yard.

Luke narrated the scene, revealing fun facts about the animals and about Montana. Fiona listened, liking how he conveyed interesting tidbits without sounding like a know-it-all.

She took a sip of her drink. "My goodness, this is delicious. What is it?"

"My own hot cocoa recipe with a hint of peppermint schnapps."

Fiona heard his phone chime. Removing it from his back pocket, he slid a finger across the screen, studied it for a moment and then laughed.

"I'm sorry. I'll be just a second." He typed out a response.

Almost immediately the phone beeped again. Head bowed, he let out a little groan. A flurry of texts and chimes ensued. Occasionally Luke would pause to chuckle or mutter softly under his breath. At one point, he looked up, peered closely at her and winked. A moment later, he slipped an arm around her shoulders and gave her a quick, friendly squeeze.

He smiled. "Sorry about this. Believe it or not, I'm normally downright negligent with my phone." Reaching out a hand, he plucked something off her neck, or maybe her ear. "You've got a little spider or something... Got it." He wiggled his fingers to let it go. Fiona didn't see anything but thanked him anyway.

"Everything okay?" she asked when he appeared to have wrapped things up.

"I think so." Smiling, he tucked the phone back into his pocket. "That was Simon."

"Oh?" A sliver of longing sliced through her, followed quickly by something close to irritation. Did she have to be reminded of him *every* minute?

"He's on his way here."

"What? Why?"

"At this point, I'm not entirely sure."

IT TOOK MORE than an hour before Simon heard back from Luke. A torturous and purposeful hour, he only realized later, for which he would someday get even with his friend for inflicting upon him.

In the meantime, a more thorough questioning of Riley revealed that Luke and Fiona had not shared a meal at the Silver Stake. Simon knew Luke would be hungry. His friend was always hungry, and they'd planned on having dinner together. A tense hour had ensued where he'd driven by every eatery in Falcon Creek. When that hadn't yielded their whereabouts, he'd journeyed all the way out to the wildlife refuge where Luke sometimes went to birdwatch and eat a to-go panini from White Buffalo's deli. Nothing. He'd headed back toward town.

He'd texted Luke again: Did you get my text?

No response. Whereupon he'd traveled every road in town. Most of them multiple times. He'd just pulled into the parking lot of White Buffalo Grocers to scan the lot once again when his phone sounded. Finally!

Luke: Which text? Thank you, my friend. What have I done to earn such a heavenly reward? Why on earth would you just push this woman toward me? I owe you. Or wait…what's wrong with her?

Simon: My text asking you to call me. AND THERE IS NOTHING WRONG WITH HER, YOU NITWIT! And I did not PUSH her toward you. This is a misunderstanding. I repeat, abort! ABORT!

Simon (one minute later): Do you understand me?

Luke: I'm looking but I don't see your earlier text... Are you sure it sent?

Luke: Not really... The only thing I understand is that I've just met THE MOST remarkable woman. I think she's into me too.

Simon: Do not touch her.

Simon: And don't tell her any of this.

Luke: Does a buddy squeeze around the shoulders count?

Simon: Yes, of course it counts!

Luke: What about an ear tweak?

Simon: An ear tweak? Double yes!

Luke: Uh-oh.

Luke: Hmm...

Luke: Oh, I see.

Simon: What uh-oh? See what?

Simon: You better not be tweaking anything of Fiona's. Where are you?

Simon (after a prolonged pause): WHAT DO YOU SEE?

Simon (thirty seconds later): Luke, I'm serious. This isn't funny.

Luke: Simon, trust me, I am not laughing.

Simon: What ARE you doing?

Luke: *sigh* Trying to decide how much your friendship means to me.

Simon: LUKE! LUKE! LUKE! YOU ARE MY BEST FRIEND PLEASE DO NOT MAKE ME HURT YOU.

Luke: Ha. As if. And do not bring up that time summer before junior year when we were haying for George Inez. That was a lucky punch and you know it.

Simon: Where are you?

Simon (one minute later): Answer me right now!

Luke: Hold on. I'm distracted… Are Fiona's eyes blue-green or green-blue?

Luke: Or gray-green? Is that a color?

Simon: Her eyes are none of your business. Do NOT talk about her eyes! Do not LOOK at her eyes? DO YOU HEAR ME?

Luke: It would be difficult not to when you keep SHOUTING AT ME LIKE A ROYAL CLASS JERK. What IS difficult for me to understand is how I'm the NITWIT when I'm the one here with her? They're gray. I think they're gray. I need to get closer…

Simon: Stop. Just stop. DO NOT get closer. I will tell you everything. I promise. And please don't tell her about this.

Luke: That's a solid maybe at this point.

Simon: Maybe what?

Luke: Maybe I won't tell her if you apologize and take it all back.

Simon: *%$)#&#@W)344! Luke! Where. Are. You??????

Luke: I'm waiting...

Simon: You are killing me.

Luke: Gray-blue is my final decision. I hereby proclaim gray-blue a color. Emailing the crayon guys right now while I wait for proper apology...

Simon: Luke, my dearest friend on this earth who I love (and don't want to injure although he's making that part very difficult) please accept my apology. I am sincerely sorry. YOU are NOT a nitwit. Clearly, I am the nitwit. Please, for the love of our longstanding friendship, stand down. I am pleading for mercy and forgiveness. Your BFF Simon ps: do NOT touch Fiona. Or tweak her. Or otherwise lay your hands on her.

Simon: Or look at her eyes.

Luke: Weak, at best. That not wanting to injure me part was both passive-aggressive and unnecessary, as was the reminder not to touch her. As was the semantics lesson. What do you think I am? Some sort of animal or best friend betrayer? Or middle-schooler? Although...

Luke: No can do on the eye thing. Only creepers don't make eye contact.

Simon: Although what?

Luke: I believe I'm going to require compensation.

Simon: What do you want? Anything!!

Luke: A new driver and 90 holes of golf. That's right, FIVE rounds on your dime. AND you have to let me beat you at least once.

Simon: Fine! Yes! Done! I'll let you beat me Every. Single. Time.

Luke: That's unnecessary. And would not be sporting. I'm not a charity case. We're at my house. But I can't be responsible for what happens before you get here. She really likes my hot...

Simon: LUKE!!! I swear I am going to

Luke: ...cocoa. Get your mind out of the gutter.

Simon: hurt you.

Simon: TY. Also, don't mention anything about my business. In fact, don't talk about me at all.

Luke: Finally, Your Majesty, a simple command. She specifically told me she DID NOT want to talk about you. So there. I don't even think she likes you and still you don't have anything to worry about. That's how good of a friend I am.

Simon barely managed to stick to the speed limit, a testament to his faith in the solid friendship he shared with Luke. And the snowy roads. It was that same attribute, combined with his abject desperation, which prompted the beginnings of a plan. Was it perfect? No. But it would buy him the time he needed to come up with a name. Or a better plan.

CHAPTER ELEVEN

FIONA MET SIMON at the door. He stepped inside, his already pliable heart softening even more as he took in her beautiful face drawn with concern. Was she worried about him?

"Simon, what are you doing here? Are you all right? Is everything okay?" She fired off the questions, cementing both the notion that he hadn't fully thought this through and that she was indeed worried.

"I'm fine. And, yes, it is." At her look of confusion, he qualified, "It will be. Colette called earlier and I need to fly back to LA for a couple of days."

"Why? Did something happen? Is it your family?"

"Yes," he said.

Behind her, Luke went wide-eyed with worry, his expression registering questions of his own.

"It's not a medical emergency or anything like that," he clarified. "I just need to straighten something out with my irresponsible brother."

Luke nodded knowingly, very familiar with the problem that was Mica.

"Oh. Okay." Fiona's expression, however, suggested a degree of perplexity. Understandably so, because how would anything less than an emergency warrant an interruption of her date. Just the word had him cringing inside. *Date. When exactly had Luke seen his first text? How well had it been going up till then? What had happened before that?* He inhaled a deep breath in an effort to quell the anxiety bearing down on him.

"Hey, buddy," Simon greeted Luke.

"Good to see you, man." Luke stepped forward and clapped him on the shoulder. "Wow," he added with a Cheshire smile, "you made good time."

Simon gave him a little glare before looking at Fiona again. "So, the reason I'm here is because I need you to help keep an eye on the Silver Stake while I'm gone."

Behind Fiona, Luke made a show of rolling his eyes.

"Of course, yes, whatever you need."

"Okay, great. Thank you."

"What can I do?" she asked.

Luke executed an exaggerated shrug, and mouthed, *What can she do?* Clearly, he enjoyed watching Simon's struggle. A struggle he knew he deserved, as much as he hated to admit it.

"I need, um, someone to open the restaurant in the mornings. As you know, Miguel has a day job, Roy takes care of his mom, and Riley spends that time with her kids and takes them to school. Michelle is off for the next three days, and I can't really depend on anyone else." This was true. Fiona was hands down the best server and all-around employee he'd ever seen. His own business and family members included.

Good one, Luke mouthed, and nodded.

"No problem."

"Unfortunately, I need to take off in the morning, so if you could come back into town with me right now I can give you a key, and we can talk about everything?"

"Sure, absolutely." Fiona crossed the room and retrieved her bag. Simon immediately felt his panic begin to subside. Now, if only Luke would agree to his plan. His friend would need convincing, and possibly another golf club. Or five. This meant he needed time to talk to him.

"Luke, any chance you could run me to the airport tomorrow?"

"Ha," Luke said, and chuckled. "The airport? No, thanks. I won't be seeing the airport for another week."

"Weren't you just telling me recently how you needed something from Golf Planet? It's right on the way and I plan on stopping."

"Oh, right!" Luke amended brightly, "I did say that, didn't I? Sure, I can take you. What time do we need to leave?"

FIONA CLIMBED INTO Simon's old pickup for the drive back to town. The vintage Ford had none of the amenities of Luke's much newer model but all of the charm. The interior was neat and tidy and, best of all, it smelled like Simon.

"Sorry about the lack of amenities," Simon told her as if reading her mind. "But I promise, it runs like a dream."

"This is beyond cool, Simon." She gave the dash a gentle, appreciative pat. "Yeah, 1968 was a great year."

"Thank you." Simon shot her a surprised glance, which transformed into an appreciative smile. "It was. I've had it since high school. It was my first set of wheels. Ned and I fixed it up, with Uncle Dean's help. A few things have been replaced, but I used original parts that we scoured junkyards to find. I like how sturdy it is and that I can fix it myself. It, um, fostered my lifelong appreciation for…old stuff." He shifted into Reverse and backed out of the driveway.

Fiona loved and hated that they had this in common. And, suddenly, a wave of sadness swamped her, surprising in its intensity. Tears gathered in her eyes and she blinked them away, glad that it had grown dark enough now that he couldn't spot them. It felt so cruel that she'd finally met a man who seemed perfect for her. Maybe she could just…

What? Waste precious time having fun with Simon when she should be thinking about the future? *You've been here before, Fiona, following your heart and not planning past next week, and look where it's gotten you.* Not where her dad thought she should be and nowhere near where her sisters were. If she was going to get what she wanted she needed to take the steps to get there.

Still, was Simon really okay with her dating his best friend? And it wasn't like they'd started dating in some organic way. Simon had set them up. Who did that? If the situation were reversed, she wouldn't be so selfless. The idea of setting Simon up with Ivy was out of the question. Then again, he was leaving soon and that probably made it easier from his perspective. Although, now that she thought back on their post-kiss conversation, maybe he didn't feel the same way about her as she did him?

She was looking for a commitment. He

wasn't. He was going back to California and made it clear that he wasn't interested in a long-distance relationship, or any kind of a relationship. In fact, his proposition had been "three weeks of fun." Was it possible that their kiss had meant nothing more to him than a sample of that fun? Regardless, he was trying to do something nice for her, and she owed it to him to at least give it a try with Luke.

"Thank you for setting me up with Luke," she told him. "He's really great."

"He is," Simon agreed. "We've been friends for a long time."

"He mentioned that."

Simon shifted in his seat and after a pause asked, "So, how did it go? Your, um, date?"

"It went really well. He's an old-school gentleman, and I like that."

"Sorry I interrupted."

"Oh, no, don't worry about it. Family is important. I would do anything for my sisters."

"And your dad?"

"And my dad," she agreed, the fresh reminder of the circumstances that had led her here making her wince.

Turning her head to look out the passenger window, she steeled herself. After all, change was hard, right? Or at least that's what people said. That cliché had never really been true for her. But then, she'd never really made important, substantive changes, had she? Until now. And her dad was right—these changes would be for the better. She was taking charge of her life. Not falling for Simon was an example of taking charge, of change. Giving Luke a chance would be another.

"Si, I LOVE YOU like a brother, you know that. But, dude, this is not a great idea," Luke said to him the next day after he'd picked Simon up for the long ride to the airport. Simon had spent the ensuing minutes filling him in on his plan, which hinged on Luke.

"Possibly not." Simon stared out the windshield and clenched a tired hand to the back of his neck. He'd been up nearly all night again trying to decide if he had lost his ability for rational thought. In the end, he'd decided to go with the devil he knew, so to speak, in the form of his best friend. He knew he was asking Luke for the favor of a lifetime, as if he hadn't already requested enough of his friend, to back off where Fiona was concerned.

"Let me just sum this up real quick, though, because it's making my head spin, quite frankly. You want me to fake date the woman you are so interested in but won't date yourself, while you are out of town in order to keep her from dating someone else?"

"Yes. Because I promised her that I'd fix her up with someone and she thinks that someone was you. If I tell her it wasn't you, then I'll have to admit that I didn't really have someone else or I'll have to find someone else very quickly. I don't want to do the former and I'm not ready to do the latter. Yet. If she finds out what happened here, I'm afraid she'll be upset with me, scrap the whole idea and reactivate her PartnerUp.com profile. Your 'dating her' will keep her from doing that and finding some loser while I'm gone."

"Thank you, I think. But how am I supposed to keep her from falling for me?"

"She won't."

"My charm is legendary," Luke countered. "We were getting along pretty great before you crashed our little party, you know?"

"I know." This was true, and part of the reason he'd spent the night tossing and turning. Guilt nudged at him because… Did he have the right to stop a possibility that might lead to Fiona's ultimate happiness? Not to mention that his best friend, who could give Fiona what he couldn't, might be the right man for her. "Just…dial it back." All Simon could do was hold on to the memory of their kiss and hope that she wasn't ready to move on from it that quickly. He certainly wasn't. He knew he had to. He would. He just needed a little more time. And some sleep. "She liked me first and we have this…"

"Connection?" Luke supplied.

"Yes, I don't think she'll be comfortable getting together with you so soon. Plus, you're my best friend. Emphasize that."

"But you said not to talk about you."

"You can talk about me, about us, like when we were younger or whatever. Just don't mention anything about my business in LA. She thinks I'm a bartender."

Luke sighed and shook his head. "This is quite a scheme you've hatched here, isn't it? I don't think I like deceiving Fiona this way."

"You don't even know her!"

"Um, I beg to differ. Fiona and I spent a lovely evening together. I know she hates the snow, adores her four sisters, enjoys traveling, hates cauliflower and has a weak spot for hot cocoa." After a beat, he added, "She's not into yoga, but she likes piña coladas and—"

"Okay," Simon interrupted flatly. "If you're about to add getting caught in the rain, then our friendship is over."

"I couldn't resist," Luke said with a snicker. "But she does like piña coladas, did you know that? That's her favorite cocktail. She loves vacationing in the tropics. You might want to keep that in mind. A lesser friend would have imagined her drinking one in a bikini."

"Luke, I swear—" Simon scowled and shook his head.

"Simmer down, I'm just ribbing you a bit. But seriously, she is…captivating, right? And did you know she likes to golf?" He delivered a meaningful look and repeated concisely, "Golf. Simon."

"Yes, I know, Luke." He could hear the self-pity in his tone.

Luke heard it, too, and laughed. "A woman you could golf with, can you imagine it?"

"Don't make this worse for me." He couldn't stop thinking about it.

Like the good friend that he was, Luke did not heed his request. "You are a fool. It's a miracle she's not already taken. I will do it, but I want to go on record repeating that this is not a good idea. I don't—"

"I know," Simon interrupted. "But it's for her own good, to keep her from making a terrible decision. You should see the guys she's been matched up with from that stupid dating site. And by her own admission, she doesn't have the best judgment where men are concerned. Besides, it's only for a couple of days, three at the most. When I get back, I'll find someone else."

"Someone real?"

"Yes," Simon ground out. "Someone…suitable." He could not begin to articulate how much he'd come to despise that word.

"Okay. I changed my mind, because *that's* the part I can't wrap my brain around."

IT WAS AN interesting sensation, Fiona decided as she sat at a dining table in the guest lodge and stared at the unopened message on her phone, to both look forward to and dread someone's text. It was from Luke, and she knew what it was going to say. Or the gist of it anyway. Simon had whisked her away so quickly there'd been no time to gently dissuade him from a second date. A part of her wanted a second date. No, a part of her *wanted* to want a second date. And she absolutely would want that if it weren't for Simon. Stupid Simon. She sighed. That wasn't fair. Or true. Simon wasn't the stupid one—she was. Peyton was right; her "romantic radar" was faulty. Meaning she needed to think about this logically.

Simon had made a perfect choice in setting her up with Luke. Luke had all the components she was seeking, and then some. She couldn't even begin to imagine her dad's delight when he found out she was dating a pilot. All of this added up to the conclusion that she needed to give him a chance. With a tap of her finger, she opened his message:

Hey you. How about a continuation of our dinner tonight? No, scratch that. I'm not going to feed you leftover lasagna. I'll cook something. Or we can go out? Your choice.

How could she resist this kind of charm? Smiling, she typed a response: Sounds good! How about we cook together?

Perfect. My place about 7ish?

She answered with a simple: See you then.

"Earth to Fiona." A voice sounded close to her ear, over her left shoulder. Startled, she turned and found a smiling Hadley behind her.

"Hadley, hi. Sorry. How are you?"

"Good morning. I'm fine. Can I sit with you?"

"Of course. Please." Her stomach pitched nervously as she gathered the apology she'd practiced a thousand times. It would be good to finally hash this out.

Hadley moved around the table, sat across from her and got straight to the point. "So, I haven't had a chance to talk to you about this pig thing."

"I'm sorry. I've been wanting to apologize in person, but Tyler thought it might be best if I waited and—"

"I know," she interrupted. "He told me. He was worried about my stress level." She let out a tiny laugh and placed a hand on her tummy. "Such a sweetheart."

Fiona had no idea where this was going so she just nodded. To keep her nervous hands busy, she slowly spun her coffee mug on the table.

"I should have told you this sooner. I thought about texting a couple of times but there was too much to say. And I wanted to say it in person, and I kept thinking I'd run into you. I stopped by your cabin a few times, but you weren't there. Obviously," she added, and then cleared her throat.

"I've been working a lot," Fiona supplied, careful not to reference the reason that so much work was necessary. "I'm sorry. If I would have known you wanted to speak with me, I would have—"

"No!" Hadley said. "My goodness, don't you go apologizing for getting a job. I could have..." She waved a breezy hand through the air. "It doesn't matter now, does it? I've been waiting for this opportunity. You're here, and so am I, and I'm glad because I have a few things to say."

"Okay," Fiona said, bracing herself.

"It wasn't your fault. I wasn't mad at you even though you may have thought that. I'm sorry that you felt so bad about this whole thing."

"Hadley, you don't have anything to apologize for. If you weren't upset with me, you should have been. *I* was mad at me."

"I think there was a lot of self-blame going around."

"Lydia mentioned that."

"Good. How about we all forgive ourselves?" At Fiona's nod, she went on, "But, listen, I know that you paid for the cake and the flowers."

"What?" She'd specifically asked that her name not be disclosed. She figured Hadley would speculate, perhaps assume, but she'd asked that she not be told.

Hadley's smile was gentle and sincere. "Fiona, this is a very small town."

"Who told you? I asked the bakery and the florist to keep my name confidential."

Her grin morphed into big and satisfied. "They did."

Fiona let out a little gasp and laid a hand on her forehead. "You tricked me?"

"I did. Sorry, not sorry."

Fiona chuckled and shook her head. "I have four older sisters—you'd think I'd know better." To be fair, she was rather distracted. She kept wondering if it was right to spend the evening with Luke when she felt the way she did about Simon.

"Yeah, it's a Tyler Blackwell trick that I've perfected. And one that makes me both proud and yet also frightened for our unborn child. Can you imagine what he's going to teach our kids after growing up with four brothers?"

"I can." Fiona chuckled through a sympathetic grimace. "Believe me when I tell you that a house of girls is no better. We developed our own share of...let's call them survival techniques."

Hadley laughed. "That's funny. Tyler likes to say it was survival of the fittest on the Blackwell Ranch. I keep telling him that term doesn't apply because they all survived."

"Not without plenty of wounds and a fair number of scars, I'm sure," Fiona said. There'd been plenty of near misses in the Harrison household, including the "rocket accident" that had resulted in Lily's dyspraxia.

"That's what Tyler says, too. He broke his

arm once after sneaking out of the house. It's actually a really sweet story. His brother Jon took him to the hospital and never ratted him out."

"That kind of loyalty does not surprise me about my cousins. For me, that's one of the best things about having sisters. Someone to keep your secrets. My sister Georgie is the absolute best at that. This one time, I snuck out of the house, and took my mom's car to a bonfire on the beach but got badly stuck before I even got there. I called Georgie. She snuck out, which she would never do, called a friend, and they rescued me. Never told a soul. Mom and Dad never found out. Then again, she and Amanda once kept a wounded chipmunk in the attic for three weeks, and I kept that a secret."

"I can't wait to meet her. She's coming for Thanksgiving, right?"

"I'm not sure. I hope so. Doctor stuff keeps her super busy." If Georgie had a fault, it was that she was a little too responsible. Too serious. Possibly, some of her busyness was self-imposed. Although, Fiona had spent her life not being serious enough and look where that had gotten her. Both of them were still single, but at least Georgie was a doctor with this incredible career. "I keep sending her photos and videos of what she's missing out on. We've all got our fingers crossed."

Hadley slid a familiar envelope across the table. "I believe this belongs to you. It was for the food, right?"

Fiona nodded but didn't touch the cash.

"How did you know how much it was? Tyler swears he didn't tell you."

"He didn't. I estimated. I've worked in the food service industry my entire life."

"Well done," Hadley said. "But, as it turns out, we should be giving you a commission. The whole pig invasion has turned out *not* to be a disaster. In fact, it's something of an internet sensation—and a profit maker. It's bringing us business."

"I'm so glad. Lydia mentioned it might be. But that part doesn't matter to me—it doesn't take back what I did. I'm still going to pay for my mistake."

"Yes, it kind of does. I appreciate the gesture. Your integrity tells me there's plenty of Blackwell inside of you. It also means that we would never accept this from anyone, and especially not from you. Fiona, you're family."

Those words were like an arrow to her heart. She wanted to embrace them, but she also wanted to earn them. And not from pity.

Reminding her that she needed to bring it on Thanksgiving.

Hadley added, "Big E would never let me hear the end of it if he knew I'd let you pay for an accident that was more our fault than it was yours. That's part of the reason I was so upset. We knew that latch was bad and I... I can be a little hard on myself sometimes." Tears filled her eyes as she went on, "Tyler and I have worked so hard on this place and the idea that an oversight like that could harm our business. I..." She stopped to sniffle.

Fiona reached a hand across the table and then stopped. "Wait... Those tears are real, right?"

"Yes," Hadley said, snuffling out a laugh and nodding. "They're real, but in the interest of full transparency it does not take much to bring them on these days. Yesterday, I cried because the bakery was out of pumpkin muffins."

"Well, that's definitely worth shedding a tear or two," Fiona joked. "Pumpkin pie is my favorite."

"Mine, too. It's the best part of Thanksgiving as far I'm concerned. With real whipped cream."

Fiona made a mental note of that and got back to the point. "But, Hadley..."

"But, Fiona…" Hadley parroted her tone while patting her hand. "Don't make me call Big E."

Fiona opened her mouth to argue, but quickly closed it again as she realized the lecture that would inspire. "Well done," she conceded with a grin. "It is absolutely no surprise to me why this place is so exceptional." Tapping the envelope, she said, "I tell you what… I'll use the money for Thanksgiving dinner."

"Nope. We already paid for the groceries."

"What? How…?"

"The Blackwell Ranch has an account at White Buffalo Grocers. Every cashier knows not to charge you."

Fiona sighed. The woman was beautiful, efficient and clever; there didn't seem much point in arguing with Hadley Blackwell. And, honestly, she could use the money for a deposit on her own place.

Hadley changed the subject. "You're out and about early this morning. Are you working a breakfast shift or something?"

"Oh. Um, sort of. I'm helping Simon out."

"Helping Simon out of what?" Tyler asked, striding into view with a heaping plate of breakfast. He took a seat next to Hadley. "Not jail, I hope?" he quipped, laughing at his own joke.

Hadley let out a playful, exasperated huff. "That joke is really old, Tyler."

Holding one finger aloft, he agreed, "Yes, but no less funny."

"Not according to your grandfather."

Tyler grinned. "That's what makes it funny."

Fiona found his smile contagious. She explained, "Simon had to fly home to LA for a couple of days, and I'm helping him out at the Silver Stake."

Tyler narrowed his eyes thoughtfully. "What kind of help?"

"Oh, uh, just opening the restaurant the next two mornings, doing the prep work and sticking around until Roy gets in."

"I see. So, does that mean you're free for dinner? We're eating at Grandma's tonight and you're invited."

"Unfortunately, no. I have plans." She couldn't quite bring herself to call it a date.

"With Simon?" Tyler asked.

Hadley admonished in a teasing tone, "Tyler, did you not just hear her say that Simon was in LA?"

"Yes, but…" He shook his head. "Never mind."

But what? She wanted to ask but didn't want to add to any speculation that might be buzzing about. "My date is not with Simon," Fiona said with a finality that she hoped would put the matter to rest, at least in Tyler's mind. "But, speaking of Simon, you're not the first person to mention this wild streak of his. What do you know about him? What was this brush with the law, and what does it have to do with our grandfather?"

CHAPTER TWELVE

"Is he here?" Simon asked Colette when he arrived at the offices of Clarke Props, Ltd. They didn't open for another hour, but his sister was already seated behind her desk outside his suite.

"Inside," Colette responded smoothly, but the expression on her face suggested the confrontation awaiting him would be anything but.

Simon entered his office to discover Mica snoring on the sofa. His brother wore a rumpled suit with one pant leg rolled to the knee, and one shoe—the other foot was bare. A lone sock rested on his chest just below his chin. For some reason only the very inebriated Mica could explain, and that Simon didn't care to learn, coins and candy were scattered all over him, as well as the floor. An empty whiskey bottle and four glasses sat on the table in front of him. He was all too familiar with the sight of a drunk sleeping off a bender.

Taking a few seconds to gather his temper regarding the conclusion he couldn't help but draw, he opened the door again and slammed it shut behind him.

Mica bolted upright and shouted, "Earthquake! Get the—" Glancing around wildly, he noticed Simon and went still. Eyes squinting in his pain-riddled face, he rasped, "Simon? What the h-h... What are you doing here?"

Simon scowled his disgust. "You know very well I don't like strangers in my office, especially drunk ones." He gestured at the table. "Were you planning on meeting Enrique Hale and his staff looking like this?" Stepping closer as he went to his desk, he inadvertently inhaled a whiff of stale booze and cigarettes. "Smelling like that? Unbelievable, Mica. You reek like a dive bar. You're turning into Dad."

"You would know, wouldn't you?" Mica retorted in a snide tone.

"What is that supposed to mean? I don't drink."

"Yeah, Mr. High-And-Mighty, I know. *Everyone* knows how you're the complete opposite of Dad. You just run off to bartend at one when Ned calls."

"Are you...serious right now? Val could have died. I owe my life to Ned and Uncle Dean and Aunt Jeanette. And the Silver Stake is not a dive bar."

"Oh, really?" Mica drawled sarcastically.

Dipping his head, he scrubbed his hands across his unshaven jaw. "You've only told me like a billion times. But you know what? No one—" He cut himself off with a soft curse and pinched the bridge of his nose. "Ouch."

"No one what?"

"Never mind. Who cares?"

"I care." Simon heaved out a sigh and leaned against the edge of his desk. "Do you want to tell me what's going on?"

Mica pushed himself to his feet. It appeared to require undue effort. "Nothing is going on. I went out and had fun last night. Remember fun? You used to have it a really long time ago. I've heard you and Luke talk about it."

"Okay, Mica, enough with the infantile sarcasm. I don't have time for it. According to Colette, you've been having enough fun for all of us lately."

"What I do is none of Colette's business."

"It is when it affects your job."

"My job?" Mica scoffed and repeated, "*This* job?"

"Yes, Mica, your job! The one I gave you. The one where you do work for me, and then I give you the money that allows you to have all of this fun. But from what I understand, only one of us is adhering to this arrangement with any degree of commitment."

Mica shook his head and glanced around absently as if he wasn't quite sure about where he was. "Since you're back, I guess I don't need to stick around for this meeting, huh?"

"Are you kidding me?"

"No."

Colette was right; he was going to have to deal with this. Somehow. But, right now, he had a meeting to prepare for.

"Yeah, go. We'll talk about this later."

"So," FIONA SAID, "the story I heard is that a sixteen-year-old Simon Clarke, with Luke Bradley riding shotgun, stole my grandfather's pickup."

"Ah." Luke stood at the island in his kitchen dicing potatoes. Grinning, he looked up and met her eyes. Fiona was glad because then she could appreciate the full scope of their mischievous sparkle. Using the knife to point at her, he said, "I've been meaning to ask Simon if you knew about that."

"Simon isn't the one who told me. I heard it from someone else. I'm pretty sure he alluded to it once, though. He said my new grandpa didn't like him, but that it was a long story." Fiona added the garlic she'd crushed to the pot on the stove, where pancetta, onions and celery were already sizzling. She gave the mixture a stir and faced Luke again. "This already smells delicious."

Nodding slowly, he said, "That doesn't surprise me that you heard about these long-ago antics. People like to talk, and memories are long in this town. And often exaggerated, too, I might add. Maybe not in this case, however. It will be delicious. You should feel special, I've never shared my mom's seafood chowder recipe with anyone."

"I'm honored," Fiona said, and started snipping the fresh thyme. "Are you saying you didn't steal it?"

"Oh, no." He gave her a slow-growing smile that wound up looking both sheepish and full of humor. "We stole it, all right."

"Like grand theft auto stealing?"

"No, more like premeditated joyriding." He chuckled, and went on. "We were stupid kids. We didn't intend to steal it. We didn't even think of it as joyriding so much as a practical joke. We knew Big E had gone to Billings for an auction and had left his pickup parked at this popular spot outside of town toward the interstate that everyone calls the wagon wheel, because it's where these roads come together in roughly that shape. You meet people there and leave a rig so you can ride together, like what you city folk might call a park and ride. But informal, right?"

At her nod, he went on. "We were going to bring it back, with the cab all muddy and the tank on empty. Again, it was something people did. And to pull off one like that on Big E Blackwell would have been the coup of the century. At least, to two enthusiastic and highly committed troublemakers like us."

He paused to add the potatoes to the mix. Fiona poured in a mixture of clam and chicken broths. Luke stirred and adjusted the temperature.

"Anyway, like any good rancher, Big E had a spare jerrican of gas strapped in the bed, so we knew we had miles and miles of empty dirt roads and four-wheeling ahead of us, which we used to our advantage. Drove for hours on the Forest Service roads, and along the river, went for a swim, then on to this field in the middle of nowhere and generally had a ball. Ran it out of gas, as planned. Lots of laughs, fun and games. But then, when we went to fill up with the gas can, it was empty."

"Uh-oh."

"Uh-oh doesn't quite reflect our sentiments at the time, Fiona, but I think you're getting the picture." He stepped over to the fridge. "You want a beer?"

"Sure," she said.

Luke retrieved two bottles, opened them and handed her one. After taking a long pull, he continued, "My family was dirt-poor, worse than Simon's, but at least I had parents who functioned. So, I didn't have a cell phone. Simon had a phone, but we had no cell service. And still, the only person we knew to call, who could truly help, was Simon's uncle Dean, who, yep, you guessed it, was with Big E. That's how we knew he was going to be gone in the first place. Before we could hike back or get within cell phone range, Big E had reported the rig as stolen."

"Oh, boy."

"You got that right. We hadn't even made it back to the wagon wheel before the cops picked us up."

"You were arrested? Did you explain all of that?"

"We were arrested, all right," Luke confirmed with a grin. "Of course, we explained. Or tried to. We'd already had close calls with the law and were in trouble at school pretty much all the time. If you didn't grow up in a small town like this one it's difficult to understand, but reputations are kinda like concrete around here. Once they get formed, they tend to stay that way. Like I said, me and Si were already, uh, *notorious*, I suppose, would be an apt word. It wouldn't have mattered what we said."

"What happened? How much trouble did you get in?"

"Simon's uncle talked Big E out of pressing charges. But we paid for it, had to wash and detail his pickup once a week all summer long and work off all that gas money. Seriously, I think we worked off enough for him to drive all the way to the end of the Baja Peninsula and back. We might have been miscreants, but we were hard workers."

Fiona's heart went out to both boys. Simon had never mentioned his troubled home life. Tyler had implied it. In addition to giving her the shortened version of this story, her cousin had revealed that Simon's father was a "raging alcoholic" and his mother "checked out." When Simon was a teenager, his parents had gotten a divorce and the family moved away. But what was the deeper story here?

"You mentioned the other day that Simon's parents shipped him off to California. Did this little brush with the law have something to do with that?"

"Oh. Uh…no." Fiona could see Luke shutting down before her eyes. Wondering how much to reveal or if he'd already said too much.

"He was already living in California by then. His grandparents sent him back here to Montana during the summers to work on his uncle Dean's ranch. And he visited at Christmas and a lot of school breaks. Summers during college he worked for Dean and wherever he could find work, including your cousin Jon's place. We'd both work two or three part-time jobs at a time. Ranching is like that—summertime offers lots of opportunities for seasonal work."

"You said his grandparents were sending him back here? Where were his parents? What was the situation with his family? My cousin Tyler mentioned some stuff, too, that suggested his home life wasn't great."

"My goodness, I am a font of information here, aren't I? Like the Clarke family historian. Except, I'm not a Clarke"

"I'm sorry. I didn't mean to put you on the spot. Is this topic off-limits?"

Folding his arms, he took a step backward and leaned against the counter behind him. His gaze was intense and felt assessing, like he was pondering something important. "How much do you like him?"

An actual thunderbolt couldn't have achieved what Luke managed with that simple question. She liked him… All of the way.

She exhaled loudly and shook her head. "I'm crazy about him. Like head over heels."

Luke remained silent, his expression thoughtful, and Fiona realized how that sounded. "I'm sorry, Luke. I want to like you. I mean, I do like you. Just not like that. I'm… He's…" *The one. And I don't care that he's a bartender. I don't care that his family situation is messed up. I don't care about what Dad or Big E think. I don't care that three of my sisters are engaged to accomplished men with "suitable" jobs. I don't care if it makes me the family underachiever for the rest of my life.*

"No." Luke grinned. "Fiona, don't apologize. I want this. I like you, too. Meaning, you would be great for Simon. There's nothing I'd like more than for my best friend to finally…"

"Finally what?" she urged.

"The topic isn't off-limits, per se. I just think you should hear this stuff from Simon. It will help you to understand him better."

"You're right. I should hear it from him. But, first, he needs to hear some things from me. I made a mistake. A big one. Even if I apologize, I don't know if he'll still want me."

Luke dipped his head forward until it rested on his chest. Chuckling, he shook his head for a few seconds before meeting her gaze again.

"Oh, Fiona, my friend, trust me, he still wants you."

"How do you…? But he set me up with you."

"Um," Luke drawled. "Yeah, not really."

"What?"

"That was an accident."

"What do you mean, an accident?"

"Do you really think he would set you, a woman who he… Well, *you*…with me?" he asked with a sheepish smile.

Fiona narrowed her eyes suspiciously as heat warmed her cheeks. What was she missing here?

He tried again. "Let me put it this way. Do you really believe any man would set up a woman he's fallen for with his best friend?"

Fiona thought for a second. "Wait, so… When you showed up at the Silver Stake it wasn't for a date with me?"

"Nope. I was waiting on a date with Simon. We were supposed to have dinner. When you sat down, I, uh… I thought you were hitting on me. Of course, I took advantage of the situation." His smile was adorable. Guilty, but adorable. "And then, in the parking lot of the grocery store, Si sent me a text letting me know it was a misunderstanding."

"So, you took me to your house knowing that Simon didn't want you to date me?"

"I did." He grimaced. "I'm sorry. I also didn't text him back right away…on purpose."

She let out a little gasp as the events of their "date" came back to her. She remembered him checking his phone in the grocery store parking lot. A long time had passed before he looked at it again. She remembered that. She'd noted it because she'd liked that he didn't pay more attention to his phone than he did to her. Then came the bout of mad texting that had Luke laughing, and then… "That's why he showed up at your house?"

"Yep. In case you have any doubts about how he really feels. He came over to make sure that we weren't having too good of a time. And notice how he scooted you right out of there?"

"And this?" She gestured around. "What is this? It's not really a date, is it?"

"Not in the traditional sense, no. He told me he would quit our friendship if I got closer than two feet to you."

"Why would he do that, though? Fake set us up after accidentally setting us up?"

"He was afraid that if you learned that he didn't really set you up you might be angry. He's concerned about you finding someone else. Or rather, he's concerned about you firing up that profile again and finding the wrong someone. He claims he's serious about the matchmaking. His plan is to find you a real date when he gets back. Someone who's *not* his best friend but who is worthy of you."

"Wow."

"I know. He's a better man than me. And the thing is… It won't work. He won't find anyone. No one will be good enough. I know my friend and he's got it bad for you."

"Wow. That's um… That's a lot of effort just for…me."

"Yes, you, Fiona. Exactly. Still interested?"

"Yes, of course. I suppose I should be irritated, but it's incredibly sweet that he cares that much about me." Enough to fix her up with someone else. Fiona felt her heart soften. And after she'd rejected him. Who did that? Only someone who really cared. She needed to fix this.

Luke stirred the chowder. "These potatoes need to cook awhile. Let's go sit in the living room and finish our beers."

Fiona followed him and took a seat on one end of the large, comfy sectional. "Jeez, Luke, now that I think about it, he really should be apologizing to you. You're the one stuck with me."

"Fiona, spending time with you is not exactly a hardship, I promise you that. Besides, it's given me time to decide if you're good enough for my best friend. How many guys get that chance?"

"And?"

"We're having this conversation, aren't we? Simon didn't put me up to this part. In fact, he would not appreciate me giving his game away."

Fiona exhaled a nervous sigh. She hoped that Luke was right that he'd give her another chance. And then what? Because they still had the matter of his living in California. She would trust her heart and play it by ear. She'd promised her dad and herself that she wouldn't do that anymore, but this felt different. This time, with Simon, she just… She knew.

"Promise me one thing?" he asked.

"Okay."

"No matter what happens, don't give up on him. Simon is…" Luke sighed. "He can be a little closed off emotion-wise. But he's the best man I know. He deserves to be happy."

"I promise," she replied immediately. That was an easy one, because wasn't she the one who'd given up on him before they'd even had a chance? She wasn't about to make that mistake again.

"Are you going to tell him how you feel?"

"Yes, when he gets back. I want to do it in person."

"Good." Luke settled against the cushions with a satisfied smile.

"Why?"

"Certainly not for my own personal agenda that includes torturing my friend a little bit more, that's for sure." His words, delivered with such contrived innocence, implied the opposite and had her believing every bit of his teenage reputation.

"Of course not," Fiona agreed with a chuckle.

"If I scooch closer, can we take a selfie? I promised Si I'd keep him updated."

It dawned on her that maybe Simon deserved a smidgen of payback for what he'd done. "Closer than two feet?" she asked with her own impish grin.

"That's the idea."

"Let's take several."

"Yes!" Luke moved to sit next to her, his arm around her. Fiona tipped her head so that it rested on his shoulder.

"Now," Luke said after snapping numerous photos, "just so that I can file it away for future reference, what is your favorite color, type of cookie and shoe size?"

SIMON WAS ON the golf course with the esteemed and ultratalented director Enrique

Hale when the harassment first started. Simon liked Enrique. The man was brilliant, funny and interesting, yet understated, humble and unassuming. Like Simon, he came from modest beginnings. Unlike Simon, he credited his success to an upbringing by hardworking, loving parents and a large, supportive extended family.

"That's good," he said to Enrique after the man teed off with a strong, straight shot down the middle of the fairway. Bonus, the man was an excellent golfer and in good enough shape to walk the course. The day was sunny and warm, and he relished the break from the Montana winter.

"Between projects," Enrique said modestly. "I've been on the course a lot lately."

Simon grinned, and said wryly, "Yeah, that's it, Enrique. I know your meek act isn't going to keep you from taking my money if you beat me."

"True enough," he said, and laughed. "I thought I was going to be meeting with Mica. Aren't you supposed to be in Montana until December?"

Simon tensed and tried to decide how honest to be. This might not be a small town like Falcon Creek, but it was a small, gossipy world they worked in, and he couldn't be sure what

Enrique had heard about Mica. Or what Mica had said to Enrique. For that matter, Simon couldn't know what havoc Mica had perpetrated around town in his absence. His brother appeared to be unraveling and Simon knew he needed to fix it.

"You were. I was, but I flew home to meet with you instead. Mica is…going through something. I'm flying back tonight and then I'll be back for good around the first week of December."

"I appreciate your dedication."

"Of course." Simon nodded. "I appreciate your business."

Enrique quirked a brow. "I also understand family. I've kept my brother-in-law on my payroll for sixteen years and I have *another* employee whose primary job is to clean up the stupid mistakes he makes. At the end of the day, family is…" Enrique paused as if searching for the right words.

Simon expected that to be *everything* or *important* or even *number one*. What he said was, "a royal pain in the butt."

Simon tipped his head back and laughed, hard. Unexpectedly relieved and heartened by the support, he wholeheartedly agreed.

They were headed to the eighth hole and discussing the popularity of CG in modern cinema when his phone buzzed with the first text from Luke. A selfie of Luke and Fiona. Cuddled on Luke's sofa.

Simon: Two-foot rule violation.

Luke: Selfie waiver.

Simon: Not a thing.

Luke: It absolutely is a thing.

Luke followed that with another of Fiona and him seated at his dining room table, bottles of beer and two bowls in front of them. Fiona had her spoon lifted as if poised to take a bite. Once again, Luke had his arm around her.

The caption read: Fiona loves my

Simon: ???

Luke: chowder. Get your mind out of the gutter.

Simon: That joke wasn't funny the first time. I know what you're doing. It won't work. Stop fondling her. And stop bothering me. I'm on the golf course.

Luke: The golf course?!? You #^&%!

Luke: You do realize you've just made things worse for yourself, right?

Luke: So, so, so much worse.

CHAPTER THIRTEEN

FIONA DOUBLE-CHECKED the email message on her phone. Sure enough, right street address. Hmm. A closer look revealed a sign pointing around the side that read Falcon Creek CPA. The neat cobblestone walk was shoveled free of snow and led to the door where an Open sign hung in the window.

Continuing inside, she found the small office empty. The reception area was neatly furnished with a plush gray sofa and two wing chairs of muted gold. Light from a tall lamp cast a cheerful glow over a coffee table stacked with a tidy assortment of magazines. The delicious scent of fresh coffee wafted from the pot still brewing atop a lovely antique sideboard.

There was a lone desk at the end of the room. Behind it, and off to the side, an open door revealed a smaller but also empty office. Fiona walked to the desk and checked for a buzzer or a bell. Another door, presumably leading into the house, was closed. She was trying to decide what to do, when that door opened and her cousin-in-law Grace hustled through. In one hand, she held a small electronic device, and in the other a coffee mug.

"Fiona? Hi! What a nice surprise. Are you here about Thanksgiving?"

Fiona wasn't sure how to handle this. To avoid the impending embarrassment, she briefly considered trying to go with Grace's assumption that she was just dropping by. But that didn't feel right.

"Actually—" she started to explain, but the ringing of the phone interrupted her. Before Grace could pick up, the device in her hand emitted a howl revealing itself to be a baby monitor. Which made sense; Grace and Ethan had an adorable little guy named Elias, after Big E.

"Nooo," Grace groaned in that mom-style tone of distress, her focus now wholly on the monitor. "I've been trying to get him down, but the poor little guy is teething." A few fussy seconds passed, and he quieted. Grace shifted her attention to the still-ringing phone, then moved, reaching out her other hand to pick up. It went silent. She sighed. The baby let out a shriek and began crying in earnest.

Frowning, she said, "Sorry, it's been one of those mornings. My sitter is running late. I'll be right back. Make yourself at home."

Fiona nibbled at her lip and briefly considered writing an apologetic note of explanation and departing while she still had her dignity. The phone started up again.

Glancing in the direction Grace had gone, she moved around the desk and answered the call. "Falcon Creek CPA, how can I help you?"

The caller identified herself as a client and asked for Grace. "Oh, I'm sorry, Grace is in a meeting right now. Can I take a message? Oh, I see. Yes, of course…" Fiona chatted, took a detailed message and said goodbye. The phone was still in her hand when the ringing started again.

"Good morning, Falcon Creek CPA, how can I help you?"

The caller introduced himself as Mac Henson, and, after a friendly round of small talk, Fiona listened while he explained why he was searching for a "top-notch" tax accountant. Fiona picked up her phone and commenced an internet search.

When he paused, she said, "Well, Mr. Henson, you've made the right call. You won't find a more knowledgeable or efficient CPA than Grace Blackwell. Clients regularly refer to her as a fiscal genius. Last year, with her knowledge of the new tax laws, she saved a Montana farm equipment company several thousands of dollars. Obviously, I can't divulge names, but another business owner gives her credit for keeping him out of jail," Fiona paraphrased from Grace's stellar online reviews.

The outside door opened revealing a delivery person. Friendly smile in place, Fiona waved him over. She signed the form on his clipboard and then mouthed a thank-you. He set the box down and waved goodbye.

"Hey, Grace," he said quietly, and headed for the exit.

That's when Fiona noticed Grace standing in the doorway to the house. Pointing at the phone, Fiona locked eyes with her and said, "That is very kind. I'm so glad you think so! Okay, Mr. Henson, let's get you scheduled for an appointment as soon as possible. Can I put you on hold for a minute?" She tapped the hold button. "A man by the name of Mac Henson would like to come in and discuss his taxes. Do you want to schedule him now? Where's your calendar?"

Grace had gone wide-eyed while she explained. Nodding, she hustled toward the desk. A quick flick of the mouse and the calendar came into view. "Right here..."

Fiona got back on the line. With her talking and Grace clicking around, they quickly made an appointment. Fiona laughed at something he said, assured him he wouldn't be disappointed and said goodbye.

"Fiona, thank you," Grace said after Fiona hung up. "I can't believe that was Mac Henson."

"Of Henson Irrigation Systems. Do you know him?"

"Not yet." Grace's smile was radiant. "I know of him, and this is beyond exciting. He has customers across the entire western United States. He could be a huge client."

"Congratulations." Fiona grinned.

"No, Fiona, you did this. Thank you. If that call had gone to voice mail and he'd called another accountant…" Grace pressed two fingers to her temple. "I don't even want to think about that."

Fiona slid the notepad toward her. "This woman, Carla Potts, also left a very long message. Oh, I forgot to write her phone number down…" She jotted it across the top. "I hope I got it all down, but I have a good memory, so if you have questions later just give me a call."

Grace frowned at the message before looking at Fiona curiously. "You memorized her number?"

"Yeah, I remember stuff like that. Don't ask me for the square root or anything. I don't do math beyond the basics, but I remember the digits."

"Thank you so much. As you can see, I really need to get someone hired around here. Which will be soon, I hope. So, what can I do for you? Did you get my text about Thanksgiving? Did you stop by to tell me I'm bringing too many people to dinner?" Her tone was lighthearted but held an edge of concern.

"No, not at all. I mean, yes, I got your text. And you are not bringing too many people. I'm thrilled you guys can make it. It's going to be a ton of fun."

"Or wait… Lydia said you were trying to track down that salad recipe that the boys like? Did Grandma Dot not have it?"

"Oh, no, Grandma did have it. I got it, thank you. I'm here because… This is sort of awkward, but I came here to apply for the job you posted. I didn't realize it was *your* business. I don't know why I didn't realize it was you. I knew you were an accountant." Fiona hitched a thumb toward the door. "I'm just going to go away now and pretend this never happened."

"What? Why?"

"Well, you know, nepotism for one. In my experience, that often causes problems in the workplace."

Grace peered at her closely like she was

trying to puzzle out her meaning. "So, you *haven't* met your family, the Blackwells, then?" she joked.

"Oops," she chuckled, and qualified, "Ranching notwithstanding. And, obviously, there are professions where a familial... weighted employment environment is beneficial if not preferred."

Grace took a moment to laugh before repeating, "A familial weighted employment environment? That is one way to describe the Blackwell dynasty."

Fiona grinned and shook her head. "Took a pretty creative shovel to dig myself out of that hole, didn't it?"

"Diplomacy is a valuable skill when working with the public."

"Oh, believe me, I know that. Years of experience in the restaurant industry taught me that and so much more."

"I can see that. I hope you're this entertaining all the time. Tyler said you were funny."

"Tyler is funny," Fiona said as warmth spread through her at the compliment. Finally she seemed to be making strides where this new family was concerned. Thanksgiving dinner would, hopefully, score her even more points.

"It will be so nice to have someone around

here who I can talk to, over the age of two. You're hired."

"Wait, I wasn't presuming that you were going to hire me. I'm horrified at the idea that you might even think that."

"I don't think that. How could I not consider you, though, seeing as how you're family?" Grace teased.

Fiona felt herself smiling. Grace was definitely someone she could be friends with. "See how complicated this could be? You haven't even looked at my résumé."

"Fiona, relax, I don't need to look at your résumé. You just had the ultimate tryout, where you scored me a big, important new client. I'm confident in this decision. When can you start?"

"Oh boy…" Fiona muttered under her breath, and added the remaining names from Grace's text to the dinner guest list. She counted, ending with "thirty-six" and not realizing she'd spoken the total aloud.

"What is the year that Jesse Owens won four gold medals at the Berlin Olympics?" Over her shoulder, a deep, familiar voice fired off the answer in a question-style game-show tone that made Fiona chuckle. And sent her heart racing.

Simon was back.

Spinning around to face him, she did her best buzzer impression, "Ehnt! Ooh, no, I'm sorry, that is incorrect. For my purposes anyway, although I'm impressed that you knew that. The correct answer is what is the number of guests attending the Thanksgiving dinner I agreed to prepare for my new family."

"What are you…? Is that a joke? You're making dinner for thirty-six people?"

"Apparently so. I know we're closed on Thanksgiving, but can I work breakfast shift on Tuesday and have Wednesday off? I'll do a double on Friday." Grace had already told her she'd like to start training her on Monday and part of Tuesday. The office was closed Wednesday through Friday for the holiday, so her new job wouldn't be a problem. She wanted to start prepping on Tuesday and cook and bake all day Wednesday.

"Of course. Who's helping you?"

"Uh, well, let's see…" She glanced down at the list she'd made on her phone. "Grace's mom is bringing a dish, Jon and the girls are baking a cheesecake, and Chance is making sweet potato bake."

"You didn't ask anyone to help, did you?"

"No, I can't. That's the point. Everyone is super busy. Katie and Hadley are both pregnant. I want to do this. It's just that the guest list has grown a bit larger than I expected. When I offered, I didn't know so many of my family were coming. That's definitely a huge yay, but also eight additional people right there. Then, when Grace and Ethan were thinking about skipping to spend it with Grace's family, I invited them all. That's another six I didn't initially account for. Boom, just like that, the guest list nearly doubled."

"Can you ask your family for help?"

"Normally, yes. But Peyton and Amanda are coming from California and Lily doesn't cook. Why are we talking about this right now? I've got it handled. Welcome back. I'm happy to see you." She hoped her smile communicated how much she meant that.

"Thank you. It's good to be back." The way he looked her over, like maybe he was drinking in the sight, gave her the courage she needed to ask, "Can I talk to you privately?"

"Of course. Let's go into my office."

SIMON FOLLOWED HER inside and shut the door. He wanted to hug her and bury his face in her neck; the feeling was both overwhelming and oddly specific. There was an ache in his chest, too, and he knew it was irrational, but it was like his heart wanted to be close to hers. Being away for two days hadn't eased his craving for all things Fiona. If anything, it had made it worse.

"So, as you know, Luke and I spent some time together while you were gone."

"Yeah, I, uh, I heard. And saw. I had no idea my friend was such a gifted selfie taker."

"He's pretty great." One side of Fiona's mouth pulled up like she was fighting a smile. "I learned some interesting things about you."

"Is that so?"

"Well, my cousin Tyler made a joke about you and Big E. Since you'd mentioned it, and Katie had already alluded to it, I asked Luke and he gave me the long story about your vehicle heist."

Simon grinned. "Good. Then you got the most accurate version."

"I asked him other questions about you, too."

"What kinds of questions?"

"About your childhood and your family."

"Gave him the third degree, did you? Luke knows it all. I can only imagine what he chose to tell you." Despite Luke's promise that he wouldn't divulge certain details about Simon's life, he felt himself tense. Not because he didn't trust Luke but because he didn't want to discuss his family.

"He's a good friend to you. He didn't say

much of anything. He told me I should ask you."

"Hmm." *Good answer, Luke.*

"He actually grilled me a bit."

"Did he?" Where was she going with this? Luke hadn't said anything about this conversation.

"Yeah. I think he wanted to know what my intentions are. He asked me how much I like you."

Simon froze. *Oh, Luke, what have you done?*

"And I told him."

"What did you tell him?" Simon asked, both fearing and anticipating her answer.

"I told him that I like you all the way. Simon, I made a mistake."

"Fiona…"

Her name was all he could manage because suddenly her arms were wrapping around him exactly like he'd fantasized. He gathered her close and buried his nose in her hair. The sheer force of emotion had him squeezing his eyes shut and focusing on every sensation: the softness of her curves, her luscious flowery scent, the warmth of her skin where it met his, the feel of her hand curled around the back of his neck, her impossibly soft lips trailing along his jaw. He hadn't been able to stop thinking about this for two days. No, that wasn't true.

He'd thought about this every single day since he'd met her, and nearly every second since he'd kissed her.

"Simon," she whispered, pulling back enough to catch his gaze. Which she held on to as she said, "I'm so sorry. I don't care that you're a bartender. I don't care what you do for a job. I just want to be with you. I know we can only give each other a couple of weeks, but if you're willing, I'm in."

At his nod, her mouth moved to his and all he could think about was how good it felt, how right it was to finally hold her. He wouldn't allow himself to think about how difficult it was going to be to let her go.

"Relax... Are you relaxed?" Simon asked in the gentle tone he favored when working with jumpy horses or nervous riders. In this case, it was all about the latter. He stood in the middle of Jon's riding arena while Mesa, with an obviously tense Fiona in the saddle, circled the perimeter.

After a spirited negotiation where he agreed to put her on the "gentlest" horse he knew where "no one" would see her, she'd agreed to another lesson at Jon's ranch. A real lesson that included her actually getting on the horse. Everything had gone well; he'd taken her through the steps of saddling a horse, then basic riding commands, safety instructions, and finally talked her into getting on.

"Do I look relaxed?" Fiona retorted, comically mimicking his tone. "With my feet strapped to a one-thousand-pound animal, who doesn't know me and whom I don't know, but that I'm trusting not to throw me against the wall and stomp on me?" She pulled back on the reins and Mesa halted.

"No." Simon walked over to her.

"You really are a good teacher, though. Did you see how I put the brakes on just now like you showed me?" Her eyebrows slid up while her chin dipped down. The rest of her remained rigid.

"I did see that," Simon said, and chuckled. He didn't think it was possible for a woman to be any more appealing than Fiona Harrison. Reaching out a hand, he curled his fingers around her calf right below the knee. He still couldn't believe that he could touch her like this. And now that he could, he couldn't seem to stop. A caress of her shoulder, holding her hand, the feel of her hair, especially nuzzling her neck, but it didn't matter, as long as he was with her. He'd never wanted to be so *close* to a woman before. Just with her, next to her, beside her, looking at her. Of course, the fact that he was leaving lent a level of urgency to his actions. He needed to be with her as much as he could.

Even though their being together presented a host of potential problems. Should he go ahead and tell her about his business in LA, about his true suitability as a partner? It didn't seem to matter now because they'd set a time frame.

But what if someone else mentioned it? That was a possibility. Would she be upset if she found out? Would she realize why he hadn't told her after their first kiss? She'd been the one to "reject him," so it seemed wiser not to draw attention to the omission. Because it didn't change the underlying, much deeper issue, that a relationship was out of the question. Marriage was something he knew she wanted. And something he didn't. But as long as she didn't bring up the possibility of something long-term, he'd be safe because he was going back to California and she was starting a new life here in Montana.

She'd even found a job working for Grace Blackwell. Another reason to avoid this unpleasant and futile topic, and make the most of the time they had together.

"It's a little bit fun, though, right?"

Gaze narrowed, lips pressed together, her expression turned calculating. "I'm going to be honest with you, Simon." She waited a beat before confessing, "No. Horseback riding is not fun. It's not *not* fun exactly, but I just don't get it. They are extraordinarily beautiful creatures, yes. Which kind of makes it worse because what in the world makes people think the horses enjoy this? If they liked it, then you wouldn't have to 'break them,' am I right? It's my theory, recently formed, mind you, that they've been repressed. Why would poor Mesa want to walk around in big endless circles with me jostling around on her back and telling her what to do? She has four legs—she knows how to walk better than I do."

Simon chuckled. "I see your point. But it makes me happy that you tried it when I know how nervous you were. I'm proud of you."

"Thank you," she answered brightly. "I'm also proud of me because I don't like to think of myself as a coward."

"Fiona, no one would ever mistake you for a coward. Packing up and moving across the country to start a new life and embrace a family you don't know—and never even knew you had until a few months ago—is the epitome of brave, in my opinion. All with a smile on your face."

"Huh. Yeah," she joked. "It sounds cool when you say it like that."

"It is cool."

"Speaking of my family and this new life of mine… There's something I need to talk to you about."

"Okay."

"Would it be okay with you if we kept this—" she gestured between them "—dating, or whatever it is that we're doing, to ourselves? And Luke, obviously. At least, until I tell my dad and Big E. I don't want my dad finding out from someone else before I have a chance to tell him, to explain."

"I don't care if you ever tell them," he said, feeling a surge of relief at the reprieve she'd just granted him. If no one knew about them, there'd also be less chance of her finding out about his life in LA.

"Really?"

He shrugged. "We've only got a couple of weeks together. I really don't want to share our time with anyone else anyway." He didn't care what Big E thought about him dating Fiona, but he wasn't sure how Fiona would feel about how Big E felt and probably, by extension, her dad. And telling her dad could raise other issues about whether he was good enough for her. Dads were notorious for quizzing would-be suitors about their work. All of that would waste energy and time, both of which he'd rather spend with her.

Smiling, she whispered, "I wish I could kiss you right now."

"Why can't you?" he countered.

"If I lean over, I'm pretty sure I'll fall off and be trampled."

"Trampled by Mesa? Who Jon and I both agree is the gentlest horse in at least the tristate area?"

"You never know. Did you not hear those warnings Abby and Gen gave me? There could be a snake hiding anywhere in this arena just waiting to pop out at her. Plus, I have no idea if you have a harmonica in your pocket and a yearning to serenade me with some blues." As if on cue, Mesa let out a whinny and pawed the ground. "See? She agrees that danger abounds."

With a chuckle, he squeezed her calf. "Okay, let's get you down from there. You don't need to be so sore tomorrow that you can't walk."

Simon helped her dismount, and she followed through with that kiss. They exited the arena with Simon leading Mesa and headed toward the barn. They were right in front of the huge metal shop where Jon kept his equipment. The large sliding doors were wide-open.

Too late, Simon realized his stagecoach was in full view.

"What the…" Fiona muttered, her gaze drifting toward the open doors. She stopped in her tracks, peering intently in that direction. "It that a stagecoach? My cousin has a stagecoach?"

Thinking fast, Simon stopped. Mesa followed suit, and he said, "Not for long. He sold it."

She slid him a curious glance and he half explained, "Occasionally, he comes across old Western items at auctions and sales. If the price is right, he buys and resells. Jon's a smart rancher, always looking for ways to make extra money."

"Huh." Fiona nodded slowly. "That does sound smart."

Tom saved him from further questioning by stepping out of the building at that moment. "Howdy, Simon," he called, striding toward them.

"Hey, Tom." Simon introduced Fiona. A quick, friendly chat ensued, quick being the key. Tom wasn't much for small talk.

He nodded at the horse. "Would you like me to take her off your hands? I'm heading to the barn anyway."

"Sure. That would be great, thank you."

Simon immediately kicked himself when

Fiona asked Tom, "Do you think my cousin would mind if we took a quick peek at the stagecoach inside?"

"I'm sure he wouldn't mind a bit," Tom said, and took Mesa's lead. "You two have fun."

"Thank you so much, Tom." Fiona smiled at the man. Winding her arm around Simon's elbow, she urged, "Come on. I know you want to see this, too."

Was this a sign that he should tell her? But what possible excuse could he give for not mentioning it sooner?

They ventured inside and Simon was immediately taken by Fiona's excitement. She circled the coach assessing and analyzing and commenting on its excellent condition.

Peering around the side, she commented, "I wonder how it's been so well preserved. I can't look at it without thinking about what an important role it played in our history— carting around people and gold and getting robbed and…bringing the news. Do you think the owner would mind if I opened the door?"

Nope, I don't mind, he wanted to say. "I don't think the owner would mind if you wanted to get inside," he answered.

An eager, hesitant smile matched her response. "I don't know… Really, you think?"

"I one hundred percent guarantee it." He

couldn't tell her right now, he decided, and spoil this moment. Especially considering the surprise excursion he'd planned for the next day. What he'd told her earlier was true. Selfishly, he didn't want anything standing in the way of their time together. Not even the truth.

"If I lived back in the day," she called out, grinning at him from the open window, "*this* would be my idea of horse travel."

CHAPTER FOURTEEN

DESPITE THE EARLINESS of the hour, Fiona awoke easily the next morning wondering what surprise Simon had in store for the day. Anticipation churning inside of her, she realized she didn't care. She was temporarily back to living in the moment and couldn't imagine anything that she wouldn't want to do so long as she was with Simon.

He'd told her to dress for a casual yet active date, suggesting comfortable shoes like sneakers, and a light jacket. Bundling up wouldn't be necessary aside from travel to and from the pickup. See? Already, she liked it.

A check of her phone revealed a text from her sister Amanda that made her heart go light:

I'm super excited for Thanksgiving! Especially dinner, not going to lie. It has been way too long since I've had Fiona food. Plus, I have sooo much to be thankful for this year. (Can you believe it? Me and Blake!) ps: What kinds of pies are you making?

Fiona: I am so happy for you! Love you. Love Blake. Love Amanda & Blake. Can't wait to see you both. Don't worry, pecan pie is on the menu.

Amanda: Thank you! (dancing emoji) For the love and the pie. Love you too! Can't wait to see you! Can't wait to see everyone.

Fiona: Me too. Have you talked to Georgie? I get the feeling she's not going to make it.

Amanda: Same. (sad emoji)

This prompted Fiona to text Georgie:

Please say you're coming for Thanksgiving. As the only other remaining single Blackwell sister, I need you. Don't make me be the 7th wheel. I love you!

"ARE YOU GOING to tell me where we're going?" Fiona asked Simon a short while later, after they'd hit the highway and headed west. To save time, they'd agreed to meet at the Silver Stake.

"I can tell you," he said, giving her an eager grin. "Or you can wait and be surprised. It's not that much farther."

"Surprise," she fired back. "I actually enjoy surprises. If they're happy ones."

"I'm confident it is. And I have another surprise to go with this surprise, and I hope it's a happy one, too." He glanced at her, readjusted his hands on the steering wheel, and Fiona thought he might be nervous.

He explained, "I finally hired another server. Riley's sister Olivia starts tonight, and I arranged for you to have the evening off. You can pick up an extra shift this weekend if you want, but I thought since you were starting your new job on Monday that you might not care? I hope that's not overstepping. I just wanted to spend as much time together as possible."

"That's great news! No, that's not overstepping. It's very thoughtful, and I'm excited to have a whole day to spend with you, too."

"Good," he said, his face erupting with a relieved smile. "I was hoping you'd say that. So, I know horses are out, but you're not afraid of flying, are you?"

"No. Unlike horses, airplanes were specifically designed to transport humans."

Simon flipped the blinker and steered the pickup onto the exit ramp. A sign for downtown pointed to the right and a smaller one indicated a school and an airport to the left. He turned left. A few miles later, he went right where a much larger sign pointed toward what Fiona could now see was a small airport. A cluster of large metal-roofed industrial-style buildings were set back from the road on the other side.

"I thought we'd go golfing."

"Golfing?" Fiona repeated in a skeptical tone as she tried to puzzle out a way this could be possible. "You mean like an indoor driving range? That would be awesome. Or wait, please don't tell me snow golf is a thing here?"

"Snow golf is not a thing. Or, if it is, I don't know about it, and not what we're doing. I was thinking of something more along the lines of Kaleidoscope Ridge."

"I wish!" Fiona said, thinking he was teasing to throw her off. She knew of Kaleidoscope Ridge, a famed course in Salty Springs, Arizona, that drew some of the best golfers in the world. "I've always wanted to golf there. I lived in Sedona for a while, and one of my coworkers used to talk about how he grew up golfing there."

Simon slowed the pickup and turned into the airport. As they approached a large hangar, two men came into view near an open bay. Fiona recognized Luke as he lifted a hand and waved.

Fiona smiled and returned the gesture. "Oh, is Luke coming, too? This will be fun."

Simon drove on, parking the pickup in a

space along the side of the building. He shut off the engine and faced her. "Luke is taking us."

"Taking us?" A mix of surprise and delight spiked through her as it all came together. "He's flying us to Arizona? We are seriously going golfing at Kaleidoscope? Today? Does Luke have his own plane?"

"Yes, to all four questions. I can't stand the thought of going back to California and never playing golf with you."

Fiona smiled despite the painful reminder that he was leaving. The problem, she realized, was that being with Simon was beginning to feel a little too right. How was she going to say goodbye? *Nope*, she told herself, *can't go there.* For these last couple of weeks, she was the old Fiona who listened to her gut and did what felt right. She'd worry about goodbye when it came. Nothing was going to stop her from enjoying every minute of this day.

"Be still my heart," Fiona said after making a beauty of a flop shot onto the green, her ball landing only a couple of feet from the hole.

"Nice," Simon told her. "That's a gimme."

"Thank you," she said, knowing he referred to the practice of picking up the ball when it lay close to the hole without bothering to tap in the final putt. "You know, I never take them."

Fiona stowed her club and they strolled up the fairway toward the green. "My best friend, Ivy, and I used to play with this couple, Justin and Sara. I swear, every lie on the green was a gimme in Justin's book. Eight feet out and he's scooping up his ball for par."

"I think I know that guy," Simon joked. Fiona walked over and removed the pin so Simon could putt.

"Very nice," she said, after he sank the ball in two attempts. "You're a pretty good putter. In my experience, men often neglect their putting skills. Or, at least, men who never play with women. Then they get surprised when they lose to me."

"Thank you," he said with a chuckle.

Fiona smiled and yielded the pin in exchange for a kiss, sank her putt for par and then continued her story. "So, one day, Ivy had had it. When Justin wasn't looking, she took his putter out of his bag and stashed it in hers. I kid you not, we played four holes before he realized it was gone. He looks around and he's like, 'That's weird, I can't find my putter? Sara, do you have my putter?' Sara's all confused and scratching her head, 'No, honey, I don't have your putter.' And then Justin's like, 'I think someone stole my putter.' Just when he's getting ready to call the clubhouse Ivy pulls the club out of her bag and says innocently, 'Here it is, Justin. You stopped using it back on the seventh hole, so I thought you didn't need it anymore.' Needless to say, that was the last time Sara and Justin invited us to round out their foursome."

Simon laughed. The round passed too quickly and with the same degree of complete and utter fun. Not only was Fiona good company, she was an excellent golfer.

After the game, they grabbed a coffee and a snack and headed into town. Salty Springs was set near the base of the mountains on the banks of the Mineral River. It had a lively history as an Old West mining settlement that became a ghost town before the beauty of the setting and the natural hot springs turned it into a tourist spot. In the 1980s, the addition of a pro-level golf course buoyed its attraction to golf enthusiasts. Smart investors then capitalized on the area's scenic beauty and the purported healing properties of the hot springs, building a gorgeous resort and spa. The quaint downtown held an eclectic assortment of boutiques, art galleries and cafés, as well as a sizable selection of antiques shops.

Like Simon, Fiona favored the latter. "Oh, my gosh, I adore these!" she exclaimed, stopping to admire an old phonograph. "My grandma had one. Mom and Dad used to play music on it on New Year's Eve and we'd all dance." Her smile was tinged with sadness, and Simon knew she was thinking about her mom.

"Simon?" A voice called from behind them. Startled, he turned to find Calliope Nettle. Calliope was a talented set designer, decent golfer, all-around nice person and one of Simon's clients whom he also considered a friend.

"Calliope, hi! What are you doing here?"

"Same thing as you, I'm guessing. Getting out of the madness for a while." She gestured around the shop. "Of course, you're probably hunting for treasures at the same time, right?"

Cold sweat prickled his back, a combination of fear and guilt sweeping through him as he realized how truly shortsighted he'd been not to tell Fiona what he really did for a living. And foolish. What was he thinking venturing into an antiques shop with her? Falcon Creek might be small, but so was the entire world these days. Obviously. What had felt like a harmless omission to save her feelings had somehow turned into a betrayal. He needed to tell her. He would tell her. If Calliope didn't inadvertently do it first.

Before he could answer, she added, "I'm

going to be working with Enrique on his new project and he told me you were on hiatus."

"I am, in Montana. I've been helping with a family emergency, which thankfully, isn't much of an emergency anymore." He introduced the two women. "We just flew in for the day. I'll be back in California at the end of the month." He knew shooting for the film wasn't slated to begin until early the next year, and he wanted Calliope to feel secure that he'd be back.

"Excellent," she said. And Simon could tell that had done the trick. Now if only he could snap his fingers and make her go away, too.

"Fiona and I were golfing this morning at Kaleidoscope," he said, trying to steer the conversation away from antiques and Hollywood.

"Oh, fun! It's a brilliant course, isn't it? The tenth hole, though, with the sand trap? I seemed to have developed some sort of jinx where that's concerned."

The two women chatted about the course and Simon felt himself relax. Golf, the ultimate topic with which to commandeer a conversation.

"I better get going, my sister is waiting. Such fun running into you," Calliope said a few minutes later, wrapping up the chat. "Simon, I'm having another holiday party again this year, second weekend in December. You'll be there, right?"

"Of course," Simon assured her. Tons of professional connections were made at industry parties. And Calliope's were a good mix of fun and business.

Smiling at Fiona, she said, "I hope you can make it, too. It was lovely meeting you." Calliope turned to go, and Simon was hit hard with a wave of relief.

Until she spun back around and pointed a finger at Fiona. "Fiona, are you an actress? Did we meet at David Bellman's wedding back in June?"

Fiona went wide-eyed. "Uh, no. I don't know who that is."

Calliope let out a relieved laugh. "Okay, good. I was hoping we hadn't met and that I wasn't failing to recognize you." Then she winked at Simon. "Good on you, Si, I'm thrilled you're not dating an actress."

Simon chuckled. They parted ways. Fiona looked confused. *Here it comes*, he thought, and braced himself.

"You've dated actresses?"

"Only a few," he answered, trying to decide how to approach this. "Nobody serious and no one famous. She was just joking."

"You must work at a place that caters to the Hollywood crowd, huh?"

"Uh, yeah, you could say that."

"Hmm. I bet you have some interesting stories."

"Not really," he said. "Mostly, I avoid dating anyone who works in the film industry." This was true. People often assumed dating was a good way to make connections, but Simon had always thought it was a better way to sever them. You never knew who was friends with who or, worse, who was related. And since Simon never stuck around a relationship for long, it wasn't worth the risk.

Fiona moved on to admire an art deco clock, and Simon decided the danger had passed. He loved seeing her like this, blissful, light-hearted, engaged. He loved feeling the same way. He'd tell her when they returned to Falcon Creek. Tonight. Or maybe tomorrow.

Luke met them in town for a late lunch, which they enjoyed at a popular restaurant with a gorgeous view overlooking the river.

Simon liked how Fiona slowly scanned their surroundings like she was soaking in every second. They were seated on the deck where large and small clay pots overflowed with bright blooming flowers.

"Ugh," she said with a cute, contrived scowl.

"I cannot tell you how much I miss sitting outside. If I sit outside in Montana, my eyelashes freeze together. Look at those geraniums. I wonder how they get them so bushy. I completely took the growing season for granted when I lived in California. I feel…regretful about that now."

Simon couldn't help but think about how much she would like his deck at home.

"So, who won?" Luke asked.

"Fiona beat me by three strokes."

"From the women's tees," Fiona qualified.

Simon scoffed. "That doesn't matter. You're better than me."

"Wait, wait, wait," Luke said. "I just…" Luke closed his eyes and held up a finger. "I'm going to need a moment to savor this."

Fiona stood and patted Luke's shoulder. "Take your time then," she teased, "I'm going to go use the restroom while Simon tells you how I birdied the twelfth. Can you order me a raspberry lemonade?"

"She seriously beat you?" Luke said after Fiona was out of earshot. "You didn't, you know, let her win like you do me sometimes?"

"I never let you win, despite what you think." Simon laughed. "But no, I didn't. Her short game is phenomenal. That, combined with solid consistent drives, and I was toast."

"Wow."

"We were wrong all these years speculating about how much fun it would be to date a woman who liked to golf."

"Really?"

"Yeah. It's way, way better. Secretly, I always thought I'd be envious because, you know, I'm good, and competitive. But no. She's a great sport about it, and just so...fun."

"What are you going to do?"

"About what?"

"About what?" Luke repeated, and rolled his eyes. "About the fact that you're in love with her. Are you going to stay in Montana for a while longer? Or travel back and forth? Take it from me, the long-distance thing can be rough." Luke's life as a pilot made him an expert in this regard.

"I'm not... I can't be, Luke, you know that. I'm not staying or traveling or making plans. We're just making the best of the time we have together."

Luke scowled. "Does Fiona know that?"

"Of course. She's the one who suggested it."

"Really?"

Simon thought. This time he went all the way back to their original conversation, the one they'd had after he kissed her the first time. He was the one who'd suggested it, wasn't he? The "three fun weeks." Then, after *she'd* kissed him, she'd essentially just repeated what he'd said and adjusted the length of time. Did that mean she wanted more? A wave of longing slammed into him so hard it left him speechless. Visions of the two of them together in California flashed before him like a series of snapshots: on the golf course, on his deck, at the beach, shopping for antiques, as his date at Calliope's party and at a hundred other events like that he had to attend. She would fit so seamlessly into his life.

Until she was no longer satisfied being only his date.

"What if she decides to follow you to California?" Luke pressed, reading his mind and snapping Simon back into the moment.

"Follow me? She's just getting to know her new family. She starts a job on Monday working for Grace Blackwell. She's not going anywhere." But, in that moment, he knew he would welcome it if she did. More than that, he wanted her to suggest it. Because what if… What if they *could* continue to see each other like this? Without promises of forever or an unrealistic commitment to a future that no one could keep.

She'd said she wanted to get married, but was that really Fiona talking? Because she'd also said her dad had something to do with that goal. Would she be willing to keep living in the moment for as long as their feelings lasted?

CHAPTER FIFTEEN

IT WAS LATE when they arrived back at the Silver Stake, but since it was a Friday night the lot was nearly full. Simon parked the pickup and turned off the engine.

Fiona stayed put and said, "Well, that was officially the best date of my life. I can't believe you arranged all that for me. Thank you."

"Mine, too." Simon took her hand, leaned over and gave her a kiss, approximately the hundredth of the day. "You're welcome, but it was a little selfish on my part." Like he was confessing, he added quickly, "I had to do it. I wanted to go golfing with you. I wish we had time for a rematch. I wish the day wasn't over."

"I'm glad you said that," she returned with a happy smile. "I'm not ready for goodbye yet, either, so I was thinking I could come inside. We can hang out in your apartment and then I'll help you close. Is that okay?"

"That would be amazing."

Simon unlocked and opened the back door. As they stepped inside, Fiona could tell immediately that something wasn't right. Bar noise had a certain sound, and this was too strident, too intense. Simon felt it, too, because instead of heading up the stairs to his apartment, he went still. Scowling, he tipped his head. They both listened—voices raised, a woman's sharp reply, and then a man rambling loudly, the words incoherent. Miguel's deep voice resonated with a certain tone, calm yet firm, that Fiona knew he used with customers who'd reached their drink limits.

"Sounds like someone's been overserved," Fiona commented. "Do you want to go see what's going on?"

A stint of angry shouting, followed by the unmistakable sound of glass breaking, propelled them both forward.

They hurried down the hall and into the bar, where Miguel's voice once again rose above the din. "No way, man. You were drunk when you got here and I'm not serving you another drop."

"What's the problem here, Miguel?" Simon asked.

The scene was chaotic. Riley stood several feet away holding an empty tray in front of her like a shield. Scowling, arms fisted at his sides, Vaughn was next to her looking ready to pounce. Miguel was moving around the bar, baseball bat in one hand, phone in the other.

A man in a rumpled suit stood with his back toward them. Knees bent, shoulders shrugged, head tipped too far forward, he did the drunken sway while gazing down at the broken glass scattered around his feet. No doubt wondering how it'd gotten there. Two stools were tipped over and lying on the floor.

"This guy is the problem, boss. Belligerent, drunk jerk came in here demanding to see you. He's running off customers with his crude language. He insulted Riley, threatened Vaughn when he interceded and then kicked over two stools. I said he was no longer welcome here and asked him if he could arrange a ride. He cursed at me and told me it was none of my business. I told him to leave, and that's when he threw the beer bottle. He says he won't leave until he talks to you. I was just about to call Scooter."

The drunk guy pivoted around, miraculously managing to stay upright, while his hips and shoulders undulated like a piece of seaweed planted on the ocean floor. Squinting in their direction, he took a few wobbly steps, threw up his arms, then flailed one out to grab the bar to steady himself.

Grinning, he slurred, "*Thh…* Si! *Issh* about time. *Whereff* you been?"

"Mica," Simon said blandly. "What are you doing here?"

"Hey! I came all *thissh* way here to Montan-a to see you…" He paused, his focus wandering a bit before settling on Fiona. "Hey, who's *thissh*?" He pointed at Fiona and then cupped a hand to his mouth and whisper-shouted to Simon as if she weren't right there, "She's *fffoxy*. Is *thissh* your girl?"

Mica? Simon's troubled brother. Fiona smiled and said, "Hey, Mica. I'm Fiona, I am a friend of Simon's. Nice to meet you."

"Hi, *Ffone-ah*," he chirped happily. *"Nice-it to-meet-you-too."* Even with Mica's glassy, half-lidded eyes and wide toothy grin, she could see the resemblance between the two men. In his intoxicated state, Mica was like a cartoon version of his older brother.

"What do you say Simon and I get you out of here? We'll go someplace where you guys can talk."

"*Yess!* Thank you, *Ffoxy Ffone-ah*! *Ffinely* someone who listen to me. *Thass* all I want. I *haff* some stuff I need to say to my big *bruthher, bru-ther, brotth-er…*" Chin dipping toward his chest, his thought tapered as he seemed distracted by something on his suit.

Giving his lapels a tug, he cried, "Hey! *Thass* not cool. Can I *haff* a nap-kin? Somebody *spilt* beer on me."

Fiona stepped to a nearby table and fetched a handful of napkins, which she then handed to a grinning Mica.

"Thank you, *Ffone-ah*. I like you." He gave her a sloppy, exaggerated wink.

Simon sighed and addressed the crowd, "Sorry about this, guys. Good work, Miguel. Riley, I hope he didn't lay a hand on you?"

Riley shook her head. "No, he didn't."

With Vaughn's help, Simon nudged and coaxed Mica up the stairs, where they poured him onto Simon's bed. For a moment, Fiona thought he might try to rally as he thrashed around and mumbled a few incoherent sentences. Instead, he pulled a phone out of his pocket and stared at it like he'd never seen it before. Then he dropped it on the floor, rolled over and started snoring.

"So," SIMON BEGAN in a wry tone, after he'd thanked Vaughn and shut the door behind him, "I think that went well. My brother seemed to really like you. He thinks you're foxy, so that's nice."

Fiona chuckled. "Well," she said with mock solemnity, "I've been secretly hoping someone would bring *foxy* back into our collective lexicon. It feels really empowering."

Wearily he crossed the room to sink beside her on the sofa. "Fiona, I am so sorry. If it's any consolation, after you leave, I'm going to roll him up in the carpet at the end of the bed, push him down the stairs, load him into the back of my pickup and dump him in a cow pasture."

She laughed. "Simon, it's okay. He's drunk."

"It's not okay. And it's more than that. It's…" If only he knew what it was exactly, then maybe he could fix it.

When he didn't finish, she agreed, "Yeah, I've picked up on that. Luke told me your parents got divorced when you were a teenager?"

"They did."

"That's when you and your sister and brother went to live with your grandparents?"

Simon hadn't wanted to do this, talk about his family. But, for some reason, he suddenly wanted to tell her. Parts of it, at least. Then, when he told her the truth about himself, maybe she'd better understand him and why he wasn't capable of a lasting relationship.

"That's correct. My grandparents, my dad's parents. I'm grateful for that—they were good people. They died a few years ago. First, my grandma was diagnosed with cancer and went shockingly fast. My grandfather had a heart attack less than a year later."

"I'm so sorry for your loss." Fiona felt a stab of sympathy thinking about the death of her mom. "Where do your parents live now?"

"My mom is in Florida. Recently married to husband number four. She doesn't drink much anymore, but she has plenty of other issues. We only talk maybe three or four times a year. My dad's last known address was Texas. He's a professional alcoholic. His life is a series of ups and downs. Truthfully, it's more dramatic than that. More like scaling a mountain, followed by a brief period of stability and then tumbling down a mine shaft. I… My family is chaos and always has been."

"I'm so sorry."

Simon shrugged a shoulder. "At least you know who I am now, right? Child of an alcoholic from a textbook dysfunctional family with emotional detachment. My entire childhood was my parents—especially my dad—getting drunk and leaving me to pick up the pieces. That was my role, and, as you can see, I was not great at it. Because I thought, hoped, that Mica had escaped the worst of the damages. He was only ten when we moved in with our grandparents. But obviously not. That's why I went back to California. He…" Simon almost said he'd screwed up at work. "He's recently divorced and that was difficult for him. And for some reason, he's gotten worse since I've been gone."

Fiona nodded but now she looked more confused than concerned. "Who *you* are? Simon, that is not who you are. And it is not your job to fix your parents, or your brother—you do know that, right? You can't fix an addict. You do not have that power."

"I know," he said, because he'd heard it all before. He understood enabling. That wasn't what he was doing. These kinds of comments used to make him defensive, but he knew now that no one could understand. He and Colette and Mica had been through hell. For most of their lives, they'd only had one another. There was no way Fiona could grasp the responsibility he felt toward his siblings. No one could.

He wanted to tell her more, but with Mica's presence here it suddenly felt so complicated. Why was he here? What was he going to do with him? How would she react? He didn't think he could handle losing her right now. It all seemed like too much to tackle tonight. Tomorrow. He'd tell her tomorrow after he'd dealt with Mica.

Exhaling a sigh, he tiredly raked a hand

through his hair. "Let's not talk about this to-night, okay?"

"You're right," she agreed with a sad smile. Scooting close, she leaned in and gave him a quick kiss. "Thank you for the best day of my life. Get some sleep. I'll see you tomorrow."

MICA FIDGETED WITH his napkin and stared out the café's window for a long moment. Then he inhaled a deep breath, heaved a deep sigh and looked at Simon. "I know I'm a screwup, Si. I'm sorry."

Simon took a sip of his coffee and set it down. He'd decided on breakfast at the Clearwater Café to avoid any of the Silver Stake employees. Plus, their biscuits and gravy were the best in town and rumored to double as a miracle hangover cure. Not that his brother didn't deserve to suffer a bit.

"You're not a screwup, Mica. You screwed up, yes. But your mistakes don't have to define you. You're a man with a good heart and a drinking problem."

Mica shook his head. "I'm not talking about last night."

The expression on Mica's face made him uneasy. "I didn't think you were."

The nervous twitch of Mica's hands and the way he was avoiding eye contact suddenly heightened his trepidation. His next statement confirmed it. "Simon, I'm in trouble."

"What do you mean? What kind of trouble?" he asked even as dread pooled inside of him.

"Bad trouble, Si. This time, I don't think it's something you can fix."

"Just tell me, Mica."

"Last week, I got a DUI."

"Why would you be driving after you'd been drinking?"

"I went to see Kelsey and—"

"You were with your ex?" Simon could already imagine what had happened. Mica and Kelsey were nearly as toxic as the parents who'd created Mica. A fight with his ex-wife inevitably set him off.

"I know what you're thinking, but it didn't happen that way. Kelsey and I have been getting along. That's the crappy part, Si! I've been trying to manage my drinking. She's been super supportive. And I wasn't wasted or anything. I only had a few…"

Simon listened to Mica's excuses, of which there were none that mattered, and felt resentment churn inside of him at this role he was forced to play in his family. Immediately he felt guilty. On a deeper level, this really wasn't Mica's fault. How could he not have issues when he'd grown up the way he had? Simon knew he was lucky to have escaped any addictions. Mica had not. Which meant it was up to him to help Mica get through it.

The selfish part of him was slammed with disappointment; he would have to cut short his time with Fiona. They'd agreed on a dating time frame and he felt cheated. They still had a week left so, maybe, after he and Mica had met with an attorney, he could come back. And then what? He didn't know. Maybe he didn't need to know, maybe they could figure that out later. The bottom line was that he wasn't ready to say goodbye.

FIONA MIGHT NEVER have figured it out if she hadn't gone to the Silver Stake the next morning. After the drama with Mica the evening before, she wanted to check on both Clarke men, see if Simon needed anything, somehow assure him that none of what he'd told her mattered. One of Fiona's longest relationships had been with an addict. A year of therapy and Al-Anon meetings combined with a ton of reading meant that she recognized enabling when she saw it. She'd try to get Simon to see it, too.

More importantly, she'd reached another conclusion that she needed to discuss—she loved him. She was in love. She wasn't going to tell him that part, but she wanted to suggest the possibility of a long-distance relationship. If that went well, she'd let him know that she was planning to move back to California. After Lily's wedding and the holidays, she was going to do that anyway. One day in the Arizona sunshine had been enough to convince her that this climate wasn't for her. She missed the sun and the ocean. The idea of living the rest of her life without those vital elements no longer appealed to her. She missed Ivy. Her dad, Amanda, Peyton—they were all in California, too. Exactly where in the state she would settle depended on what Simon had to say. Butterflies danced in her stomach.

The place wasn't officially open yet, but the door was unlocked. After a quick search, she decided he must be upstairs. She was on her way there when a man in a worn baseball cap entered and stopped just beyond the threshold. Removing his leather gloves, he kept them bunched in one hand, but made no move to take off the hat or the thick plaid wool jacket he wore. That, and how he methodically scanned the room, suggested he was looking for a person and not a meal.

"Hi," Fiona said. "Can I help you?"

"Yeah, uh, my name is Colin. Is Simon around?"

"He's not in yet. Do you want to have a seat

and wait, or can I give him a message from you?"

Colin shifted on his feet and readjusted the cap on his head. "Well, I've got a delivery for him, but I'd like to ask him something before I proceed."

"Oh, well, you can go ahead and unload it if you want. I can accept a delivery for the Silver Stake."

"No, sorry, ma'am. It's not for the Silver Stake. I'm supposed to be on my way to California. I picked it up out at the JB Bar Ranch, you know, Jon Blackwell's place?"

"I sure do. He's my cousin."

"Yeah?" Colin smiled, looking more at ease. "Heck of a nice guy."

"Yes, he is."

"Well, you probably know about it then. It's the stagecoach."

"Stagecoach?" Why would Simon be having Jon's former stagecoach delivered to California?

"Yes, ma'am, for Clarke Props, Ltd., Simon's movie prop business."

"I see." But she didn't. Not at all. His…business? Fiona tried to process what Colin had inadvertently revealed. "Um, let me see if I can find him." With that, she headed upstairs and knocked on the door. No answer.

She texted: A guy just arrived here at SS to talk to you.

Simon: You're there?! Great. I'll be back in five minutes. Can you meet me in my apartment? I need to talk to you about something.

She sent him a thumbs-up emoji and went back down the stairs, where she relayed the news to Colin. Confused, head swimming, she felt incapable of making small talk, so she invited Colin to take a seat. Back upstairs, she went inside Simon's apartment to wait.

Other than the pillow and the neatly folded blanket resting on one end of the sofa, there was no evidence of last night's episode. Fiona took a seat, opened a new browser on her phone and launched a search for Clarke Props, Ltd.

CHAPTER SIXTEEN

"WHERE'S YOUR BROTHER?" Fiona asked Simon when he came through the door. The stage-coach delivery was going to be delayed. Colin's father had had a heart attack and he'd stopped to see if he could wait a few days or if he needed to hire someone else to transport it. Simon had told him to take all the time he needed.

"I took him to Ned's this morning. But I'm so glad you're here. I need to talk to you."

Simon stepped closer. She was so beautiful. All he wanted to do was tell her so, kiss her and take her in his arms. Unfortunately, they needed to have the conversation he'd been dreading.

"There's something I'd like to discuss with you first."

"Are you okay?" he asked, after sitting next to her. She seemed tense, unsettled. "I'm sorry about last night with Mica. He's, um, he's got some issues I need to help him work out."

"This isn't about Mica, Simon. Your brother

is not you. Besides, Mica might have been drunk, but at least he was honest."

That's when Simon realized that she knew. "What do you mean?"

"You know what's funny? I've been sitting here waiting for you and trying to figure out how I missed it. There were so many clues…" She gave her head a disgusted shake. "But, as usual, I didn't want to see them. You know what's ironic—and probably a coping mechanism? I keep going back to the fact that it was the stagecoach that finally delivered the news." She choked out a bitter laugh.

"Fiona—"

"Please don't say anything yet…" Tears pooled in her eyes. Tipping her face toward the ceiling, she took a deep breath, and he could see the pain and anguish as she fought the tears. Regret sliced through him, sharp and deep. He'd done this to her, and it was unbearable. He wanted to move closer, put his arms around her, beg for forgiveness. Another part, the wiser, more tentative part, realized the gesture would be much too little and way, way too late.

Then, seeming to steel herself, she blinked away any last hint of sadness and firmly captured his gaze. "Originally, I came here this morning to tell you that I've been thinking about moving back to California. To see if you'd want to stay together if I did that. I was thinking I could even get a job at the restaurant where you work, and we could see how things went. No pressure. Just…stay together. I can't even believe I was going to suggest it…" she said on a weak sob. "I was so certain you were different. It will be okay, I told myself. Simon is nothing like the guys you usually date. He would never use you or intentionally hurt you."

He was ready to beg. "Fiona, please, if you'll let me—"

"I don't even know who you are." She lifted her phone and held it a few inches from his face. The mobile version of his website stared back at him. "You own this really cool business in LA called Clarke Props, Ltd., and you didn't tell me?"

"I was going to tell you," he repeated. "And apologize."

"When?"

"Fiona, I am so sorry."

"No, I don't want an apology *now*. I want to know when you were planning to tell me."

Simon didn't respond, because to say *today* sounded completely far-fetched. And honestly how could he explain without sounding like the heel that he was?

She said, "*When* did you plan on telling me?

Like right after you kissed me goodbye one last time? 'Oh, by the way, baby, I'm not really a bartender.' Or, 'Hey, yeah, funny story, sweetcheeks, I own my own successful movie prop business in LA. You'd love it, it specializes in antique and vintage items.' Or maybe you planned on texting me after you got home? You know, just to clear the air with the woman who you enjoyed a few fun weeks with? But I'm guessing never. I doubt that I would have ever heard from you again.

"What a laugh you and Luke have undoubtedly had at my expense. Sweeping me off my feet, flying me to Arizona in his stupid cool airplane and making a fool of me. This makes it so much easier to believe the stuff I've heard about you. You're just as despicable as your reputation."

Simon felt himself wince as that rebuke hit its mark. "No, I'm not. You don't understand…" How could he convince her that he hadn't intended to deceive her? Not in the way that she believed. He knew he was stalling, but he found himself asking, "When have I ever called you *baby* or *sweetcheeks*?"

"You may as well have! Your dishonesty makes me feel just as cheap and disrespected."

She was right. He hadn't meant to make her feel like that. He'd been trying not to hurt her because selfishly he'd *wanted* to be with her until…it had to end. He'd known it would happen, but he didn't want it to be like this. That's when he realized he didn't want it to happen at all. Luke was right; he was in love with her. But how could he fix this now? She had to understand and forgive him.

Desperately he said, "I never lied to you, not directly."

"What are you—in middle school? You led me to believe that you were a bartender in LA. You did not tell me that you own your own business. And it's not like it never came up! All those conversations about antiques, Falcon Creek's history, the stagecoach, the *antiques shopping* where we ran into your friend, who I can clearly see now is one of your clients. All of which makes me feel like the biggest fool on the planet. But that isn't even the worst part—you kept this huge part of yourself a secret. I thought we had so much in common. I thought we had this connection that was… I am such an idiot. But you know what? That part is my problem. I give my heart away too easily. That's why I should have stuck to the profile."

How could she even think that? "That profile wasn't working, and you know it."

"Neither did your matchmaking! Which you also lied about."

"I didn't want to find someone for you. I wanted…" *You*, he wanted to say but couldn't bring himself to do it. Because if he'd been brave enough to admit that then, maybe they wouldn't be here now. He needed to accept that this was over. With his issues, his responsibilities to his family, it was bound to end anyway.

"Why didn't you tell me? Why did you let me get attached to you, to this person who isn't even real?"

"Because—" He stopped. Frustration boiled inside of him. The irony—the truth—was that he'd never felt as "real" as he did when he was with her.

"I'll give you my theory and you can tell me if I'm right. You were afraid that if I knew you had all the qualities I was looking for in a partner that I'd want to marry *you*, is that it?"

"Yes," he answered, and then rushed to explain. "Initially, that was my fear. I'm not interested in marriage. In my family, when you get married you may as well hire a divorce attorney at the same time."

"Whatever," she said doubtfully. "So, that was just perfect for you, wasn't it? When I told you I didn't care about your job and suggested we spend these last couple of weeks having fun and not worrying about the future? You were happy to be with me as long as there was an end in sight? An expiration date."

"Yes, but, Fiona, that was before I—"

"Save it," she interrupted with a stop-sign hand. "Please, do not tell me you have feelings for me. I'm not interested in any more of your lies. Do you remember our meet-cute? That's what I've spent these last few days thinking it was. I was so happy to finally get one, even if it didn't last forever.

"Do you remember what you said?" She went on before he could answer, "You said, 'Fiona, one thing I am not is mean. What I am, however, is honest.'" She held up two fingers. "Two lies. Right there. You are mean and you are not honest! For the record, I would *never* marry you, Simon. I don't even want to be near you. Because number one on my personal list of suitable attributes is honesty, and that most definitely does not describe you."

"Fiona, please, let me explain. I didn't mean to lie to you. I mean, I didn't *want* to lie to you. I don't know..." He hesitated, not knowing which direction to try to get through to her. "It's that thing where the longer you go without saying something, the harder it gets."

She scoffed, a look of pure disgust twisting her features.

"I thought about telling you when we were looking at the stagecoach… And then I decided it didn't matter. But then in Arizona, when we ran into Calliope, I realized it wasn't fair for you not to know… So I decided to tell you, but I didn't…" None of these excuses sounded legitimate when he said them out loud, not even to his own ears. "I don't even understand it myself, why I didn't just tell you."

"I do." She stood and picked up her bag. "I understand it perfectly. You can't even be honest with yourself about your family. You think your dad and your brother are the ones with the problems. You think because you're not an addict that you've somehow escaped the dysfunction. You need to face *your* issues where your entire dysfunctional family is concerned. You're an enabler, Simon. A lying, excuse-making enabler. How could I ever expect you to be honest with me?"

FIONA'S ENTIRE BODY was trembling. Her hands were shaking so badly she could barely get the key in the ignition. Too many emotions were boiling inside of her. Unwanted emotions: anger, sadness, regret, humiliation. Even her teeth were chattering. Okay, that last part had to do with the fact that she'd fled the scene without her jacket and then driven away without letting her car warm up. All the things her new life in Montana had been designed to avoid, as well as the surprises that she'd found here, had coalesced into a perfect storm inside of her.

Unfortunately, anger was winning the day. Of all life's emotions, it was the one she most despised and was the worst at dealing with. Which was why she normally avoided it at all costs.

The upside though, she soon realized, was that it kept the tears at bay. Simon did not deserve her tears. She made it all the way back to the ranch and into her cabin without crying. Once inside, she dropped her bag on the floor and tossed her phone on the nightstand. Kicking off her shoes, she cranked up the heat, climbed under the covers on her bed and waited for the shaking, which she could no longer blame on the cold, to subside. It did. Slowly she became aware that the anger still remained. Eating away at her insides. She needed an outlet.

Her mind drifted to her childhood, and she yearned for the light blue aluminum baseball bat from the many games she'd played in the yard with her sisters. So she could hit something. Like Simon's precious pickup. Which, she realized, had been another clue for oblivious Fiona to not decipher.

A devious chuckle escaped her. Yeah, that's all she needed, to destroy something else she had to pay for. It might be worth it. Instead, she focused on her breathing as she stared at the wall and waited for the intense emotions to pass. Vaguely she registered the buzzing sounds coming from her phone. *Simon.*

She could throw the phone against the wall. It would be better if she could throw it at him. Both options would result in expensive damages and entail climbing from beneath this snuggly down-filled cocoon. That last one she was definitely not ready to do.

Two hours passed with more texts, including three from Simon and, still, not a tear. But as the shock wore off, she realized there was a fair amount of guilt mixed in with her anger. She shouldn't have called him an enabler and said that stuff about his family. It was true, but she'd said it in anger because she'd wanted to hurt him. Not well done on her part. And precisely why feeling anger was so nasty—because she always said things she regretted and failed to say things she later wished she had. But he'd blindsided her. Honestly, with other men she'd dated, she could always see the end in sight. Usually she was relieved when it finally arrived. But this… This was a level of hurt and betrayal that she couldn't seem to process.

Ivy was right that this move to Montana had been an impulsive, grief-driven decision. To make matters worse, she couldn't even talk to her sisters or her dad. Especially not her dad. Her family didn't know that she'd been seeing Simon. Which reminded her that she didn't have a lot of room to talk, did she? She hadn't been honest with them, either. She'd even asked Simon to keep it quiet. No, that was different. She'd never been dishonest *with Simon*. The opposite, in fact. Ironically, her honesty about marriage was the reason he hadn't told her about himself in the first place. But it was still not a legitimate reason to *keep* lying to her.

Her phone buzzed with a text from Georgie:

7th wheel, ha-ha! So sorry I can't make it for Thanksgiving :(Amanda told me you were cooking and I'm sad to miss it. Any chance you could FedEx me a piece of apple pie? I'm extra sorry and super sad I won't be there FOR you and even out the wheels. #eighthwheel #SingleSisterSolidarity I love you, Little Fee!

Well. That did it.

A sob welled up deep within her. Burying

her face in the fluffy down pillow, she didn't even try to stop the flood. Suddenly relieved, she welcomed the tears. At least she knew she was still capable of crying, of feeling something besides anger. That consolation didn't last long, however, because on the heels of the most intense anger of her life came the most awful sadness.

"AH, MAN..." LUKE said with a shake of his head as Simon finished filling him in on the details of Mica's arrest. "I'm sorry, Si. Your brother really let himself down. Driving drunk?"

"I know."

"What are you going to do?"

"Right now, I need to get him back to California. I already called my attorney."

"Do you need me to fly you?"

"No, but thanks, Luke. I'm packed. We're leaving now. I'm going to pick up Mica from Uncle Dean's and hit the road."

"Wait, you're *leaving* leaving. As in driving back to Cali to stay?"

"Yep."

"What about Fiona?"

"It doesn't matter. It's over."

"You told her?"

"She figured it out before I could. Colin

stopped by with that stagecoach I bought from Jon and she figured it out."

"Uh-oh. No wonder you look like you've been bucked off a horse, boot caught, and then dragged around by your ankle. I thought you were just upset about your brother. I take it it didn't go well?"

Simon felt a fresh twist of pain right in the center of his chest. Like there was some sort of serrated blade in his heart, and with every thought of Fiona it would work its way deeper. Previously, an unfamiliar sensation. He wondered absently if he should be concerned about his health. But that would entail caring about it, and right now he really didn't.

"You could say that."

"You want to talk about it?"

"No. She doesn't understand, and I can't expect her to."

"Understand what, exactly?" Luke asked.

"That my life, my childhood, precludes marriage as an option for my future. I can see now that I screwed up by not simply telling her that to begin with, but I did. And now it's too late."

That's when he realized why this feeling was so unfamiliar. Luke was right—he loved Fiona. He'd never been in love before. This ache in his heart was worse than any pain his family had ever wrought.

"But it isn't. And the stuff about your family doesn't matter, either," Luke countered.

"Luke, you know my family's history."

"I do. But no one in your family has a problem with marriage, Simon. Except for you."

"Yeah, and that means I'm the one who won't end up getting divorced and hurting people."

"By people, you mean you, right? *You* won't get hurt? I got news for you, buddy—relationships hurt. Relationships of all kinds. You can't avoid it. You just have to hold on to the notion that a little pain is worth the reward."

When he didn't respond, Luke added, "Simon, in case you missed the message there, Fiona is your reward. You need to fight for her."

Simon heaved out a sigh. "Luke, I know you're trying to help. But I don't want to talk about this anymore. I also know you like Fiona, which is why I'm here. Can you...you know, watch out for her? I know it's over between us, but I still can't stand the thought of her ending up with some jerk."

"Gladly." Luke nodded, but Simon could see the disappointment on his friend's face. How did he keep disappointing people he cared about when all he tried to do was the opposite? "Just for the record, I think you're almost as big of an idiot as your brother."

CHAPTER SEVENTEEN

SIMON, WITH A dejected Mica trailing behind, found Colette waiting in the living room of his house when they returned from the appointment with Mica's attorney. Simon collapsed into his favorite chair, a comfortable recliner. The familiar scent and feel of the worn leather elicited a modicum of relief to the overwhelming sensations swamping him. His head was spinning. Fear for his brother was a heavy weight. Guilt churned on two fronts, Fiona and Mica. But the worst was how his heart hurt from missing Fiona.

He was exhausted from yesterday's travels and the relentless, emotionally draining conversations with Mica. They'd arrived home late. He'd barely slept before getting up and heading straight to the attorney's office this morning for an early appointment.

"How did it go?" Colette asked.

"Simon can fill you in," Mica said. "I'm going to go lay down."

Simon watched his brother trudge up the

stairs to the room he'd been inhabiting in the months since he and Kelsey divorced. As terrible as his brother's actions had been, Simon couldn't help but feel a stab of sympathy.

Which reminded him of the sibling who didn't cause such conflicting emotions. Forcing a smile for Colette, he said, "Thank you for making sure my house was clean when I got back last night. I can't tell you how much I appreciate it, Colette. I don't know what I'd do without you. Do I tell you that enough?"

"You tell me that plenty. Right back at ya, brother." Colette gave him a gentle smile. "It was the least I could do. I know Darlene only comes on Tuesdays, which meant Mica had plenty of time to wreak his usual havoc all over before he left here." Darlene was the woman who cleaned his house one day a week.

Squeezing his eyes shut, Simon shook his head and pinched the bridge of his nose. "Seriously, Colette, he's our brother. How can he be so...?"

"Inconsiderate, irresponsible, self-centered, reckless, thoughtless, manipulative—"

"Okay," Simon interrupted when she showed no signs of slowing down. "Yes."

"He's spoiled. We spoiled him."

Simon chuckled disbelievingly. "That's not

what he says. On the drive home, he told me
he was neglected."

"Ha," she barked. "Ridiculous. After Mom
and Dad sent us here, Grandma and Grandpa
spoiled him, and so did we. Mom and Dad neglected him, yes, but they neglected all three
of us. But we felt the worst for Mica because
he was so young. We tried to make up for it
and ended up spoiling him."

Some of this was true. Mica had only been
ten years old when their parents had essentially
abandoned them.

"I also learned that he's angry because I
used to leave him in the summers to go to
Montana. Did you know that?"

"Yes," Colette said with a roll of her eyes.
"He's mentioned that in his drunken ramblings.
He's also upset with me because I didn't take
him to the beach whenever he had the urge to
go surfing. Apparently, there was some *wave*
back in the day that was *epic*. All his friends
were there, and he missed it because I wouldn't
give him a ride."

Simon couldn't help but chuckle a bit at that.

"Never mind that I was working so that he
could buy whatever new surfboard or skate-
board he wanted. Simon, he will say anything
to get what he wants from you. It doesn't work
with me anymore—all that expensive therapy

has paid off. Grandma and Grandpa are no longer here, Mom and Dad are AWOL like they've always been. That leaves you."

"But, maybe… What if it's true? What if by going to Montana I contributed to his abandonment issues? Kelsey leaving him pushed him over the edge and then I left for Montana *again* when he needed me most."

"Are you serious?" She huffed out an irritated breath. "He is no longer a child. You are his brother, not his parent. Mom and Dad abandoned us, *all three of us*. And I was here for Mica when you were gone. Grandma and Grandpa were here for Mica. Your taking off in the summers doesn't have anything to do with how Mica turned out. There's no way you could have made the kind of money you made in Montana staying here and working fast food or some other minimum wage job. You had a college education to pay for. Besides, you loved it. You needed that time away. Mica always thinks the grass is greener. If only he'd had this or that… He's the definition of entitled. We should have made him get a job when he was a teenager."

When he didn't respond, she added, "Do you realize that the only job he's ever had has been working for you? And he sucks at it."

Simon started to say something else but

stopped and thought. A part of him wanted to argue, to blame himself. But a deeper realization was too busy setting in.

"We'll circle back to this," Colette said. "For now, tell me what's going on. Mica looked like he was going to his own funeral."

"I'd probably look similar if I thought I was headed to prison, too."

"Prison? What are you talking about? I thought a first offense DUI was a misdemeanor."

"Normally, it is. But did you know that Kelsey was injured when it happened?"

"No. Well, Mica said he bumped into a pole in the parking lot of her condo and Kelsey got a scrape and a bruise."

"Try five stitches and a neck injury."

Colette's eyes went wide as the shock registered. "No," she whispered. "He did not mention that."

"They kept her in the hospital all night worried about head trauma. When you get a DUI that causes an injury it elevates the seriousness of the crime. As well it should. It creates what they call a wobbler, meaning it can be either a misdemeanor or a felony. They charged Mica with a felony."

Saying it all out loud brought back the sick

feeling that had overtaken him in the attorney's office.

"Oh my…" Colette covered her face with one hand. "He could have killed someone."

Mica could have killed someone. The realization was like turning on a switch in his brain. Colette was right. Luke had been trying to tell him for years. And Fiona… Fiona had called him out in the starkest, most honest of terms. He could no longer continue on this path, bailing his brother out, fixing his problems, making excuses, giving him money, a job. Enabling him. He'd been so focused on escaping his dad's behavior that he'd somehow adopted his mom's. Fiona was right—he was an enabler.

The help Mica needed was the professional kind, and only Mica could make it count.

"What are you going to do?"

"I'm not sure. But for the first time where Mica is concerned, I know what I'm *not* going to do."

FIONA KNEW HER dad would be proud, and her sisters, too, if any of them were actually aware of what she'd managed to accomplish with a broken heart. And it turned out that her first day working for Grace, while not the most exciting of jobs, did provide an adequate distraction from the shattering of her heart.

Between the night before and this morning, she'd ignored, without throwing her phone—another secret source of pride—seven texts from Simon and two from Luke. Easy peasy. Especially with her phone off and tucked inside her bag, which she'd stored inside a cabinet behind her desk.

Grace spent the morning outlining her expectations and training Fiona in various tasks around the office. She learned the computer basics, how to accept payments, take notes in the computer and reviewed scheduling procedures. They discussed answering the phone, although after her "audition" the week before Grace pretty much gave her free rein where that was concerned. She provided typed instructions and/or spreadsheets to accompany some of the more detailed undertakings. Since she'd never had an assistant before, she decided they'd play "the rest" by ear.

Fiona had no idea what the rest could possibly be, but she appreciated Grace's thoroughness, kindness and flexibility. If only she'd had a server's handbook when she'd first started in the restaurant business. She kept busy and, with the noon hour fast approaching, had yet to encounter a problem she couldn't solve.

Waiting for the most important appointment of the day, Fiona was double-checking the schedule when he came through the door. At least, Fiona assumed it was Mac Henson because his name was on the schedule and she'd put it there. This man was younger than she'd imagined and much better looking. Medium tall with a fit, stocky build, he looked like a boxer or a martial arts aficionado. Messy, dark blond hair suggested he'd been wearing a hat until very recently. Stepping close, he studied her with eyes the color of dark amber.

"Hi there, can I help you?" Fiona asked in her friendliest tone. She knew securing this account was important to Grace, and she wanted to make a good impression.

In a quick, assessing motion, his gaze traveled over her, and Fiona had the feeling he liked what he saw. Slowly his mouth curled up at the corners like he was holding tight to a smile and maybe a secret. "I am sure you can. My name is Mac Henson."

"I thought it might be," Fiona said, returning his smile.

His gaze latched on to hers and narrowed. "Are you by any chance the woman I spoke with on the phone last week?"

"That would be me. I'm Fiona."

"Fiona," he repeated slowly as if committing

it to memory. He reached out a hand and she shook it. "It is *really* nice to meet you. After I hung up, I realized I didn't get your name. Which is not like me. I checked my notes several times and couldn't believe I'd overlooked it. That's what a smooth talker you are. I was hoping you'd be here."

"Oh, thank you, I think." Fiona wondered if he was flirting. And if so, that in itself was a testament to his skill. She'd met a lot of flirts in her line of work and the best ones left you feeling both flattered and curious. Like Simon. The liar she no longer cared about and was determined to extricate from her mind.

"You're welcome. You were very convincing regarding Grace Blackwell's skills. I can only imagine how much business you generate for her."

"I'm glad to hear it, Mr. Henson. I'm certainly hoping to be an asset around here. This is my first day on the job." Fiona was aware that someone had come in behind Mac, but she didn't have a clear view and she wasn't about to look. She needed to focus on charming Mac Henson. Besides, Grace didn't have another appointment until two this afternoon, so it was likely a delivery person or an existing client dropping off paperwork.

"Please, call me Mac. This is *not* your first day," he countered in a playful tone.

"It is."

"But I talked to you on the phone last week."

"You did. But I wasn't technically an employee yet. I was here for an interview, and Grace had to step away from her desk for a few minutes. The phone rang so I answered it. You, sir, happen to be the very first appointment I've ever scheduled." And with those words, she realized what a nice meet-cute this would be. If Simon hadn't ruined that for her, too.

"Lucky me," he said.

"Indeed, because you're about to meet with the best CPA in the state of Montana."

"So, Fiona, are you—"

"Mac Henson, as I live and breathe," the new person said, walking closer. Familiar voice, she realized, a fact that was verified when Luke stepped up beside Mac and waved. "Hi, Fiona."

Mac shifted to face him. "Hey, Luke. How are you?"

The men shook hands and began talking football.

Fiona was grateful. It gave her time to get her bearings. What in the world was Luke doing here? If he thought she was going to listen to him plead Simon's case, he had another think coming. Then she decided that before she got too indignant about it, she should check the schedule to make sure he didn't have an appointment. Which, she quickly confirmed, he did not.

Grace's office door opened, and she and her client, Mrs. Helmut, emerged. They exchanged goodbyes, and Grace said, "Hi, Luke, how are you?" and then "Mr. Henson?"

"Hey, Grace," Luke offered with a friendly wave. "Doing good."

"Hello, Mrs. Blackwell," Mac said, and reached out a hand to Grace.

"Please, call me Grace."

Mac said, "I realized after I made the appointment that you're married to Dr. Ethan Blackwell, the vet?"

That led to a discussion about Ethan's care of Mac's favorite horse, and Fiona couldn't help but notice that Mac was decidedly less "friendly" with Grace. Polite and earnest, yes, but no playful half smile or lingering eye contact for the married Blackwell in the room. Definitely, he'd been flirting.

Grace directed Mac toward her office. With a last, thorough round of eye contact, he smiled at Fiona and strolled away. Grace made to follow, then stopped and looked back at Luke with a little frown. "Do we have an appointment, Luke? I don't usually see you until February."

"Nope," he said, and pointed. "I'm here to take your new assistant to lunch."

"Oh? That's nice. Perfect timing. I don't have another appointment until two. Go have fun."

Cringing on the inside, Fiona waited until Grace shut the door to scowl at Luke. "Luke, what are you doing here?"

"You didn't answer my texts. I was worried."

"Well, as you can see, I've been busy. And now you know I'm fine."

"Can I take you to lunch?"

"I packed a lunch."

"Please?"

"No." She punctuated it with a scowl.

"I know you're mad at me."

"Yes, I am."

"I'm so sorry. What was I supposed to do?"

"Hmm, I don't know…" she drawled in an exaggerated tone, tapping a finger to her chin, looking up and around before locking a glare on him. "Maybe not lie to me?"

"I know…" Luke let out a painful-sounding sigh. "But he's my best friend."

"Exactly. Neither of you can be trusted."

One finger came up as if in protest. "That is technically inaccurate. However, under the circumstances and with the extent of your current knowledge about us both, it is a fair assessment on your part. Although arguable on mine."

Fiona scowled more. "Don't give me that philosophical gibberish, Luke. He lied. You were complicit. That equals no trust."

"But if you look at this situation from Simon's perspective, I can be trusted. Plus, I'm the one who encouraged you to give it a try with him, remember? I told you more of the truth than I should have. I risked making him angry because I think you're right for him."

"Are you even kidding me? *More of the truth?* No wonder you two were in trouble all the time if that's the kind of defense you're employing."

He laughed. "I like you, Fiona. I liked you from the first moment you sat down at my table because you thought I was your date. I know we don't know each other that well, but I thought we were friends."

Fiona felt herself thaw slightly. "I thought so, too."

Gaze intense, he said softly, "You promised me something, remember?"

"Of course," she snapped, hating that the question made her fidget. She'd promised not to give up on Simon. "But when I made that promise it was without full knowledge of who he really is."

"That's what I'm trying to tell you, Fiona. You don't know who he really is. And I think, if you did, it might change your perspective. When I asked you to make that promise, I suspected that at some point the situation between you would reach this critical juncture. And just so you know, Simon has never gone to such lengths for anyone."

"You mean, he's never lied so well?"

Luke sighed. "I may have been complicit in Simon's deception, but I didn't agree with it."

"Fine."

"Fine…?"

"I'll go to lunch with you if you promise not to lie to me."

Luke went squinty-eyed, shifting his weight from one foot to the other as he seemed to consider the implications of that kind of commitment. Fiona almost laughed. "I promise not to abuse the privilege, Luke, and ask you anything embarrassing. I want to know about Simon."

"Great." He looked relieved and nodded. "I agree to your terms."

SIMON STARED AT the two-word text from Luke and felt the last of his hope evaporate: Mac Henson.

Until that moment, he hadn't even realized he'd been holding on to any. But the painful sensation radiating through his body assured him he had been. What had he done in life to deserve this kind of misery? Admittedly, he'd been confused and troubled in his youth, but he'd never been a bad person, never had malicious intent.

Staring at his phone, he waited for more information. But did he really need any? He knew perfectly well what it meant. Mac Henson was perfect for Fiona. He had all the criteria she was looking for, and then some. And Mac Henson was not his best friend who he could ask to step aside. He couldn't think of a better worse person for her.

Accepting this fact would be easier if he hadn't just experienced some sort of life epiphany. He could see things so clearly now. He'd written his parents off a long time ago and believed they no longer had a hold on him, on the choices he made. He'd reveled in his professional success and the fact that he'd risen above his family's dysfunction. What a crock. In reality, he'd been coddling Mica because of it, trying to compensate for what his parents had done to him to keep his little brother from experiencing the same pain. All while trying to keep his own fear at bay.

It had taken Mica's accident, where he could have killed someone, for Simon to finally recognize what was wrong with his own behavior. Well, that and hard truths from the people who loved him. And Fiona, who he loved.

Until his doorbell rang, Simon would have said this day could not get any worse. Already running later than he'd like for work, he wasn't expecting anyone and considered not answering. He looked outside. Standing on his porch were the last two people he expected to see.

Simon opened the door.

Big E Blackwell said, "Si Clarke. I can see now I got the right address."

"Big E, hello." He realized he was less surprised than he should be. Then again he was almost numb emotionally.

Big E gestured at his companion. "This is Rudy Harrison. Rudy, Simon Clarke."

"Pleasure to meet you, Rudy." The men shook hands, then Simon gestured behind him through the door. "Would you guys like to come in? I've got coffee, iced tea and lemonade, I think?"

"We would," Big E said, and the men followed Simon inside. "Nice place you got here."

"Thank you."

"There was a short time in your life when I might have bet against you ever owning a home at all, much less one this impressive. In fact, the word *homeless* comes to mind. Or maybe even *inmate*. Coffee would suit me just fine, thank you."

Simon laughed. "Yeah, you and me both. I owe a debt to my grandparents and Uncle Dean and Aunt Jeanette for never giving up on me. And you, too, for not pushing the issue with that whole pickup episode. I caught some breaks, that's for sure."

"Well, you paid for that mistake. That's how we get stronger in life, isn't it? By admitting the wrong we've done and doing our best to correct it if we can. Or at least try and compensate for it. I happen to be an expert in this area."

"I believe you're right about that." The difference, he could see now, was that Uncle Dean, and Big E with regards to the pickup incident, had made sure Simon owned his mistakes. Uncle Dean had never made excuses for Simon the way Simon did for Mica.

"Please, have a seat." In the kitchen, Simon poured coffee for Big E and glasses of iced tea for Rudy and himself. After delivering the drinks, Simon sat on the sofa and waited.

It didn't take long. "You're probably wondering what we're doing here."

Simon grinned. "I figured you'd get around to it when you were ready, Big E."

"We've been out of town on a mission. We're on our way back to Falcon Creek for Thanksgiving and were in the vicinity. I've heard on good authority that you've been courting my granddaughter." He waved a hand at Rudy. "Rudy's daughter."

"I bungled an attempt to do so, yes, sir."

"Not very smooth, huh?"

"No."

"I heard about that, too. Which is the reason we stopped by."

"FIONA, GOOD YOU'RE BACK," Grace said, walking through the door of her house and into the office. "There's something I need to talk to you about."

"Okay."

"Um, how was lunch?"

Fiona quirked a brow and joked, "You want to talk about my Cobb salad?"

"No," Grace said on a chuckle. "I was trying to decide how to ask if you and Luke are dating?"

"No, we're not dating."

"Then I have something potentially very... interesting to discuss with you." Grace lifted her chin and sniffed the air. "You made fresh coffee? What a treat." Heading to the sideboard, she poured herself a cup.

"Well, it's a treat for me that you buy the good stuff. How did your meeting with Mac Henson go?"

"Funny you mention him." Sauntering back over to Fiona's desk, she sat on the chair across from her. Her smile was approximately a mile wide. "That's what I want to talk about."

"I'm guessing from your smile it went well?"

"Oh, yes, it was great." She waved a breezy hand. "I wooed him with my riveting tax talk. Gonna save him a bundle. But that's not the interesting part. He was asking about you."

"Was he now?" Fiona couldn't help feeling validated that she'd nailed the flirting thing. And she was flattered, since he seemed like a nice guy. Then again, what did she know about nice guys? Luke had laid out quite a case for forgiving Simon. She'd learned quite a bit at lunch. Simon's upbringing explained a lot of his behavior. But she had no idea what to do with the knowledge. She could maybe understand why he hadn't told her initially. Especially given that she'd blurted out the marriage confession when he was so adamantly anti-marriage. But after they'd started dating, he should have come clean.

In the big picture, it didn't change the fact

that he hadn't cared about her enough to be honest. Once again, she'd jumped into a relationship based on how she *felt*. The difference was that this time the damage to her heart was deep. Invasive and all-encompassing. *Scarred for life*. She'd heard the expression forever without understanding exactly what it meant.

"Yes, but don't worry, I didn't tell him much. Nothing too personal. Not that I know anything all that personal, but you know what I mean. I told him that you are new to Montana and newly a Blackwell. And…"

"And?"

Hopeful grin in place, she explained, "And I asked Ethan about him and he says Mac is an awesome guy, excellent businessman, takes great care of his horses, loves his dog, et cetera. Mac asked if you were single and made it very clear that he'd like to go out with you. So, I was thinking, if you're interested, I could play matchmaker?"

CHAPTER EIGHTEEN

TWELVE YEARS AGO, the last thing Simon would have ever imagined was that someday he'd be discussing his self-sabotaged love life with Big E Blackwell and a stranger. Especially if they'd told him that the love interest was Big E's granddaughter and the stranger's daughter.

Even more surprising was Big E's response. He expected the man to warn him away, lecture him, possibly even swear. Instead, Big E leaned back in his chair and heaved a loud sigh. "I get it, son. Don't be too hard on yourself. It took me a few tries to figure out the woman I belong with was the one I let go too easily."

Simon nodded, his heart twisting with pain and regret. "Well, I don't need a few tries to know that I belong with Fiona. This is a mistake that will stick with me for the rest of my life."

Rudy's expression was a bit more skeptical. His questions were like an interrogation. "You met Fee in a bar, isn't that right?"

"Yes. When she came into the Silver Stake for a PartnerUp.com date."

"And then you talked her into working at that same bar?"

"It's a restaurant, too. But, yes, I did offer her a job."

He scowled. "She was trying to find a better job, something more…"

"Yeah, I know," Simon fired back, not caring if he sounded touchy and critical. "But I don't see how it's better if she's not happy. She waitresses because she enjoys it and she's amazing at it. That's the best kind of job as far as I'm concerned. I know this is difficult for you to hear, but she's doing all of this for you. She's trying to find a better job, a better guy, and make what she thinks will be a better life in Montana." He waved a wild hand. "For you. She's trying to be better—for you. When she's already perfect just the way she is."

Rudy glared, his mouth opening but then closing again. Simon expected another angry response. But it was a day of surprises. Teary eyed, Rudy finally nodded. "You're right. I did that. I want…" He cleared his throat and added, "I wanted the best for her. Fiona is so kindhearted, maybe too much so. She sees the best in everyone, goes out of her way to be open and caring to everyone, but doesn't always think about what she wants. I thought if I pushed her a little, she might fight harder for what she wants. I didn't realize that what she wants and what I want for her are two different things."

Simon nodded. "I understand you wanting the best for your daughter. I want the best for her, too."

"Do you think that's what you are? The best thing for her?"

"I do now," Simon told him confidently. "I know I'm not good enough for her, but who is? Trust me when I tell you I've spent a lot of time thinking about that question. She's the best person I've ever met. You raised an amazing human, Mr. Harrison. I feel honored to have known her at all. She makes me want to be a better person."

"Please, call me Rudy," he answered with a smile. "And thank you. It's nice to hear that right now, that nurture had plenty to do with how my girls turned out."

Simon felt a stab of sympathy for the man. He was trying to find the girls' biological father. The notion of another man taking his place as their father must be terrifying. "I guarantee it did. She thinks the world of you."

A man of action, Big E leaned forward and asked, "What's your plan, Si?"

"No plan. It's too late."

"Too late? You only left Montana a couple of days ago."

"There's someone else."

"What?" He nearly shouted the word. "Don't tell me she reactivated her PartnerUp.com account? That was a disaster. Rudy and I have owned our part in that."

"Yes, it certainly was. But no, it's even worse than that." Simon chuckled bitterly. "It looks like she found someone more… Someone…" He gritted the word out through clenched teeth, "Suitable."

"Who?" Big E demanded. "I haven't heard about this."

Mac Henson might be the definition of that word, but Simon couldn't bring himself to say his name out loud. Simon slid his phone from his back pocket, activated the display, pulled up the text from Luke and handed it over.

"Mac Henson," Big E read out loud, and Simon felt himself cringe. "Good guy. I'll admit that could be a game changer, if it's true. But unless they got married in the last twenty-four hours, which I doubt, seeing as how Fiona is busy preparing a Thanksgiving feast, then you've still got a shot."

"I don't know…" Simon said, his gut knotting in an uncomfortable yet all too familiar way. But now he recognized it for what it was. Fear. And hadn't he recently established that fear had dictated his actions, his life, for too long? He wasn't about to let it stop him anymore. Not where Fiona was concerned. "How am I going to get her to talk to me? She won't even respond to my texts."

Big E grinned and rose from his seat. "I don't know the answer to that, but what I do know is that any teenage boy who'd have the guts to commandeer Big E Blackwell's pickup for a joyride is certainly man enough now to figure it out."

LATE IN THE morning on Thanksgiving Day, Fiona stared at the curdled eggnog on the stovetop before her and tried not to cry.

"Please," she whispered, "don't let this be a sign foreshadowing a disastrous dinner."

She'd already overslept. Which had incentivized her to prod the eggnog along by cranking up the heat. She shouldn't have tried to shortcut a new-to-her recipe on a holiday. She really wanted to make this day special for everyone. With Lydia's help and her own subtle inquiries, she'd compiled an interesting list of family favorites. Including Big E's passion for homemade eggnog.

Did she have time to start over? Maybe.

Tears burned the backs of her eyes. So irritating how every little thing made her want to cry. She didn't have time for this. Squelching her tears, she told herself that's what she got for going and getting her heart broken right before she had to prepare the dinner of her life. No matter how charming and sweet Simon had appeared to be, she never, ever should have listened to her heart. But she'd also accepted that her plan to make a Montana match had been flawed, as well.

She was through with matchmaking, which was why she'd declined Grace's offer of setting her up with Mac Henson. Grace had understood and been incredibly kind when she'd also confessed that her job at Falcon Creek CPA wasn't going to work out long term, either. After Lily's wedding, she was moving back to California. That much had been decided before her untimely heartbreak.

Time to stop dwelling on this and move on to the stuffing. Ha. Yep. Exactly like she needed to stuff Simon in the past and move on with her life. And then she'd get the potatoes boiled, mashed and in the slow cooker. With that task completed, she wouldn't have so much to do in the final minutes before dinner was served when she needed to be focused on gravy preparation. Gravy stressed her out the most. People had strong opinions about gravy, and she didn't want to get it wrong. Extra incentive, Tyler loved mashed potatoes and gravy.

So did Simon. She'd learned that in Arizona. The nice thing about this holiday prep was that it had kept her from dwelling on Simon. She'd hardly thought about him at all.

Tuesday, after working half a day for Grace, she'd headed into the guest lodge's kitchen, where she began prepping for dinner, peeling, chopping and mixing pie dough until nearly midnight. Back aching, feet on fire and nearly every inch of her dusted with flour, she'd headed to her cabin, taken a shower, collapsed into bed and then started again at dawn. She'd spent all day Wednesday cooking and baking. Admittedly, she may have gone slightly over-board, but she had no choice because when she stopped moving, when she went still for even a few minutes, that's when she started thinking about Simon.

Simon. Who she no longer felt any anger toward. Butcher knife in hand, she chopped off the end of a celery stalk, startling herself as the sound reverberated through the kitchen. Okay, very little anger. Definitely, her anger was now at a manageable level.

Rewarded for her efforts, the pies had all

turned out beautifully: three pumpkin, Hadley's favorite; two apple, in case Georgie surprised them; two pecan, for Amanda; and an absolutely stunning lattice-topped sour cherry, Jon's favorite. And the rolls she'd baked for Lydia were a veritable masterpiece. The yeasty, buttery scent cheered her considerably. As did the fact that Peyton and Matteo, and Amanda and Blake had all arrived late the night before.

Main dishes were on task. The lodge's kitchen was well stocked and included a state-of-the-art roaster, where the two dry-cured, smoked, bone-in hams that she'd special ordered were now heating. The kitchen had large double ovens, so she was set for the simultaneous roasting of the two turkeys, which had three more hours before they were slated to go in.

Side dishes needed assembling. While chopping celery for the stuffing, she scanned her list, trying to determine if she had time for another go at the eggnog. "Turkeys brined—check, cranberry sauce—check," she muttered as she confirmed every detail. "Corn bread baked, sprouts washed, salad done, special surprise for Ben—check, odd fruit salad for my cousins—check…"

"What's an odd fruit?"

Fiona hadn't heard anyone enter the kitchen

but recognized the voice, and the sensation it stirred inside of her. *Simon.* Her pulse leaped and took off racing. What was he doing here? She turned toward him, searching his face for the answer. When his impassive expression didn't yield anything but curiosity, she explained, "That would be the mandarin orange, pineapple, raisin, mmm…walnut, marshmallow and lemon gelatin concoction I made for my cousins. Lydia told me about it. Apparently, their mom used to make it for Thanksgiving when they were kids."

"That is both the most disgusting and the sweetest thing I've ever heard." He continued forward until he was standing close. "Then again, it doesn't surprise me at all because that's what you do, isn't it? You find ways to make the people you care about happy. Even if it's at the expense of your own happiness."

"Simon…" His name was all she could manage because her heart had climbed into her throat and was crowding all the space.

"Fiona, we have a lot to talk about. And I know that right now is not the best time."

Nodding, she tried to swallow down the knot of emotion. "That is true. I am incredibly swamped here." She motioned at the bowls, utensils, measuring cups, ingredients and various containers covering the countertop. "I'm running late and I…" *I will not cry or throw this measuring cup at his head.*

"I can see that."

"What are you doing here?" she asked again.

Eyes searching hers, his smile turned hopeful, almost eager, as he said, "If you tell me where to find an apron, I'll show you."

FIONA ALMOST CHICKENED OUT. Was it crossing a line? Assuming too much familiarity? It was something she'd do to one of her sisters, and yet she didn't know her cousins all that well. In the end, it was Grandma Dorothy who pushed her over the edge. She'd come into the kitchen while Fiona was staring at the dish, took one look and busted out laughing. That was all the encouragement she needed.

Here goes. "Thank you all so much for being here today," she announced to the crowd seated in the guest lodge's dining room. Thanks to Tyler and Chance, four long tables were neatly arranged and draped with harvest-themed linens. They'd even set the tables, poured drinks and lit the candles. Hadley had surprised her with gorgeous centerpieces constructed of colorful mums, fountain grass and greenery. Fiona was so touched she nearly cried, and then silently blamed Simon for her overly emotional state.

Dinner was ready to be served. Almost.

She went on, "And thank you for trusting me to prepare this special meal for you all. It's an honor, truly." Turning her palms inward, she placed them over her heart for a second before removing them and continuing, "I am grateful. Thanksgiving is my favorite holiday. I like it because it's focused on two of my very favorite things—family and food. Luckily, I've always had a bounty of both to be grateful for. My family means everything to me. No matter what's happening in my life, they're always here for me. Until recently, when my sisters and I lost our mom, and she could no longer be here for any of us." She took a deep breath and continued.

"As you guys know—" she looked around the room, slowly making eye contact with Jon, Ethan, Ben, Tyler and Chance "—losing a parent is a blow to your heart that leaves a type of pain that I'm unable to describe." She turned to glance at Grandma Dot and Big E. "I can only imagine how it feels to lose a child. The death of a loved one is…excruciating. And it… changes you. But so does their love, the love they left behind. And we were so lucky to experience that love, right?" She thought about kids like Simon and Mica never feeling that from their parents and nearly cried again. Out of sympathy, this time, and not anger.

"I wish my sisters and I could have known your parents, and I wish you all could have known our mom. Her heart was so good and so big, and her love was endless. She would have given it to every single one of you." Fiona gestured around the room. "Seriously. Every new family member and friend in this room would have felt Susan Harrison's love. The world was a better place, an easier place, with her in it. And while we have to figure out a way to navigate this world without her, I'm grateful for the new family my sisters and I have gained to help us do that."

She looked at her sisters, reached up with both hands and touched the earrings her mom had given her on her eighteenth birthday. "The first day of the rest of your life," she'd told her, "should be remembered forever." That had been their mom's thing, special earrings for her girls to mark the most special events in their lives. Fiona fought back tears while her sisters all mimicked the gesture. Lily's eyes were shining. Amanda was dabbing at hers. *Oh, Fee*, Peyton mouthed, before pressing a hand to her mouth. Despite the tears running down his cheeks, Rudy wore a proud smile.

Then she turned to the man who'd made it

all possible, "Big G, thank you for inviting us all here to get to know our Blackwell family and to learn about our Montana heritage. For me, one of the best parts has been gaining a new grandfather. And now, I couldn't imagine a better new family to be a part of.

"To show my appreciation, I've tried to make sure that everyone's favorite Thanksgiving dish is represented. Thank you, Lydia, for helping me figure out what those dishes are. And a huge thanks to Grandma Dorothy for tracking down the recipe for a certain salad that I'm hoping you Blackwell brothers will especially enjoy.

"And on that note, I think we're about ready to eat. But first, cousin Ben, I'd like to present you with your special entrée." Fiona picked up the small covered casserole dish in front of her and carted it to the next table, where Ben sat with Rachel on one side and their daughter, Poppy, on the other. Placing the dish before him, she said, "I didn't want you to miss out on what all those *regular* people are eating for Thanksgiving dinner, so I made you your very own…"

"Pad thai," Tyler called from the next table. "Please say it's pad thai." He was laughing before she could even remove the lid.

"Pad thai," she confirmed, revealing the contents.

"Priceless!" Chance cried, erupting with laughter and fist-bumping Tyler across the table. Ethan guffawed.

"Enjoy it, Ben," Jon called in a voice that could only be described as gleeful. "That's all you get."

Laughter rang out from all around the room.

Gaze narrowed intently, expression unreadable, Ben peered at her so closely for a few seconds that Fiona grew nervous. Until she noticed his lip twitch. Face breaking into a smile, he reached for the chopsticks she was now offering, and said, "Well played, cousin Fiona." Beside him, Rachel was laughing so hard she couldn't speak. "And I guess we won't be requiring any further proof that you are truly a Blackwell."

"LITTLE FEE, IF I only had this eggnog to drink and that corn bread stuffing to eat for the rest of my life, I'd die a happy man." Big E leaned back in his chair and winked at Fiona.

"That is quite a compliment, Big G," Fiona said. "I'm glad you like them."

Truthfully, she was thrilled. She tossed an appreciative glance at Simon, whose help had ensured she had time to make that second batch of eggnog. For which she'd used a thermometer. His smile was gracious yet enigmatic. They'd spent hours in the kitchen together but hadn't talked about anything other than the food. Fiona knew she couldn't put off the conversation much longer. And now that dinner was complete, she found that she wanted the conversation that way, too. Over. Because even if he was here to apologize, that was the only thing they could be.

She forced herself to focus on the words she'd said, how grateful she was for her family. Satisfaction slowly settled into her as she absorbed the conversation, laughter and compliments swirling around her. She'd done it. Presenting Ben with the plate of pad thai had broken the ice, and she was pretty sure the "odd salad" had forever endeared her to all five Blackwell brothers. Lydia was touched that Fiona had used *her* nana's recipe for yeast rolls with honey butter. Katie seemed delighted with the homemade cranberry sauce.

Everything had turned out perfectly. Almost. The brussels sprouts were slightly overdone, and the turkey was a bit bland. But the gravy had turned out so good that she could hope no one would notice the turkey's shortcomings. Experience had taught her that the cook was always her own worst critic. And, from the fun everyone appeared to be having, the meal was perfect enough.

"It's all about the mashed potatoes and gravy for me," Tyler reiterated. "These mashed potatoes taste like Lydia's, which is *the* highest compliment. And this is the best turkey gravy I've ever had. You know, Simon, you could get the recipe for Ned and he could serve it as soup at the Silver Stake."

"Gravy soup?" Simon responded drily. "That does sound appetizing."

Tyler said, "Hey, all I have to do is put a photo of it on the guest lodge's Instagram and the next thing you know #gravysoup is sweeping the nation."

"As long as it's not #pigblitz I'm okay with it," Hadley quipped.

"Me, too," Fiona said, laughing. A few weeks ago, if someone had bet her she'd be joking with Hadley about that disaster she'd have lost all her savings—again.

"I like the ham," Abby chimed in. "I've never had ham that tastes this good."

"You never eat ham," Gen pointed out. "Because you love pigs so much."

"That is true." Abby's face twisted with thoughtful consideration. "But this is delicious. It's a real quan-dar-y. Is that the right word, Mom? Quandary?"

"It sure is," Lydia assured her. "Very nice use of it, too."

Twin sister Gen frowned. "Why isn't it a… *quan-er-dairy-whatsit* for you to eat steak then?"

Adorable, precocious cousin Rosie had the answer: "Because beef is our business. It's what we Blackwells do best, right, Big E?"

That generated another round of laughter and a loud "Amen!" from Gen, who reached out and fist-bumped her cousin.

"That is a fact," Big E agreed, beaming with pride at the aspiring ranchers in his midst.

"Some of us Blackwells," Katie agreed. "That is true. Some of us are pretty darn good at guest ranching and wedding planning, too."

"And veterinary medicine," Abby said, parking her smile on Ethan. So cute how the girl worshipped her uncle.

"And singing!" Rosie smiled at Chance.

"And riding horses!" Gino, Peyton's soon-to-be stepson, chimed in.

While the kids went on ticking off all the things the Blackwells were good at, Big E leaned close and whispered, "It's been said that some of us are pretty good at matchmaking, too."

CHAPTER NINETEEN

"I WISH GEORGIE was here. She is coming for the wedding, right?" Fiona sliced the pecan pie and then looked from Lily to Amanda for confirmation. Beside her, Peyton was busy dishing out pumpkin pie. Dessert was a serve-yourself buffet, and, with the rest of the family and guests settled in the dining room or watching football in the lobby, the Harrison sisters met in the kitchen and gathered around the island to share a quieter moment. Happy sounds carried in from the other rooms and made for pleasing background noise.

"Yes," Lily answered. "She said she'd be here."

"She'll be here," Amanda added confidently. "She wouldn't miss Lily's wedding."

Fiona nodded and scooped a slice of pie from the dish. She handed it to Amanda and waited impatiently for her to take a bite.

"Of course she'll be here," Peyton confirmed. "Let's talk about you for a minute." She spooned whipped cream onto a slice of pumpkin pie and slid the plate across the counter to Lily.

"Okay, sure," Fiona smiled. "What about me?"

"Specifically, your hot cowboy sous-chef." Peyton gave her the big-sister, eyebrows-up "give it to me straight" look. Lily and Amanda laughed. "Is he a PartnerUp.com match? Because...wow."

"Simon," Fiona supplied. "His name is Simon. No. He was, um, my boss at the Silver Stake."

"Oh, that's just great," Peyton teased. "You became romantically involved with your boss? You might want to ask Matteo if that's a good idea." Everyone laughed at the reference to Peyton and Matteo's rocky beginnings.

"Well, I...we..." Fiona stammered, her stomach tightening nervously. "That's not really what he does. He was just here to help his cousin run the place while his wife recovered from an accident. We sort of dated for a while and then he... *We* broke it off and he went back to California where he lives. I didn't know he was going to show up today, but I think Big E might have had something to do with it. I'm not really sure how he feels or what's going on."

"Can't keep his eyes off you, if that's any

sort of clue," Amanda supplied between bites. "What does he do? Is he really a cowboy? This is the best pecan pie I've ever had, Fee."

Fiona smiled gratefully at the compliment before glancing toward the doorway. Yearning flooded through her. Despite her misgivings, she wanted that to be true. But what had Big E done? Had he put Simon up to this?

"I heard that he's a bartender," Peyton added, and the confident look on her face had Fiona wondering where she'd gotten that information.

"I heard he was a juvenile delinquent," a grinning Lily supplied like she was revealing that he was a rock star.

"Who told you that?" Fiona peered at her, knowing full well it could have been anyone seeing how Lily was a comfortable part of Falcon Creek now. "He wasn't a delinquent. He was a wild teenager who exercised bad judgment. Is this about him stealing Big E's pickup? Because that wasn't—"

Amanda let out a sound that started like a gasp and ended on a chuckle. "He stole Big E's pickup?"

"He was a teenager, he and his friend Luke," Fiona attempted to explain. "It was an accident. They didn't mean to steal it. They were just taking it for a joyride, and they ran out of gas." Flustered, she changed course. "He's been both, a cowboy and a bartender, but he's neither anymore. He used to be, and he was doing those things here temporarily... Does it matter what he does for a living?"

"Absolutely not," a concerned-looking Peyton said, and patted her hand. "Not if he makes you happy. But when we filled out your profile, you specifically said you wanted to find a guy with a real job, a man who was serious about his career. A 'businessman' or a 'professional,' I believe were the exact terms you used."

"Bor-ing," Lily chirped in a singsong voice. "Trust me when I tell you cowboys are..." After a thoughtful beat, she settled on, "Not boring."

They all chuckled. Amanda said, "Yeah, yeah, we know, and Conner is pretty dreamy. Fiona, Simon seems very sweet to me. And watching you together, it's obvious that you're...close. Why didn't anyone know about him?"

"Because I didn't think there was a future for us," Fiona partially explained. "It was a relationship with an end date. He lives in LA. I knew he was going back to California, and I was determined to start a new life here."

"Why no future? Because of the long-distance thing?"

"Not really," Fiona said, and sighed. "Actually, yes, that was a factor but not the only issue. It's complicated..." She fidgeted with a pot holder left on the counter. "The breakup was about his job, his real job. He lied about it. I think he's here to apologize, but I don't know if I can forgive this kind of dishonesty."

"Uh-oh," Lily said. "What does he do? He's not a professional gambler, is he? Or a fire dancer? Remember that guy?"

"It wasn't the fact that he was a fire dancer that bothered me," Amanda commented drily. "It was the fact that he was a *perpetually unemployed* fire dancer who wound up setting Fiona's apartment on fire that I took issue with."

Fiona chuckled at the memory because she'd been quick with the fire extinguisher and what else could she do now but laugh? "Simon actually owns his own business, a prop rental company. He specializes in vintage and antique items for movies and other productions. Like airplanes, cars, equipment, that type of thing."

"Well, now," Amanda said. "That is beyond cool. You guys must have fun talking about all that old stuff."

"That is the complicated part. I didn't know that's what he did when we were dating. I thought he was a bartender. And he let me believe he tended bar in LA because he was afraid that if I found out that he was a successful businessman that I'd get too attached to him."

It was a rare moment when silence and any combination of Harrison sisters were in the same room together. Fiona waited while they processed this information.

Not surprisingly, it was Peyton who finally spoke. "I think I get it. He found out about your dating profile and the fact that you were husband shopping?"

"Yep. And he's not interested in marriage."

"And you weren't interested in a man who didn't have a career-type job," Peyton supplied. "You didn't think it would last, either. That's why you didn't tell us about him."

"I wanted to tell you. But I didn't want Dad to know I was already falling into my old habits. Or Big E. The job thing wasn't working out, either, and I just… I wanted to prove I could change. I wanted everyone to be proud of me."

"So, essentially, you were dishonest, too, in a way?" Lily pointed out.

"I don't think you need to change," Amanda stated. "You are like the nicest person I know, and I'm not saying that because you're my sister. You have such a kind heart, Fiona. And you shouldn't change for anyone. You just need to figure out what you really want. Seriously, marry a fire dancer if he makes you happy. Just not that last one. He was a poser."

They all chuckled. Peyton wound an arm around her shoulders and gave her a gentle squeeze. "I agree with Amanda, and Lily has a good point. Maybe you need to be honest with yourself. Listening to your heart has always served you well. Where you run into trouble is when your heart tries to make everyone else happy before you. Including these less than stellar, albeit *fiery*, romantic entanglements you've had in the past." They all laughed, and Peyton added, "Amanda is right—you need to try making yourself happy and the rest will fall into place."

"Like maybe your hot cowboy-bartender-antiques dealer," Lily added with a wink.

Peyton and Amanda were right, and Lily did have a point. It hadn't exactly been her most shining moment when she'd asked Simon to keep their relationship a secret. It felt so good to be advised and consoled by her family again. Fiona felt tears spring to her eyes. But they were right; it was time to decide for herself what she really wanted.

"Now, if that isn't the coolest job title ever," Amanda proclaimed. "And speaking of him, we need to get back to some earlier details that were skimmed over." She pushed her plate across the counter. "I need more pie, and details. In that order."

"You got it." Fiona smiled and dished out another slice. Peyton topped it with a dollop of whipped cream and handed it to Amanda. "I know this is a lot to process. Which details, Amanda?"

Amanda grinned. "The details where Simon stole Big E's pickup."

THE BLACKWELL MEN insisted on doing the dishes. Neither the Blackwell nor the Harrison women argued. Tyler and Chance hadn't been kidding when they said there would be two televisions. A football game played at one end of the lobby where the comfy furniture had been arranged for optimal viewing while doubling as a corral. The sofa, love seat and chairs were arranged so the youngest of the Blackwell brood could frolic in the middle. Here, Jon, Ben and Ethan watched football and embraced toddler duty, occasionally swapping out a little one here and there to Grandma Dorothy, Peyton or whoever was wandering by.

A Christmas movie was on another smaller television at the other end of the room where Lydia, Katie, Hadley and Amanda played cards at the table with the older kids. The other adults mingled in groups, chatting and drinking coffee while seconds of dessert made the rounds.

With the crowd content and settled, Fiona grew increasingly uneasy. Simon showed no signs of approaching her to have that talk. Nor did he seem intent on leaving without having it. She saw no evidence of any bad blood between him and Big E. On the contrary, Simon was currently seated between Rudy and Big E watching the game.

Finally she decided she couldn't take it for one more minute. She removed her phone from her pocket and sent him a text: Do you want to meet at my cabin in 15 minutes?

She watched as Simon slipped his phone from his pocket and glanced at the display. Then he looked up and, like he'd been aware of her watching him the whole time, locked his gaze onto hers. It wasn't difficult to read his lips: *Yes*.

ONCE INSIDE FIONA'S CABIN, she and Simon began speaking at the same time.

"I talked to your dad…"

"I talked to Luke…"

They stopped, and then immediately did it again.

"Big E said…"

"My sisters think…"

Simon chuckled a little and remarked, "Sounds like everyone has been talking except us."

"Including you and Big E?"

"Yes. He and your dad paid me a visit in California."

"Did he force you to come here and make amends? Like he did with his pickup?"

"What? No! Fiona, I told you it's not like that. We're…fine. A little better than fine, actually. I owned up to my mistake back then and paid for it. Big E respects that. The surprising part is that, apparently, he respects me, too. More than I would have imagined, which is a bonus."

"What about my dad?"

"Your dad seems like a great guy. He only wants you to be happy. They both encouraged me to come here and talk to you."

Fiona nodded and managed a wobbly smile. Staring at each other, they both remained silent for a few seconds before Fiona blurted, "I'm sorry for what I said about your family and for calling you an enabler."

Simon went wide-eyed. "No, Fiona, don't be sorry about that. It's all true."

"I know, but I shouldn't have said it in anger.

And I don't have any right to talk about your family. I don't even know them."

"Well, I think the snippet of Mica that you witnessed combined with my behavior and our conversations were enough to get a pretty good idea. And, in this case, you did have a right because it impacted you. I hurt you, Fiona."

"Yes, you did. And you made me *really* angry. I don't think I've ever been so angry with another person in my entire life. I have four sisters, and not even the worst fight with one of them can compare."

He winced. "I deserved it. I hope I never do it again."

At his reference to the future, Fiona tried desperately to keep a lid on the hope that was already bubbling inside of her. "Me, too."

He drew in a quick, sharp breath and squeezed his eyes shut. When he opened them, she thought she could see the same spark of hope she felt reflected there. "Fiona, I'm so sorry. That day I kissed you… I was terrified when you told me that the next person you dated you wanted to marry. So, I let you believe what you already thought. From what you told me, if you thought I was a bartender, then I would be safe from…"

"Marriage. I know. Luke explained about your family's marriage curse."

Simon nodded. "Luke has been a busy boy."

"I love Luke," Fiona said. "And you should, too."

His smile was crooked but heartfelt. "Believe me, I do. And I am looking very forward to getting… Paying him back for some things. Anyway, that's why I didn't say anything then."

"I get that. And later?"

"I absolutely should have told you later after we decided to start seeing each other. You were right—I was a coward and a fool. I thought it would keep me *safe* from you wanting me too much, but I didn't anticipate how much I would want you. I never expected to fall for you like I did. And now, I'm a miserable foolish coward who is telling you the truth."

Fiona felt her heart ache with a mix of longing and terror. "But now I'm…scared."

"I know," he said, and took a tentative step forward. "I don't blame you."

Without thinking, she stepped toward him. "What do you want from me, Simon?"

"Whatever you can give me. I love you, Fiona."

"What? Simon, no… Please, don't say that." Tears gathered in her eyes, but this time she couldn't stop them.

"Wait." His hands came up to lightly grip her shoulders. "Why is that a bad thing?"

"The idea of you loving me and me loving you and never having a…a future is awful."

"You love me?"

"Of course I love you. Why else would I have been so angry?"

"This is good." His face erupted with a smile that was so joy filled it distracted her for a few seconds. Sparkling blue eyes pinned on hers, he said, "This is so much better than I hoped for. Big E said…" He removed his phone from his pocket and began tapping on the screen.

"What did Big E say?" Fiona asked. "You're texting? Right now?"

"Big E is a very smart man. Luke," he said by way of explanation. "I'm texting Luke." Holding his phone, he waited a few seconds before nodding and stuffing his phone back into his pocket. "He's ready." Reaching out, he snagged her hand, planted a kiss on the back and entwined his fingers with hers. "Are you ready?"

"For what?"

"You'll see."

She didn't have to go far. Outside the cabin, Simon's stagecoach pulled up. Luke was driving, and two horses were secured with long lengths of leather reins and silver loops. It had been washed and polished so that it gleamed and looked even grander than it had in Jon's shop. And just completely…wrong. Disappointment rushed through her followed closely by a flash of anger. She turned to face him. "Simon, I don't—"

He squeezed her hand. "Wait, I know what you're thinking but, please, hear me out."

"Fine. What am I thinking?" she challenged, trying not to sound snappish but knowing that she failed miserably. She didn't care. Because, seriously, what was this?

"You're thinking, how could Simon possibly imagine that the ultimate symbol of his lies and deception could be a romantic gesture?"

"Oh," she conceded. "Maybe you do know."

"I couldn't stop thinking about what you said, about the stagecoach and how it had delivered the news. I don't want there to be this… dark and unhappy reminder between us. Something we didn't mention or that we were afraid to discuss. Every time you saw a stagecoach, you'd remember what I did.

"I've lived like that my entire life, not talking about problems, letting fear rule my actions. I don't want that for us. I want you to be a part of my life, Fiona—my real life. I want to be a part of yours. This is who I am. And for the rest of our lives, when you see a stagecoach, I want you to remember this—how I tried to make it right. I'll always make mistakes. With my screwed-up childhood, that's a guarantee. But thanks to my uncle, and a few other people—your grandfather being one of them—I know the right thing to do is to own them and try to make amends."

She had to interrupt him because she was sort of stuck on one key phrase. "For the rest of our lives?" she repeated.

"If you'll have me. Fiona, will you—"

"No, Simon, I won't." At his look of devastation, she took hold of his shoulders and quickly clarified, "I mean, definitely yes! Eventually. But all I need right now is to know that a future is possible."

Eyes twinkling, his mouth curved with that mischievous smile she'd come to crave. His arms came up to encircle her. Dipping his head, he nuzzled her neck, and she shivered when he increased the pressure, hugging her tight against him and tucking her inside his jacket. She wanted to tell him he was mistaken, that she wasn't cold, that it was his touch that made her tremble. Only his. Forever. But then he whispered, "Fiona, when I'm with you, I feel like anything is possible."

Fiona savored his words, let them sink into her. Then she shifted so that her body was flush with his. Smiling against his mouth, she whispered, "Is that so?"

"Yes, it is. For you, I will make anything happen."

She closed the remaining distance between their lips, pouring everything she had into the kiss. She loved him and she wanted him to know, to feel every bit of it.

A moment later, she pulled back far enough to ask, "What do you know about this stage-coach here? Do you think the owner will mind if we climb inside? I want to tell this guy that I love him inside of a stagecoach because I think it would make a perfect memory. Every time we see a stagecoach, I want him to re-member it."

Letting his forehead fall against hers, he breathed her name. When he looked up, his blue eyes were shining. Clearing his throat, he whispered softly, "I am a hundred percent positive the owner will not mind."

CHAPTER TWENTY

FIONA FILLED TWO tall glasses with ice and poured in the tea. Crossing through the kitchen, she exited out the French doors and onto the sprawling deck that fronted Simon's house. The sun was shining. The sun, whom Fiona had missed like an old friend.

They'd arrived in California three days ago so Simon could tend to his business and check Mica into an alcohol rehabilitation facility. His attorney had assured him that Mica's case would most likely result in a diversionary program. Simon had made an appointment with a therapist to try to understand his issues and discover what his role was in his brother's recovery. Fiona was waiting until after the holidays to find a job and an apartment. She'd insisted on remaining at Falcon Creek CPA until Grace found a replacement, but Grace wouldn't hear of it. Fiona only acquiesced when Grace informed her that the next best candidate after Fiona had taken the job.

Saying goodbye to her sisters had been difficult, but it was so much easier knowing they were all happy. With Peyton and Amanda both settled in California, she knew she'd see them often. And they'd all be together again soon for the holidays and Lily's wedding. With Georgie, too.

A long talk with her dad, including his blessing where Simon was concerned, had also made leaving easier. Rudy admitted to being thrilled that she'd be so much closer to him in San Diego.

"Seventy degrees," Fiona said, setting both glasses down on the table fronting the sofa. She took a seat next to Simon. "In case you hadn't noticed, it's not snowing."

"I did notice that," he said.

"I think this is my favorite thing about your house," she said, and gestured at the outdoor space he'd created complete with cushy sofa, two chairs, a dining table and a built-in grill.

"I'm glad you like it." She knew that he knew that she would.

She exhaled a happy sigh and gazed up at the clear blue sky. "What was I thinking, leaving this place?"

Simon looped an arm around her shoulders and tucked her in close. "I believe you were thinking that you were going to find your perfect Montana match."

"Which I did," she said. "He just happens to reside in California, where there is very little chance of a snowstorm, thank goodness."

Simon pushed her hair over her shoulder and planted a kiss on her temple. "Speaking of your new, new life in California, I have an idea to run by you."

"Listening. Amenable. For future reference, you should note how open I am to ideas when they are suggested beneath the warmth of the sun."

"How would you like a job working for Clarke Props? Mica has quit, and he says he's not coming back after rehab. I agree it could be good for him to make his own way in the world. We'll see. I want you to know that I'm not offering it to you because you're my girl-friend. You know as much as I do about antiques, and I've seen how hard you work and how good you are with people."

"That's incredibly sweet."

"Are you interested?"

"Yes."

"Yes?"

"I accept."

"That's it? I don't have to talk you into it?"

"You just did." She'd been to work with him every day, and from what she'd seen, she liked everything about his business. And he was right—she worked hard and knew she would be a good fit. "I would like very much to work for you. Thank you."

"Well, that's awesome." He leaned over and sealed his words with a kiss. Fiona didn't argue. *See, amenable.*

Then she said, "My second favorite thing about your house is that it's technically located in Malibu and not LA." Still a bit awestruck by the stunning view of the ocean, she gave it an appreciative scan. The beach was an easy ten-minute walk. "Which is only a little over an hour drive to Santa Barbara. I cannot wait for you to meet Ivy. Thank you for taking the time to have lunch with us tomorrow." They were driving up the coast to see her the next day.

Simon shrugged a shoulder. "She's important to you. That makes her important to me."

"Which reminds me." Fiona reached for her phone where it sat on the table by her glass. "She sent me another video this morning."

Simon nodded toward the laptop on the table. "Interesting coincidence. I have a video to show you, too."

"Okay, me first," Fiona said. "So, there's this hero in San Diego…" She trailed off while she pulled up the video.

"A kitten hero?" he joked, and leaned in. "I

need to see this." By now he was well aware of her fondness for cute kitten videos.

"No, funny guy, a man hero." Fiona chuckled and kissed his cheek. "Don't worry, I'm not going to make you watch the whole thing. I'm sending it to my dad. The guy saved this family, but no one knows who he is. It happened near San Diego and they're looking for him. My dad knows a lot of people." She held up the screen so Simon could see the man's face. "Recognize him?"

Simon studied the image before shaking his head.

She typed out a quick text to Rudy and hit Send. "Your turn." She lifted a hand and waved him on. "Ivy sets a high bar. I hope you can compete."

Laughing, he opened his laptop, clicked around and then set it on her thighs. "It's not kittens or heroes, but I think you'll like it. I hope so anyway."

The video was taken from ceiling height, and she immediately recognized the interior of the Silver Stake. Only a few seconds ticked by before Simon stepped into view. A bar towel hung over one shoulder, and she recognized the denim shirt he wore. He made a thorough scan of the place. Fiona felt herself smiling when he moved to stand in front of his laptop and started tapping away because she'd seen him do that a hundred times.

"What is this, security footage?" she asked.

Beside her, Simon nodded. "Wait for it…"

Suddenly, on-screen Simon looked up, closed his laptop and walked off-screen to the right, toward his office, she assumed. A moment later, Fiona watched herself enter the scene and climb onto a bar stool. Her gaze nervously darted around before focusing on the entrance. She recognized the outfit she had on because she'd taken great pains in deciding on what to wear for her first date in Montana. Also, the first time she and Simon met…

Fiona gasped and clapped a hand over her mouth as she realized what was unfolding before her. "Simon…" she whispered. Her hand found his and squeezed, but she couldn't tear her gaze away from the screen. She was still facing the door when Simon took his spot behind the bar again. His eyes traveled over her, and she could almost hear his deep voice asking what he could get for her. They talked, and he served her coffee. The film ended, freezing on a still shot of Simon leaning over the bar, very close, a faint smile in place and whispering next to her ear. Right before her date entered the bar.

"Our meet-cute." She set the laptop aside

and threw her arms around him, their laughter mingling as she hugged him tight and kissed him repeatedly. Drawing away slightly, she said, "I can't believe you thought of this. I am overjoyed. This is hands down the most thoughtful thing anyone has ever done for me. I didn't think you'd be able to top the golf trip. Or the stagecoach. At least, not this soon."

He delivered a scorching kiss before pulling back to search her face. His satisfied, appreciative smile sent sparks shooting through her bloodstream. "Do you remember what you said that day? How you said that you wanted to remember the moment forever. How cool it would be to be able to show our kids someday."

"Of course." *Our kids. Someday.* Such otherwise simple phrases, yet coming from Simon's lips, they meant the world. She wondered if she'd ever get used to it, how it felt to be loved like this.

"I know you said that you didn't need to be married to be with me."

"That's right. I don't," she answered softly. And she didn't. It was enough that he was even thinking of it as a possibility. That he was here with her now, sharing himself and making plans for them weeks and months in advance. They were having lunch with Ivy tomorrow and going to Calliope's holiday party, and then back to Montana until Lily's wedding and staying through Christmas. They were going golfing with Luke in Arizona over New Year's, and Simon had been talking about a trip to Hawaii in February. Where he promised to present her with the best piña colada she'd ever tasted. He was all in and she knew it.

"What if I told you that I do?"

"Simon, I realize now that I only wanted to get married to make my dad happy. I mean, I only wanted to get married that quickly to make my dad happy."

"So, do it now to make me happy, to make us happy. Fiona, now that I'm…free, it's all I can think about. I want to be yours and I want you to be mine. For forever. I want to *be* married to you. What do you say?"

"Okay." She nodded. "I say yes. I want that, too!"

"That's it? Just yes, and you've agreed?"

"Yes."

Simon kissed her again. Then he sank back into the cushions and said, "That's it. Every important conversation that we have for the rest of our lives we will have in the sun."

EPILOGUE

"AT LEAST IT'S not snowing," Rudy said. "I've discovered that these old bones do not like the cold."

Big E chuckled and flipped on the blinker. "Fiona has rubbed off on you."

"I like to think it's vice versa," Rudy said with a smile, his heart squeezing tightly inside of his chest. He was so proud of his youngest daughter. Not only had she figured out exactly what she wanted out of life, she was going for it. He felt bad about the part he'd played in temporarily leading her astray. But, as always, she'd forgiven him without a second thought.

He had Simon to thank for helping him realize that, too. That, and for making his Fiona shine with happiness once again.

"Speaking of our youngest California girl, she sent us another one of those videos." Pulling out his phone, he reread the message that accompanied it:

This guy reminds me of you! You'll always be my hero and my dad. (No matter what or who your search might find.)

Rudy swallowed down the knot of emotion and tapped on the link. Words flashed on the screen: "Have You Seen This Hero?"

A reporter at a news desk appeared and said, "This video was taken outside of San Diego..." The footage began to roll with that slightly jumpy, not-quite-clear quality often present in the amateur cell phone filming of an action scene. The camera zoomed in on an upside-down car at the bottom of a shallow ravine, an accident, Rudy quickly realized as the smashed car came into focus. The reporter confirmed it, relaying that the "single-car accident would likely have ended in the most traumatic circumstances if not for the actions of this Good Samaritan."

The narration continued as smoke and steam billowed from the wreckage. Suddenly a man ran into view and disappeared behind the vehicle. Flames joined the smoke, upping the intensity a millionfold. Rudy found himself holding a breath. Long seconds passed, and then the man appeared again, carrying a small person in his arms. The camera zoomed in to show him gently deposit the child on the ground. He sprinted back toward the car and returned with a second child. Then again, with a woman. The last time he was moving more slowly, his arm wrapped around a man's waist half carrying, half dragging him along. Just as he turned to glance up the hillside, the camera panned around to catch the arrival of emergency responders.

Fiona said the video reminded her of him, but the man, and his actions, reminded Rudy of his daughter Georgiana. What had happened to his daughter that she no longer wanted to treat *people* and, instead, spent her days staring into a microscope? Not that medical research wasn't important, too, it was just that it wasn't what Georgie had always aspired to.

When the camera refocused on the survivors the rescuer was gone.

The video flashed back to the car engulfed in flames while the reporter added, "A spokesperson with the highway patrol is crediting the actions of this mystery man with saving the lives of the Frye family. CPR was performed on Scott Frye…" A witness was interviewed. A grainy close-up still-shot of the hero appeared while the reporter gave a physical description and the following nugget, "One witness said she believes the man was driving a commercial truck." The segment wrapped up with, "Have you seen this hero? Highway patrol and San Diego police are asking anyone with information on the identity of this man to please call the following number..."

"Elias, pull over."

"What? Why?"

"I need to check something, and you need to see this."

"I get the gist from here, Rudy. You can show me later. I'd like to watch that baby goat video again, too. You know, the one where they're playing with the kittens?"

"Nope. Pull over. We're going to San Diego. Fast." Rudy rewound the footage until he found the still photo and took a screenshot. Bless Fiona for teaching him that useful trick.

"What in the world are you talking about?"

"I think I know this hero." Rudy reached for a file folder and removed a photograph. He compared it to the photo on his display. "And his name is Thomas Blackwell."

* * * * *

For the next installment of
The Blackwell Sisters,
don't miss Montana Wedding
coming next month
from acclaimed author Cari Lynn Webb
and Harlequin Heartwarming!

And for more Harlequin Heartwarming
romances, please visit
www.Harlequin.com today!

Get 4 FREE REWARDS!

We'll send you 2 FREE Books plus 2 FREE Mystery Gifts.

Love Inspired books feature uplifting stories where faith helps guide you through life's challenges and discover the promise of a new beginning.

FREE Value Over $20

THE WESTERN HEARTS COLLECTION!

19 FREE BOOKS in all!

COWBOYS. RANCHERS. RODEO REBELS.
**Here are their charming love stories in one prized Collection:
51 emotional and heart-filled romances that capture the majesty
and rugged beauty of the American West!**

YES! Please send me **The Western Hearts Collection** in Larger Print. This collection begins with 3 FREE books and 2 FREE gifts in the first shipment. Along with my 3 free books, I'll also get the next 4 books from The Western Hearts Collection, in LARGER PRINT, which I may either return and owe nothing, or keep for the low price of $5.45 U.S./$6.23 CDN each plus $2.99 U.S./$7.49 CDN for shipping and handling per shipment*. If I decide to continue, about once a month for 8 months I will get 6 or 7 more books but will only need to pay for 4. That means 2 or 3 books in every shipment will be FREE! If I decide to keep the entire collection, I'll have paid for only 32 books because 19 books are FREE! I understand that accepting the 3 free books and gifts places me under no obligation to buy anything. I can always return a shipment and cancel at any time. My free books and gifts are mine to keep no matter what I decide.

☐ 270 HCN 5354   ☐ 470 HCN 5354

_____
Name (please print)

_____
Address   Apt. #

_____
City   State/Province   Zip/Postal Code

Mail to the Reader Service:
IN U.S.A.: P.O. Box 1341, Buffalo, N.Y. 14240-8531
IN CANADA: P.O. Box 603, Fort Erie, Ontario L2A 5X3